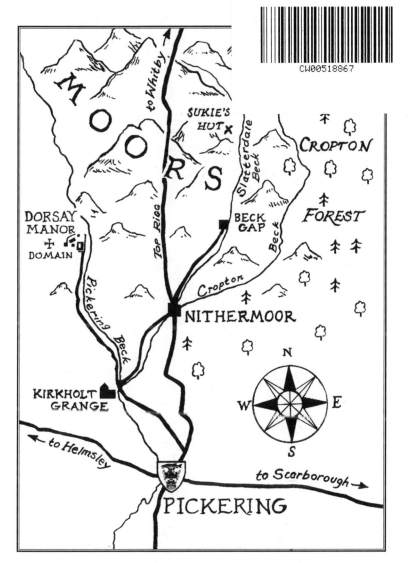

Map of Slatterdale region, 1396–1431

SYCORAX

J. B. Aspinall

PETER OWEN
LONDON AND CHESTER SPRINGS

PETER OWEN PUBLISHERS
73 Kenway Road, London SW5 0RE

Peter Owen books are distributed in the USA by
Dufour Editions Inc., Chester Springs, PA 19425-0007

First published in Great Britain 2006 by
Peter Owen Publishers

Map on half-title page drawn by Nick Pearson

ISBN 0 7206 1278 0

Printed in Great Britain by Windsor Print Production Ltd

For Frances

Of its own beauty is the mind diseased
                                    — Byron

Contents

Preface   *9*

The Trangressions and Penance of Brother Edmund   *13*

A Journey to the Territory of the Fiend in Slatterdale   *21*

The Ale Wife Alys and the Beginning of the Investigation   *28*

The Young Gentleman and the Shepherdess   *40*

Brother Denys Betrays Secrets of the Confessional   *51*

Brother Edmund Makes a Report and Receives
a Reprimand   *56*

The Arrest of the Witch Sukie   *63*

The Interrogation and Condemnation of the Witch Sukie   *71*

The Sojourn of the Witch Sukie in Pickering Gaol   *79*

The Ordeal of the Witch Sukie in Pickering Stocks   *91*

Brother Edmund Is Drawn to the Ale House in Nithermoor   *98*

Mumping Night and the Bewitching of Brother Edmund   *105*

The Homecoming and Wedding of the Witch Sukie   *114*

The Comportment and Gruesome Death of
Watkin Trothers   *123*

The Comportment and Gruesome Death of Abbot Fabian   *132*

The Flight of the Witch Sukie and the Advent of
the Fiend Sycorax   *142*

Mayhem Is Wrought by the Fiend Sycorax in Pickering   *152*

Brother Edmund at the Trial of the Witch Alys   *161*

The Expedition Against the Fiend Sycorax, 1414   *175*

What Befell the Expedition at the Lair of the Fiend   *183*

The Retaliation of the Fiend Sycorax   *195*

The Triumph of the Fiend Sycorax, 1414   *201*

The Bewitching of Brother Edmund and the Hanging
    of the Witch Alys   *206*
The Expedition Against the Fiend Sycorax, 1431   *219*
The Triumph of the Fiend, 1431   *226*
Winter at Byland   *235*

Preface

HE SYCORAX MANUSCRIPT never achieved book form even by medievalstandards. We can speculate about Edmund of Byland's failure to finish it by using clues he furnishes in his last contributions. Discouragement, spiritual confusion, mental instability and terror all seem to have played their part in bringing him to abandon the work. On the other hand, the fact that he did not destroy the text suggests that the matter was taken out of his hands, as foretold in his second interview with Prior Jocelyn (page 205 of this edition).

One presumes that the manuscript remained at Byland in the same form in which it was discovered four centuries later in the archives of the See of York: that is, as a large number of separate folded sheets, unnumbered and disarranged, in a leather wallet secured with straps. The 'properly written and illustrated volume' which Edmund mentions, both in his introduction and elsewhere, as being intended to emanate from his document, has never been found, nor any reference to it. In fact there is no historical evidence to corroborate the Sycorax manuscript. None of the events are reported elsewhere and the names of important personages such as abbots seem to have been changed.

There have been several editions of Edmund's Latin text: the latest of which – *The Sycorax Codex* (Otto Baluth, Ocean Palisades Press, 1983), hereafter referred to as 'the *Codex*' – seems definitive and has guided my procedures.

It includes a literal translation and an exhaustive commentary. Since my own approach is not scholarly but aimed at producing effective literature I have made a number of adjustments to the text as postulated by the *Codex*.

Professor Baluth asserts that it is impossible to be confident about the order in which Edmund wrote the manuscript, it being a 'thicket of shuffled palimpsests'. There is evidence that some of it was written as investigations proceeded, whereas other passages were inserted at a later date with the benefit of hindsight. The *Codex* imposes a degree of coherence by confining all Edmund's autobiographical material to the notes and appendices, leaving the history of the witch Sycorax uncluttered. I have preferred to construct a narrative that reflects Edmund's consecutive experience: his personal problems and adventures intertwined with the facts about the career of Sycorax as he gathered them. To achieve this I have had to take liberties with the original text, without, I hope, altering the gist or intent.

I have also added passages of my own invention. Some of these give background detail, to make the medieval world more accessible. Others extrapolate the characters, particularly Edmund, and interpret motivation. It would be nice to think that my additions are not only compatible with the rest of the text but so seamlessly interpolated that the forgery cannot be detected without use of the *Codex*!

I have removed several passages of conventional piety – and countless brief expressions of the same – judging them irritating to most modern readers, but have tried to retain enough to be representative of Edmund and his epoch.

Translation presented a number of difficulties, some solved by cheating, as a comparison with the accurate translation in the *Codex* will show. While I have avoided anachronisms, I have chosen a 'modern' rather than 'medieval' idiom because it is less contrived and more accessible. At the same time I have tried to preserve something of the cadence of Edmund's Latin.

The chapter headings I use are mostly taken from marginalia to Edmund's main text in what seems to be a different hand.

The speeches which Edmund records in local dialect present as sturdy a challenge as Latin. They could not be understood by a modern reader without use of the glossary in the *Codex*. I have translated them into a hybrid of northern peasant which I mean to seem exotic without being too baffling. I apologize to those whom this annoys. The direct speech which Edmund renders in Latin I have translated into the formal style of the bulk of the text. It is usually conversation between ecclesiastics.

J.B. Aspinall
Gascony, 2006

The Transgressions and Penance of Brother Edmund

I AM EDMUND OF Byland. I surrendered my surname to God when I came here as a novice in 1413.

The younger son of a yeoman tenant of this abbey, I learnt Latin at grammar school in York and at one time seemed likely to progress in scholarship and make my people proud of me. But even before I had fully attained manhood I was a hapless sinner, given to drink and fornication. This disqualified me from the Chantry school in York and returned me disgraced to my father's estate where for two years I wallowed in further lewd and drunken godlessness, until the scandal arising from my conduct and the exasperated intervention of my father constrained me to submit to God and enter this abbey. The fact that I took refuge here (though under a degree of compulsion) for the protection of both my body and soul is the first major irony supplied by my history for the sardonic entertainment of Satan.

At the time when I lost my surname I also hoped to discard all my antics in Satan's dominions, for I had come to fear both the temporal and spiritual consequences of such error. In general, for many years, I found tranquillity here, in duty and abstinence. But the lovely, soothing ritual of the abbey never managed to dispel a sinful residue of my adolescent self, a poison smuggled inside me. Sixteen years later Satan was still able to use me as a duct whereby he might bring his monsters into the holy haven: when I was sleeping, or if I had been swallowing this abbey's excellent wine, or was otherwise made unwary. Sometimes even when I was at devotion they posed and leered before me and my brain was helpless to exclude them.

Peasant lasses I blithely swived in my youth came as succubi and incubi, shameless and shaming demons. There was Nell with her gap-toothed grin, Malkin spry as a weasel, Nance who gave such raucous grunts of greedy glee. They all came smiling to lean over me or squat under me, hoisting their skirts from their pudenda. Notable among them was Luce, her auburn hair and pale, soft belly, with whom I had been taken *in flagrante delicto* and beaten almost to death by her husband, sub-tenant of our water meadow.

After years of confession and countless trifling penances, along with the conscientious consumption of lentils, lettuces and other known depressants of lust, had failed to prevent recurrence of these filthy visitations and end my torment, I undertook, with the prompting of Abbot Fabian, a more vexatious and time-consuming penance: a history of the Slatterdale witch, Sukie Trothers, later known as the Fiend Sycorax.

I daresay it seems a bland sort of penance: scratching out a book in this snug room, within sound of the bells and peacocks, the wind in the tall elms of Byland, safe from need, plague, wolves, trulls and whatever else folk are enduring out yonder. So I begin by pointing out what Abbot Fabian explained to me when he first broached the notion: that my penance and the book would together be worthless if the task did not involve an unusual degree of toil and even suffering. Rather than concocting some artificial hardship, such as inscribing the entire work left-handed, so disciplining my soul at the expense of the project, we decided it best that I punished myself as I benefited the book, by the rigour of my research.

My labours at my Byland desk with ink, parchment and candle are the least arduous aspect of my penance. In pursuit of the full truth I have suffered discomfort and peril, both physical and spiritual, in places where no godly or learned man would willingly be found. I have consorted with half-wits in sunless vales, drunkards in pig-huts, crones in the gutters of wicked towns. The worst of the hellish visions I confess and atone would be shrugged off as nothing – tolerated with the morning's hangover – by the boors out there on Satan's acres. Whatever it once was, my nature is now delicate, scholarly and refined: it has been as painful for me as for the holy man among the heathen of the Danube, to be sequestered with those yokels among the hovels of the North Riding of Yorkshire, enduring their belches and farts, the vomit-provoking stench of their proximity and the humiliation of their sodden familiarity. North Riding men of the vulgar class, whether in town or demesne, seem to count it obligatory to drink their flat, muddy ale all day long until unconsciousness prevents them. Their women are slovenly and immodest, only saved from harlotry – if then – by listlessness.

Remembering my disgusting secret self, I can endure contact with more blatantly disgusting humanity: but it is not the only hazard out there, nor the worst. God is in the Church and in those rare homes and hearts that have ousted the domestic fiend; the rest of the earth is pitfalls to Hell. The North Riding, in particular, even before the rise of the great Fiend Sycorax, was full of ancient evil: goat-footed demons and camouflaged goblins. I do not speak only of metaphor, of spiritual peril. There is a local tradition of fiends that have material impact: a red-eyed serpent that can drag you down through the rustling underbrush into the earth; a great bird that swoops to carry you kicking away; a black wolf that prowls the gorse moors and bracken slopes, ready to lope off to Hell with a sinner in its slobbering jaws. Satan can bite you to the bone in this terrestrial interim as well as claim you for eternity. Hildebrand tells of a German bishop who had a hundred men-at-arms to guard him day and night in case the fiends of Satan should bear him bodily away.

But worse than any fleshly peril is the hazard into which I have plunged my soul in search of Sycorax. The fact that my task began as a quest for spiritual benefit is the second great irony with which my life has gratified the Fiend.

It all seemed very different at the outset, only a year ago. I can remember the cool fingers of the Abbot stroking my tonsure, as I knelt before him in shame and self-pity at my ignominious transgressions. Leaning from his stool to chastely embrace me, he let out a little moan of compassion. In his bleak private cell, after that confessional, we discussed the details of the project which was intended to be my purgation but which was to bring Abbot Fabian to a terrible death and myself to the brink of Hell.

'You entered the abbey young, Brother Edmund, and have no memory of the world out yonder except as an ignorant sinner. Now that you are strong in devotion and obedience it will benefit you to confront that world again. Once you are confident that you can repudiate its evil squalor it will cease to torment your spirit with obscenities that you were once unable to resist.'

He paused, but I said nothing. I wanted to say that I felt weaker and more sinful than other men – not fit to be let at large beyond the safety of the abbey. But I could not reject the Abbot's confidence in me, nor refuse the ordeal he proposed.

'Your spiritual need, dear Brother Edmund, though close to my heart, is not the only reason that I have chosen you for the task – or chosen the task for you. You are the most scholarly monk in Byland if I do not include myself. I rejoice to have a kindred intellect in my care, even if that intellect resides in such troubled flesh as yours, which is why I have not hesitated to offer you such friendship and esteem – indeed, partiality – as is not incompatible with our stations and the rules of our order.' He squinted his pale old eyes in the light begrudged by the narrow window and smiled at me almost coyly. 'I am confident that you are fully qualified for the task I confer on you, not just by virtue of your literacy but because your keen wits will enable you to avoid the superstitious ignorance which affects so many of your brothers.'

It was not the first time Abbot Fabian had confided his views to me. His was a lonely and unpopular eminence at Byland, partly because of the stringency with which he had applied the Cistercian discipline and stamped out abuse.

'I find it regrettable that no original literary work has ever been produced in Byland. While our abbey has a valuable collection of documents, they are all copies of scripts that reside in other abbeys. I realize that this attitude of mine is eccentric within the Cistercian order. It is certainly not shared by any of your brothers here. Our rules have always promoted the virtues of physical toil and by this have avoided some of the abuses rife in more scholarly orders, but we have thereby become prone to other shortcomings.'

I said, 'Satan is ready to make a weakness out of an asset as soon as we blink.'

He poured me another minute measure of gooseberry wine. 'There is a body of opinion among the Fathers of the Church that original composition is an act of pride unbefitting a monk, who can best show his obedience by the faithful transcription of established authority.'

I said, 'I will eschew the pride of original authorship, Father, and be a humble collector and recorder of the testaments of others.'

He nodded approval. 'I am keen that such a book should be particular to Byland not merely because it is composed here but also because it treats a local event. I suggest that the subject might be some local holy personage whose words are instructive and deeds exemplary, so that the book can be of interest and devotional value even to abbeys outside the shire.'

Sadly, when I set myself to examine the Abbot's proposal I was confronted with facts which he was unable to refute. The North Riding of Yorkshire, as I have already indicated, is one of the most godless tracts in Satan's world and almost entirely populated by brutish sinners. Those with any claim to virtue have been discouraged, if not corrupted, by the prevailing nastiness: the best have seen fit to undergo the ordeal of life with prayer and submissiveness in the relative safety of holy ground, avoiding the Devil rather than wrestling with him and sheltering from noteworthiness as well as from temptation. The virtuous having adopted such a low profile, I thought it best, with the rueful approval of Abbot Fabian, to make wickedness the topic for my labour, so that if I could not give an example for those who aspire to Heaven I could warn sinners with a glimpse of some of the workings of Hell.

The Fiend Sycorax was so recent a scandal that her fame and power were still current in the region and the end of the story not yet known. This both attracted me to the topic and assisted my account by providing me with many witnesses to events, from those who knew young Sukie Dobson forty years ago to children visited by nightmare at the last full moon. It is a tale that corroborates the doctrine of the Church by illustrating the urgent danger to us all from the power of Satan working through the weakness of a woman. It is also a tale typical of the age in which we live, because at this time witchcraft is as widespread and flagrant as were any of the great heresies that in past centuries challenged the diligence of the Holy Inquisition. Thousands of moonlit sabbaths are celebrated throughout Christendom every week, with obscenity and blasphemy. Countless respectable country wives are versed in the witch's lore of herbs, use love-charms and potions, and at night put out little bowls of cream for the ancient demons that visit their sleep. Even as I write this account there is news of a witch in armour leading the armies of France to victory against our English forces, with the approval not merely of the French soldiery but of the Dauphin of France and his court and even of many French churchmen that have sold themselves to Satan and taken the side of the French. It seems that in Satan's world great nonchalance is being shown towards both God and Satan!

These grand matters of state may seem a far cry from Sukie Trothers and the plight of Slatterdale, but our wisdom, as well as our destiny, must begin at home. It is essential that we use what we know best to inform ourselves and each other of the dangers, under the guidance of Mother Church and in submission to the Will of God. The case of Sycorax is a microcosm of the entire assault of Satan upon God's purpose for man. By studying this matter in the great detail available we may gain an inkling of issues otherwise too vast for our understanding, as one might augur the whole calamitous harvest from the examination of a single diseased plant. So each of us may be helped to avoid damnation and shorten our sojourn in Purgatory and the whole of Christendom may avoid the wrath of God and the great plagues which have afflicted us.

Much of the history of Sukie Trothers is no more amazing than that of any prey of Satan, but before the story is over you will read of events that are bound to strain your credulity. It may be hard for you to credit that I have rejected large quantities of spectacular and implausible material, accepting only such as was verified by several witnesses, or came from witnesses I esteem reliable, or is in accordance with proven and established authority. If my judgement in such matters should be brought into question I would ask you to remember that, though devout, I am no mystic but disposed towards reason and logic. If there is a flaw in my account it will be that I have underemphasized the miraculous and looked for mundane explanations. I also fear that in the tone of my book and my commentary on events I may sometimes shirk my duty from soft-heartedness, letting my compassion for the silly woman Sukie Trothers hinder my detestation of Satan's darling Sycorax.

When I dare to comment or interpret during the narrative that follows I trust that I do so with reference to the word of God as made manifest to me through the authority of the Church. If I err, as mortal man must, I am hopeful that my superiors will pity my simplicity and seek to correct the error rather than castigate the man.

As well as the history of Sycorax I shall relate my own adventures and suffering in pursuit of the truth. This is not from pride or the need for attention; nor does it otherwise contradict the assurances I gave Abbot Fabian about my motives. I am happy to know that another book is to be produced from this text, by another hand than mine: a properly written and illustrated volume that will reside in a library long after this present text is destroyed and my contribution forgotten. I am content if all reference to myself is removed from that official history.

It was in fact Abbot Fabian himself who suggested that I should include an account of my own experiences in the history of Sycorax. It should reassure my readers that I invent nothing, simply giving an account of what I have seen and heard: but this is not why the Abbot suggested it, as shall be seen later in this text. The third great irony, the third prong of Satan's pitchfork, is that in the course of my search for Sycorax I have myself become a witness to her story and she has become a terrible part of mine.

A Journey to the Territory of the Fiend in Slatterdale

HE ONLY PERSON in Byland Abbey who had had even indirect dealings with Sukie Trothers (née Dobson) was Brother Denys, but I hesitated to approach him, though he would have been a logical starting point for my investigations. He was an educated man and had been held high in esteem by the previous abbot, to the extent of being an obedientiary entrusted with care of the library, but he had been relieved of this post soon after the succession of Abbot Fabian twenty years ago. At that time the mortal sin of sodomy was rife in the abbey. As well as by precept and objurgation, Abbot Fabian had excised the vice by transferring or expelling some monks, eclipsing the influence of others.

Far from resenting his demotion, Brother Denys had remained one of the few monks who spoke admiringly and gratefully of Abbot Fabian, dating his own salvation from that purge. It was not therefore from diplomatic delicacy, or any suspicion that he might resent me as the eventual usurper of his librarianship, that I hesitated to approach him. The problem was that in recent years he had seen necessary to do penance by delineating his old offences in ignominious detail, not only to God in the confessional but to any who could find no means to avoid being an audience. In any case I already knew – from past exposure to his self-castigating reminiscences – that a certain Brother Simon (transferred by Abbot Fabian to Rievaulx) had been a more immediate witness to the events known to Denys and would surely be less tedious and embarrassing to interview. I decided to keep Brother Denys in reserve and commence my investigations at the birthplace of Sukie Dobson in Slatterdale.

*

My throat was dry with trepidation as I peered out through the abbey gates that April morning. In Byland we are even less reclusive than most Cistercian communities: monks frequently leave the premises, usually travelling to the sheep granges and other properties that the abbey has purchased or been bequeathed since its foundation. Occasionally my duties as librarian had provided scope for contact with other abbeys, but I had always contrived to avoid these opportunities. My sense of my own vulnerability to Satan, fully justified by the lamentable history of my youth, had ensured that I had neither budged from holy ground nor clapped eyes on a woman for sixteen years.

Riding a couple of plump white stots we took the north road from the abbey: a wagon track that skirted Sawton Moor to Helmsley Castle, where we crossed the River Rye and met the main thoroughfare through the Riding to Pickering and Scarborough. Northwards, on our left, moorland rose purple and yellow towards the Cleveland Hills, while to the south, once we had passed beyond the range of the Hambletons, there was the great plain of the Derwent stretching towards York.

I came myself from the Vale of York and had little notion of the district into which I was heading, other than that the route was one infested by outlaws as well as by the snares of the Fiend. The Abbot had given me the services of a sturdy young lay brother, John, to guide and protect me. But it was not merely the intrepid face of the lad and his weighty bludgeon that eased my anxiety. My physical and spiritual insecurity was effortlessly offset by the crisp spring day, the skylarks singing and a juvenile sense of release that was giving the commencement of my penance the semblance of a holiday.

The bulk of the day's journey was the fifteen miles of main road between Helmsley and Pickering castles. The curiosity of the children in the villages through which we passed made me think that there is not normally a lot of traffic on that road. Once we were met by a wagoner bringing baskets of salted lampreys and live lobsters for our abbey and that of Rievaulx. Once we passed a load of woollen bales heading for

Scarborough. We lunched at the roadside on the oatcakes and watered wine provided by the abbey kitchens.

I was favourably surprised by the cheerful and well-nourished appearance of such people as we saw until we came to Pickering, the aspect of whose denizens was more compatible with my notion of Satan's kingdom. The streets were infested with hard-faced thugs of both sexes and all ages. Ancient paupers brandished stumps of hands removed by leprosy or the law. Their rags revealed their sagging teats or testicles and their cold old thighs of speckled bone. Shaggy children played football with a shaggy bundle that looked like the head of a child. There were trollops with shameless eyes and a great gruff chorus of insane mirth came from an ale house in the middle of a workday afternoon.

The boldness of my early morning humour was dashed, and I found it comforting to reach the order and piety of Kirkholt Grange, one of many sheep farms owned by our abbey in the Riding. Here, five miles from Nithermoor and the mouth of Slatterdale, it had been arranged for me to spend the night.

Prior Jacobus flattered me with a cordial welcome such as one might give a visiting dignitary and at refection questioned me diligently about my purpose in Slatterdale. He also spoke at length of the horrors visited on the region by Sycorax during her supremacy and of the destruction of the force at last sent out against her: stories that were common throughout the Riding and which I shall recount later.

'Slatterdale still belongs to the Fiend Sycorax,' he said. 'It is entirely her kingdom and Satan's. There is no priest beyond Nithermoor and if any Christian souls still abide there they do so at their peril.'

It was clear that my task would involve more than one trip to the region of Slatterdale – which would be preferable to spending an extended period outside my abbey – and I had decided to proceed as far as possible chronologically, beginning by gathering information about the family and youth of Sukie Trothers. Prior Jacobus was unable to give me any information on this but advised me to journey to Nithermoor and make enquiries there. He also proposed that I take a lay brother with me: not John, who was off back to Byland in the morning, but Colin, a native of Slatterdale, who would be useful both as a guide and a translator of the local dialect which the Prior declared unintelligible.

I was given lodging in a guest room rather than the dormitory. This permitted a sense of my importance – or at least the importance of my mission – to mingle agreeably with the permissible alleviation of the monastic rule and the exhilaration of travel which had survived both the unpleasantness of Pickering and the reiteration of the terrible legend of Sycorax. It was only when I had settled seriously to prayer that I was able to become sufficiently sober and humble to remember my shame and penitent's purpose, abjuring both vainglory and the cheating comeliness to be found here and there in Satan's realm. In particular I chided myself and prayed God's mercy because of the feral eyes of a Pickering wench that had looked back at me over her shoulder. That done, I went to bed and sank at once into a sweet and dreamless sleep such as was rarely vouchsafed me in the abbey.

Colin had no horse but led my stot by the bridle or walked beside me. Neither did he have a cudgel, and he was a skinny little fellow who looked as if he would be able to offer me very little protection against robbers and other menaces. He did, though, beguile our climb into the hills with chatter that I found informative:

'I aren't a lay brother, rightly speaking, Feyther, just a shepherd what works for bread and bed. And I aren't a Slatterdale lad, I aren't one o' yon sheep-shaggers. I'm from Nithermoor, sithee. But these times Nithermoor's full o' yon Slatterdale lot what run from t'witch while half proper Nithermoor folk've buggered off. Aye, there's nowt in t'dale now, nobody at Beck Gap, not a shepherd. There's not a sheep in Slatterdale beyond t'Nithermoor pastures. It don't bother me, though, coming back up Nithermoor, for I were nobbut a bairn when there were all that flapdoodle wi' t'witch. I've cousins up yonder yet, but most of us family buggered off along wi' t'others.'

Nithermoor crouched at the junction of Slatterdale Beck and Pickering Beck, where the track came out of Slatterdale to join the ancient ridgeway that ran northwards over a moorland wilderness to Whitby. It was an untidy village of mud and wattle dwellings, swarming with pigs and scabby dogs. The clothes of the humans seemed made of dung and their skins were grey as drudgery. It was clear that to people of Nithermoor Pickering would represent a glittering metropolis full of savants and modish sophisticates.

Colin pointed at a hovel that looked no more inviting than the others, though a garland on a stake outside proclaimed an ale house. 'The grub there's famous grand and what's more it run by us cousin, so thoo's sure to be safe and welcome.'

Though I had taken only wine sops for breakfast I proposed that we push on into Slatterdale, approximately four miles to the hamlet of Beck Gap where Sukie Trothers was born and grew up. I felt it was logically where I should begin my investigations, even if there was nothing left to see there. I also had an impulse to invade the territory of Sycorax while my spirits were high and the sky bright. And a large part of my motive was to stay in the open air for the time being, rather than commit myself to the stinking interior of a Nithermoor hovel.

I regretted my decision as we climbed alongside the beck, between the moors and forest. For Slatterdale was an eery and discomfiting spot even then, fifteen years after the catastrophe. Across the beck in the royal forest were many acres of black and palsied trees, evidence of the great fire that had accompanied the other horrors. A sheet of cloud like grey metal had covered the sun as we came into the dale. The track was strangled with gorse and bramble, so that it was clear that nobody ever passed that way: there were not even sheep tracks in the swart tangle of the moorland slopes. A hawk hung in the sky and other birds were silent.

Most dispiriting of all was the change in Colin, who was supposed to be unbothered by Slatterdale, yet whose jaw had dropped and eyes boggled when I proposed venturing beyond Nithermoor. The garrulous, chirpy lad of the morning now slunk silently alongside like a dog with its tail tucked into its haunches. He no longer led me by the bridle, since I needed to manoeuvre my steed through the obstacles on the climbing track, but he either kept hold of my stirrup or scampered to join me whenever I left him, all the while looking fearfully at the looming moor, the stricken forest, the iron sky.

I was conscious that I represented for the lad the authority and security of Holy Church, although I was well aware of my unsuitability for such a role. Not only was it impossible for me to permit a retreat until we had reached Beck Gap which I had declared the object of our foray: I felt it my duty to seem blithe and exude a trust in heavenly protection which I was far from feeling. Remembering the tales of what Satan and Sycorax had done to those worthier and more confident, I fervently repeated prayers inside my head and was not sorry when we arrived at Beck Gap, although it was a source of further perturbation.

It was a hamlet of three dozen wattle huts, ruined and empty. The dilapidation seemed worse than you would expect from fifteen years of no tending and various weather. And there were items – a rusty ploughshare, a child's hobbyhorse, the skeleton of a pig in a sty – suggestive of a place made bleak by pestilence rather than orderly migration. Most disturbing of all was an iron crucifix that had been wrenched from the stone shrine over the drinking trough at the entry to the hamlet.

Colin flushed and started as I raised the cross and propped it on its plinth. I could see he regarded my act as an impudent challenge to the resident powers of evil.

'Heyoop, Feyther . . .'

His voice died in a croak. He had given up all pretence at composure and was clearly on the point of taking to his heels. His fear communicated itself to the horse he had held for me to dismount, which shifted, let out a snort and rolled its eyes. It also affected me, so that I was glad to have the excuse to retreat out of consideration for the lad. Not for anything would I have investigated the interior of any of the huts in Beck Gap.

As we wound back down the dale I praised his fear of fiends as being wise and well justified but instructed him to try to temper it with a little more trust in the power and mercy of Christ and His Saints. He listened to me only fitfully, looking back fearfully from time to time as if he was aware that we were being followed. Disdaining to either follow his example or question him about it, I could only hope that each time he looked round he saw nothing.

The Ale Wife Alys and the Beginning
of the Investigation

ITHERMOOR SEEMED ALMOST welcoming. Colin's spirits revived immediately we were out of the dale, and this time I was less inclined to shrink from his suggestion that we dine at the hut under the ale stake. Colin wanted us to use the tavern as the base for our enquiries and proposed that we slept there, but I was determined to return for the night to the secure, austere comfort of Kirkholt Grange. I was also minded to introduce myself as soon as possible to the parson of Nithermoor, with a view to using his modest chapel as my interview room and headquarters. All the same, for want of an alternative, I agreed to try Colin's cousin's fare.

This led to a number of pleasant surprises, such as the day had so far shown little sign of providing. The first was that the interior of the tavern, a two-bay cottage constructed on three pairs of crucks, was both unexpectedly roomy and cunningly ventilated, the smoke from the central fireplace going straight to the roof hole and swirling out round the cowl of thatch. It had also been swept clean and carpeted with fresh straw; the only stink was from the piggery at the back which also served as latrine, and it was a subtle stink this cool spring day, compared to most peasant dwellings. Another agreeable surprise was that unlike the ale house in Pickering this was empty in mid-afternoon; our meal was taken in privacy but for a fat dog, a pregnant cat and an old codger eking out a stick of ale.

The food was what the ale wife and her family would eat later in the afternoon: mutton porridge with turnips and wastel bread. Perfect in quality and generous in quantity, washed down with potent creamy ale, it would have featured as the most pleasant and surprising aspect of Nithermoor had it not been for the ale wife herself, Colin's cousin, Alys.

I was apprehensive about speaking to a woman: for sixteen years, since my entry into Byland, they had existed for me only as the lubricious goblins of my involuntary reveries. I had striven to erase them from my spirit, or to focus on those models of womanhood that served as a corrective to my awareness: Rosamund Mowbray, who was awesome and exclusive as a monstrance; my mother, whose tearful tenderness used to balm the bruises of my father's wrath.

Alys was a limber woman with the grace of a fairground dancer or acrobat. She was wearing no kerchief and her brown hair was cut short in peasant fashion: this seemed to emphasize her fine throat and the elegant poise of her head. Her skirts were mired and her apron stained, yet among the muddy squalor of Nithermoor she was fresh and vivid, with her deep-grey eyes and sanguine lips, like the only coloured item on an unfinished picture. Her attractiveness was further enhanced by the sway of her hips and the set of her shoulders, the swag of her perfect breasts and the way her dress and apron seemed draped, as if on statuary, to coyly indicate her belly, buttocks and thighs. She had a baby swaddled in wool which she dandled on her arm, or laid in a crib in a curtained recess, or suckled behind the curtain if it wailed. Once she came away from this mission displaying a lovely naked shoulder as she adjusted her dress a little too late for absolute modesty.

I questioned her during the meal and afterwards while Colin was gone at her suggestion to round up various Slatterdale ancients that were to testify to me. She was wed to Jackin, who was working the field strips on Long Acre with her father. The family slept in a separate building, snug in winter above the manger. 'Me mam minds our hut an' pigs an' chucks an' whatnot.' Jackin's father was farrier on the manor farm, and his family also had sizeable field strips and flocks on the common, so it was a lucrative marriage all round. 'But me and Jack dunnut give a fart for that, we're fair capped wi' one another an' that's a fact.' She thought she maybe had the easiest job in the family. 'Pourin' ale and gobbin' wi' folks is softest work in our hut, though oftentimes I'm still toilin' when t'others of us is abed, way after curfew, selling sticks of ale to silly buggers what've no 'ome to go.'

Her physical attractiveness was complemented by her manner, which was a delightful blend of the sprightliness suitable to an ale wife and the show of modesty befitting a wife and mother. She spoke freely and pleasantly to me, as to a friend and equal, but without impertinence. She greeted pleasantries with a deep, mischievous chuckle and was merry and droll of speech from time to time but without any of the coarse persiflage that often seems compulsory among the churls.

I asked her if she was a good woman that went devoutly to pray and confess. Then she shocked me by announcing frankly, even mirthfully, that she went to church when she must but otherwise left religion to those with more wisdom and leisure than she had. I concluded that she had fallen into neglectful error and was remonstrating gently with her on the topic when Colin arrived with the first clutch of informants.

Our trip up to Beck Gap had put Colin in considerable awe of me and made him eager to assist my enterprise. Not only had he brought me several elders of a village that seemed to have more than its share (life-expectancy in Yorkshire is not high) but he had made arrangements for other witnesses to come along as they finished work that evening. This had the effect of countermanding some of my decisions, since the ale house had become my base and I was to be interviewing until after sunset, making a return to Kirkholt Grange impracticable. Which was clearly to Colin's liking: when he was not acting as my usher and interpreter (the Slatterdale dialect was not as grave a problem as Prior Jacobus had foretold) he drank and chatted with Alys; the cousins got on well together on a level of affectionate flippancy and he evidently had a taste for the ale she purveyed.

I drank several cups of ale myself, grateful that Abbot Fabian had provided me with a purse of pennies for my provisioning. I had to confess that the ale house had considerable advantages over the church as a base for my project. For one thing it attracted more informants, since Colin had let it be known they would be rewarded with a stick of ale after the interview. Furthermore, the presence of Alys had modified my attitude to Nithermoor, and I was no longer horrified at the prospect of spending the night there. My main regret was that I did not have the chance to communicate with her or even observe her as much as I would have liked, occupied as I was with my informants.

They took their place in turn, at Colin's bidding, opposite me at the table that contained my writing materials and, later in the evening, the lanthorn that furnished the only source of light in the ale house interior. Rather than try to write what I was told I used a system of mnemonic scribbles, trusting in the strength and order of my memory. I had made it clear via Colin that I wanted, on this occasion, only information about the early years of Sukie Trothers – everybody in Pickering and Slatterdale was eager to deluge me with stories, mostly hearsay, of the miraculous and terrible events of her later years. I was also careful to reward each regardless of the quantity or quality of their information: others, sitting on a bench or standing in the shadows, were listening as they waited to testify and I did not want the prospect of reward to influence what they said.

Most of their testimony was dross. Some, influenced by later events, emphasized the weirdness of the child Sukie, even recounting credulous examples of her supernatural powers, small precursors of her malevolence. Others who spoke of her as a quiet, unremarkable lass were more credible but so bland and vague as to be without interest. From both these factions I gathered and verified some basic facts: Sukie Dobson was born at Beck Gap half a century ago, the third of seven surviving children of impoverished peasants. She grew into a sour, lanky girl with brown hair and green eyes who was not seen much in Beck Gap because she mostly lived as a shepherdess on the ridings. Taking to witchcraft young, she was still a teenager when she first came to the notice of the authorities. Tom and Ibbie Dobson, her parents, were now dead. Her brothers and sisters were either dead or had disappeared from the Slatterdale region, with one exception.

Trissie March, a tall, angular woman, was Sukie's sister, two years younger. She claimed to be ashamed of the association but spoke with a relish that made one suspect she revelled in the notoriety of her sister and the attention it bestowed. Her testimony fell between the two poles I have described and seems entirely credible: neither proposing any miraculous or spectacular behaviour, nor claiming that Sukie was a conventional, undisturbing child.

'Yon were allus weird, like – traipsin' about wi' a gormless gob or perchin' up trees an' rockin' and croonin'. Mam allus reckoned yon were daft as 'er granny.' Trissie had not liked Sukie much and assumed this was reciprocated. 'Yon were gruff if she opened 'er gob at all. She kept on 'er tod but'd allus have a mutt or a mog for a pet. She'd stroke toads an' poison snakes an' bumbledores. Onetime she fixed smashed wing of t'barn owl wi' t'wooden slat and nursed t'bugger till it were fit to fly. She got on wi' none on us kin but t'owd granny as she took after in name and nature.'

Granny Sukie, though seemingly free from Satan in her youth, had become the local doctor and weather forecaster, regarded by the peasants with a mixture of respect and disapproval. 'She were summat to see an' all, wrinkled as if she were pickled, an' 'er toothless chops an' 'er blind white eye.' Ibbie Dobson, who submitted at least in principle to the doctrine of the Holy Church, hated her mother and was embarrassed by her. She had kept to family tradition by naming a daughter after her mother, then was appalled when the child became adoring of the grandmother and obsessed by her heathen lore. There was constant strife among the females of the Dobson family, with the two Sukies, each in her own way, too tough for Ibbie to handle. Even though domestic power had shifted down a generation old Sukie still had the hex on her daughter. 'T'owd granny could allus put shits up

Mam just by t'squinny of her good eye.' Young Sukie was sullen, disobedient and reckless of punishment. Ibbie got no support from Tom. 'Dad were owd easiful, a sot what believed in nowt and saw 'arm in nowt.'

Dobson family life was further embittered by brother Ellis, a year older than Sukie. 'We all on us favoured, folk allus said, wi' us long necks an' shaggy locks.' Ellis devoted a lot of his energy to making his sisters miserable: snatching their titbits and gobbling them down, breaking their playthings and tossing them into the beck, kicking and gouging, groping and jeering. Yet the lasses neither formed an alliance against him nor complained to their mother. 'Yon Sukie wanted nowt to do wi' none on us an' Ellis made me believe he'd do murder if I told.'

Eventually, expensively, Ibbie won the domestic war. 'Mam wouldn't face thoo down, sithee, but were a schemer and sulk what never let go of a grudge. Both yon Sukies went to tend muttons on t'top moor or river riding. They wintered up yonder in t'low 'ut and never saw much of us till t'owd granny were borne down for burial. After that Sukie went back up dale on 'er tod, where it were 'er notion of 'eaven, sithee, wi' mutts and mogs and muttons around 'er instead of 'er own kind. As for me I were glad to be shot of 'er, but I'd of sooner it were Ellis, for after she'd buggered off 'e'd only me to torment.'

Trissie used to be sent to provision Sukie once a fortnight: relieving her so that she could spend two nights at home, go to church and be shriven. 'It were grand to get off from Ellis but I were shit scared up there in t'dark wi' Sukie's fuckin' mutts whimpering for 'er all night through.' Ibbie confessed to Trissie now and then that her conscience troubled her that her daughter, who had taken so young to her grandmother's impermissible eccentricities, was now living godless and alone in the wilds. 'Yet it were plain enough Mam didn't want the bitch-bag back in Beck Gap.' After a while Ibbie was able to console herself with the fact that Sukie had a boyfriend – Gib, the Nithermoor miller's lad, who visited her in her solitude – and there was every prospect that she would get pregnant soon. Marriage and childbearing might knuckle her down to obedience and piety.

Gib the miller, bald and fat, a regular toper at the ale house, was brought to my table by Colin just as I thought I had nobody left to interview. He spoke of his long-ago summer affair with Sukie Dobson without any of the shame and horror expressed by Trissie March, but in a matter-of-fact way, with the candid aplomb a fellow will use in a tavern when describing his business to another.

'We first paired off at ewe lettings wake when her cousin Joan went wi' t'brother, Dodge. It were Dodge wi' t'sly eyes as lasses fancied, afore t'owd sow killed him, but Sukie an' me made up foursome.'

Once a week Gib delivered a sack of milled barley for the pigs of Beck Gap; then he would climb the dale on his mule, leave it tethered at Stonecross Nab and run a mile down the riding to Sukie. He usually took her a gift: she preferred something practical like a knife or a rabbit pie. They fornicated in the bracken if the weather was fine, or if it was raining they went into the drystone hut that Sukie used as living quarters. On alternate Sundays, when Sukie stayed on the ridings, Gib did the whole journey of seven miles on foot.

Sukie was a difficult lover, he said, then seemed stumped when I asked for examples of this. But he was merely summoning his memories into order.

She was weird and disconcerting: would laugh suddenly in the middle of nothing or unaccountably weep when everything seemed well. She talked to herself unashamedly even when not alone – 'Sod it, Sukie lass, what's to be done with um?' – and often spoke of herself in the third person – 'Sukie baint too capped wi' yon.'

More serious were her wild and unpredictable swings of mood. She would be fond and limp and lavish with endearments, then suddenly turn on Gib viciously, jeering at his stupidity and his appearance. 'I were a plump, pink lad as she said put 'er in mind of a scrubbed pig.

She'd reckon she were more in love wi' Fart – as were 'er name for yon big black dog she kept.' She would fondle the creature's thick pelt and let him slobber his tongue on to her face and hands, while she informed Gib how much handsomer the dog was, how much more intelligent, deep and trusty than her human lover.

She could also be maliciously, unamusingly playful, flexing her quicker wits at the expense of a lover who bored her. Some of it was mere teasing mischief: asking him how far it was to Normanby, a place of her invention, knowing he would venture a guess rather than admit ignorance. Some was heavier stuff: telling him she was pregnant and would kill herself, then laughing at his distress. 'I should of give 'er some knuckle to learn 'er respect, but I were too gentle-natured for us own good them days.'

Gib had three brothers and no sisters. He knew little about girls and assumed they were all more or less as weird as Sukie, until he got a whiff of what others said about his Slatterdale shepherdess. 'Everybody but me knew she were 'alf daft.' Then he became embarrassed about the trysts and kept them as secret as he could, but neither this shame nor her exasperating behaviour were enough to get him to break off the relationship until their copulation grew increasingly unsatisfactory.

He was evasive on this last topic, almost certainly because I was a monk and he felt that frankness would be indelicate and disrespectful to my cloth. 'When all went well yon were a sprightly lass but a touch over-eager and off-putting, sithee. If owt were amiss she were bloody impossible.' I gathered that their temperamental incompatibility had been fatal to their carnal function. This baffled me, because Gib, as he described himself, sounded very like the sort of young sinner that I had been. I had never had the slightest difficulty in fornicating with wenches I scorned in the depths of my soul and who for all I know fully reciprocated this contempt.

He had not seen Sukie for six months when he heard of her arrest. By the time she came out of gaol the Nithermoor mill had given up deliveries of barley to Beck Gap. Gib rarely went up the dale, never saw

Sukie again. Thirty-five years later he seemed able to disassociate her from the terrible figure of Sycorax and think of her with rueful humour, wistful for the sinful folly of youth. 'She were mostly a fair to middling shag, saving your reverence, Feyther, but as awkward, wilful and contrary a lass as it were impossible to abide. Yet she could be gentle, too. She'd tell me 'er dreams, sithee, stuff about flying on Fart with 'is fur between 'er thighs, over the treetops and thousands of rivers. Daft. We was daft and young up yonder among the bracken and woollybacks. It makes me wishful now. It's queer to think that she's a famous witch and I'm a fat old codger dribbling ale.'

I intended to remonstrate with Gib the miller over what I discerned as a heedless stance towards sins which would put him in danger of damnation unless properly repented and pardoned. But before I could summon my eloquence I discovered that he had quaffed what was left of his drink and gone, apparently without taking advantage of the free stick of ale which was his reward.

During the evening Alys's family had installed themselves at the next table: her husband Jackin, a blackavized, quiet lad and her more garrulous parents who were grey, wizened and grimy like the bulk of Nithermoor. As they ate their porridge pudding, which contained considerably less mutton than had been served to me, they had taken a lively interest in the interviews I was conducting, to the extent of interrupting (though they were not Beck Gap folk) with titbits about Sukie's later, more spectacular career. Colin had protected me: 'Feyther Edmund wants to put it in his noggin a morsel at a time', which was quite a pithy summary of what I had explained to him earlier. While consuming a second meal of mutton and turnips (which I declined) he distracted the family from my activities with an account of our trip to Beck Gap that day, putting emphasis on my daring – in particular my heroic replacement of the crucifix – so that I was gratified to see all of them, especially Alys, regarding me with fresh esteem.

Then the baby had been brought out to be passed among them and became the focus of attention. But now they were vanished, Colin, baby and all, as abruptly as Gib the miller. The pots had been cleared from their table. Alys, as fresh and amicable as she had been all day, was chatting with two craggy old churls who were her remaining customers.

These sudden developments informed me that I had drunk too much of Alys's potent ale during the afternoon and evening, not keeping a sufficiently wary count while my attention was focused on my informants. It was now after curfew time, but my lanthorn still blazed and the door was wide – the law was clearly not enforced in Nithermoor. The lamp's light fell candid on to the page before me where I had inscribed, in the course of my interview with Gib the miller, a series of ornate squiggles which I would never begin to understand.

I carefully stuck my quill, at the second or third attempt, into the inkpot and rose clumsily to my feet, my calves making the bench topple behind me. Alys came over and put a tactful hand under my elbow. She was proficient at handling drunks.

'Coom, Feyther.'

'Brother. Call me Brother Edmund.'

I left the writing materials on the table and allowed her to guide and support me into the adjacent dwelling, aware of her soft warmth through the drunken blur. She must have left her customers in darkness, for she lit me with the lanthorn past a platform strewn with sleepers to a curtained recess that was the counterpart of where the baby had been kept in the ale house. My saddle bag was there and a clean straw pallet.

'Sweet dreams, Feyther.'

To my shame I caught hold of her hand. It was calm and strong.

'Alys,' I murmured. 'You're a lovely princess prisoned here among these muddy churls.'

She disengaged her fingers and gave the contralto chuckle that was characteristic. 'Don't mind me, Feyther. I'm nobbut made of t'same shit and piss as t'others.' Then she was gone and I was in darkness.

*

Despite my sixteen years in Byland, I remembered enough of the lasses I swived in my youth to recognize that Alys was as superior to them in all respects as my own attitude was improved. For I was able to almost entirely discount the lascivious aspect of her attractiveness and to respond to her beauty as one might to the loveliness of a child or the blue-robed statue of Our Lady in the abbey chapel. I was of course aware that to be susceptible to any earthly beauty is to make oneself vulnerable to Satan, yet could not think my feelings towards Alys more culpable than, for example, Abbot Fabian's delight in the monastery garden in summer. If there was an amorous tinge to my admiration, it was not the carnal lust I once felt for such as Malkin or Luce but more like the pure and fervent emotion I used to experience at the thought of unattainable Rosamund Mowbray, daughter of the Lord of Strensall. Alys the ale wife was a vulgar slattern compared to regal Rosamund, but from the point of view of a devout monk she was as remote as any troubadour's paradigm. I was also reassured by the fact that she was a feeding mother, a condition proverbially unattractive to the lubricious male. All the same I resolved to discuss the matter with Abbot Fabian when I made my confession.

Then, as I remembered Abbot Fabian, contrition hit me like a thunderclap. God's mercy and the Blood and Agony of His Son on the Cross made me sober. I fell to my knees, knowing I would not sleep until I had prayed, reflected, repented, submitted my spirit to the will of my Maker as well as I could without the guidance of a superior. I realized that I had followed no observances all day since Prime at Kirkholt Grange. Abbot Fabian had absolved me of the stricter monastic observances, in so far as I found it necessary to neglect them in pursuit of our project, but I was horrified by the ease with which I had sloughed away the pious habits of sixteen years: failing to experience the slightest memory of the bells that call to devotion at the appointed hours. This forgetfulness seemed much more terrible than my innocent dalliance with Alys, or the tipsiness which was a popular transgression among the monks of Byland.

When I left my monastic refuge at the bidding of my Abbot to seek out Sycorax and use her for our devout purpose, the mission was more perilous than either I or Abbot Fabian realized. While I was invading the territory of Sycorax, she was invading my soul. Only two days away from the rule of the abbey, I was no longer recoiling in horror from the ugly profanity of the Riding. I was behaving as uncharacteristically as if I had been bewitched: neglecting my devotions, drinking to excess and being over-attentive to the enticements of a daughter of Eve.

The Young Gentleman and the Shepherdess

ABBOT FABIAN LISTED my transgressions in a different order of seriousness, not sharing the relaxed view of my encounter with Alys which I strove to justify.

'I am guilty of failure, Brother Edmund, if you are still naïvely given to admiration of the lewder sex, after sixteen years of God's grace in the abbey and tormented strife, under my particular and partial tutelage, against the advent of filthy apparitions. When I came to authority here the beastly sin of sodomy was rife – as a consequence I have been too lenient with more natural sinners such as yourself, who wallow in foul flesh no less than the sodomites but prefer to spill your sin into the dank den ordained for procreation.

'It was thought by the ancients such as Plato the Greek that women were fallen or failed males: those men who failed to attain in the higher life – the cowardly and those who lived badly – returning to the world as women. They are more lustful than men, according to Hippocrates of Cos, because of the loose and porous quality of their flesh and they suffer from uterine suffocation if they do not have intercourse or masturbate. Isidore of Seville derives the word *femina* from *fiery* – denoting lustfulness – and has observed that the elephant is without sexual desire until the female picks mandrake and shares it with the male: an emblem of Eve's implication in original sin. Albertus Magnus goes so far as to say that every woman should be avoided like a poisonous snake or horned devil.

'I should not have to instruct you that for a man of God who has forsworn Satan's world it is no more permissible to seek carnal gratification with women than with men. In fact it is feasible that a man may more easily (thus perhaps more excusably) fall into error with another man; for there are many legitimate sympathies and interests – physical, intellectual and aesthetic pursuits – which can bring man to intimacy with man, whereas the only attraction of woman, apart from her breeding function, is as a receptacle for ignominious lust.'

The long rivalry between the abbeys of Byland and Rievaulx, recently exacerbated both by grazing disputes and differences of doctrine, was a hindrance when Abbot Fabian asked permission of Bernard of Rievaulx for me to visit there and gather information (mostly from Brother Simon who had once been a Byland monk). Abbot Bernard replied that he disapproved of what he understood to be our project, deeming it impious, dangerous and incompatible with the Cistercian rule. He also declared himself in sympathy with Brother Simon's wish to utterly shun the sins and sorrows of the past and be born anew within the Church.

The account which immediately follows is therefore that of Brother Denys of Byland, uncorroborated by Simon of Rievaulx. Originating in confessions made by Simon to Denys when the latter was chaplain on the Dorsay demesne, it is also based on later discussions when the monks were at Byland, before Simon's transfer. The fact that there is more detail than in some of the other information I have gathered about Sycorax is partly due to the degree of access I have had to this informant, but also to Brother Denys's predilection (already mentioned) for morbid detail both in personal confession and general reminiscence. I cannot speculate how authentic these details may be or how far even basic facts have been distorted in their transmission.

It was the third time that Simon had defied the interdiction and ridden out alone across the ridgeway, beyond the parkland limits, so it was proper that calamity should have befallen him, because three was a fatal number. There were three in the Trinity, three crosses on Golgotha, three prongs on Satan's pitchfork. Simon had a private devotional habit which he thought was original, of counting threes and multiples of three: when praying, chewing, drinking, scratching his head, pacing in an enclosed area . . . He sought the number for spiritual purposes and avoided it in any carnal context. From his experience he had amassed a convincing number of instances of third events proving crucial and had forgotten or ignored the times when chance had let another number be decisive. That retribution was now following the third offence was confirmation that nothing was accidental: the most humdrum happenings were blows and manoeuvres in the battle for Simon's soul between the Prince of This World and the King of Heaven.

Simon could see a sheet of bright unbroken orange. A horizontal line, like a scratch on ice, was intermittently visible, fading and looming to the pulse of a noise like a distant multitude at prayer. Gradually the line became stable and permanent. The upper edge spread like liquid into the blue shape of ferns against an orange sky. The background noise was the sound of many insects.

Lifting his eyelids he saw the scene in detail and naturalistic colours. He was descending a pathless slope through a grove of bracken. The ancient plants were above head height, so that nothing could be seen but ferns and sky. Simon moved warily, limping crab-wise, parting the foliage with his left hand and treading down the stems with his left foot. He did not want another accident. His right hand held the reins that made the horse grudgingly follow him. Rabican was wincing and snorting and dipping in three-footed progress, holding his right forefoot in the air.

The tumble had injured Simon less than the horse: the lad had twisted his knee, bruised his head and loosened a couple of teeth. He could taste blood. The wide sleeve of his jacket was ripped and blood had seeped through the left knee of his woollen hose. But these physical consequences were unimportant compared to the chagrin and anxiety that was overwhelming him.

He could probably avoid a thrashing if he lied. He could say the horse had been startled by something – a boar or a wild dog that had wandered through the pale into the park – and had bolted with its helpless rider far into the shirelands. Rabican's nervous, headlong nature would make this story feasible, as would Simon's character and reputation: as poor a horseman as he was an unlikely delinquent.

Simon had never been seriously thrashed. Richard Dorsay kept a length of plaited rope with which he intimidated his wife, children, servants and animals, but it was employed almost exclusively on his elder son Roger and almost as a token of respect. Simon was perceived by Richard and others in contrast to Roger, pensive and fastidious and suitable for the Church.

He stopped and turned, aware of the horse's discomfort. Holding his palm under the quivering muzzle he patted the white blaze on the animal's forehead. Rabican rolled a reproachful eye at the boy.

Setting off again, Simon felt his heart gripped with panic. A few minutes ago he had been galloping along like an armoured paladin, raised above the earth and immune from its threats and demands. Now he was lost with a lame horse, groping blind through the enclosing menace of bracken, feeling distinctly vulnerable with only a dagger for defence. There were bandits in the shirelands who would murder for much less than Rabican's expensive trappings and Simon's well-woven clothes.

And there were demons everywhere. He had heard the local stories of the giant bird, the black wolf, the serpent with eyes of blood. Brother Denys had instructed him in more orthodox doctrine that was every bit as alarming: away from the altar and pious hearth the world was Satan's. You had to ride through it briskly and do penance if its beauty beguiled you. At all events you must not tumble in the midst of it and leave yourself at its mercy.

The bracken was an ideal place for an ambush, secular or satanic. Simon was relieved to emerge into a field of meadow-grass that sloped down to a modest river. He assumed it was the Slatterdale Beck that bordered the Dorsay demesne on the west, but he did not know this place. Trees ran along the beck and the opposite slope was mostly woodland. There were several dozen sheep in the field, munching the grass and looking tranced by plenitude. Butterflies, meadow blues and brimstones and fritillaries, swooped and staggered. The insect noise diminished as soon as he was out of the ferns, and he could hear birdsong. The sheep were silent.

But these background details made little impression, because there was something in the foreground to cause Simon's relief to turn to instant terror. The black wolf was before him, as if the mental act of remembering its existence had evoked the Fiend. Standing massive six yards from the sudden edge of the bracken, it had been listening to Simon's approach and awaiting his appearance. It was black all over except for the teeth and lolling tongue and golden eyes. It let out just one deep and truculent WOOF then remained supernaturally still and silent, more like a cat than a dog, ready to pounce if Simon either advanced or fled.

Rabican swayed back and snorted with terror, hopping sideways on his good forefoot and almost wrenching the reins from Simon's hand. Simon put his other hand on the hilt of his dagger without it giving him a lot of confidence. He stood like the black wolf, frozen, incapable of movement in case it should precipitate an attack.

Then a piercing whistle like the screech of a hungry goblin crossed the meadow. A girl was perched up on the drystone wall of a sheepfold, her arms around the triangle formed by her raised knees, her face turned over her shoulder to witness the events on the edge of the bracken. She whistled again then called out in a clear, cool voice:

'Hee, Fart!'

She got down from the wall. The dog bounded to her and writhed around her sycophantically without presuming to touch her. It was joined in this by a smaller dog, a sheepdog that had appeared from somewhere and caught the excitement, yapping. Ignoring them both she climbed the slope to confront Simon.

'Now, little master. Are thoo a sprite?'

He stared at her stupidly. She was not a notably pretty lass. Her long neck and upright stance, as she stood directly confronting him with shoulders square and feet apart, combined with the interrogative tilt of her eyebrows, gave her the look of a predatory bird. Lank brown hair fell on to her shoulders. The woollen dress she wore, exactly the same shade of grey as the sheep, left her shins and forearms bare and was belted with string.

'Are thoo a sprite?' she asked again. 'An elf-lord, hm?'

Now that he understood her question he was baffled by it. He knew that many peasants had blasphemous pagan beliefs. To an ignorant shepherdess his appearance – his neat, slight form and pretty face and silky blond hair, the fine cloth of his garments and the splendour of his steed and its caparison – might be exotic enough to suggest the supernatural. What was baffling and shocking was her obvious lack of fear, or even abashment, in the presence of what she seemed to believe might be a fairy – a sort of demon. Her demeanour was perky and challenging.

Another source of bafflement was that she did not know him. Simon did not remember having seen her before: there were a lot of peasant girls on his father's demesne, whom Simon only saw when they came to church concealed in their Sunday hoods. But it was amazing that she should not know him – or Rabican, for that matter.

'Or are thoo a castle lordling come to shag poor shitty Sukie?'

There was mirth in her green eyes and he understood at last that she was being flippant and ironical. He failed to summon a retort and she went past him to where the horse stood shivering. Rabican did not protest as she ran her hands around the injured fetlock, squatting down to examine it. Simon saw how her hips and buttocks distended the grey sheath of the dress.

'Sprent it fettle,' she announced, rising. 'Shift yon clobber off ov 'im.'

Then she strode off purposefully towards the stream. The dogs went with her: the sheepdog, sober again, beside her, the wolf-dog bounding off and returning and flourishing the black banner of its tail.

Simon intended to go after her, or order her to come back to him, but her authority was so casual and absolute and his own morale so chastened by calamity that he finished up following her instructions.

He removed Rabican's saddle, keeping an eye on the girl as he did so until she had disappeared among the stream-bank foliage. He did not remove the bridle and reins because he wanted to keep control of the animal. Taking off his own coat he sat on the saddle with the reins in his fist and waited, among the heat and birdsong and chombling sheep and pestering insects, assuming the shepherdess had gone to fetch help.

Since puberty Simon had seen little of his mother, who spent much of her time sewing and spinning, enclosed with a couple of female attendants. Richard Dorsay was of the fine old school of fatherhood who thought male children should have little to do with the cissyfying influence of womenfolk. While his daughters were instructed in the female virtue of submissive industry, the boys not at school or farmed out into some grander household were taught valour and chivalry by Richard and religion by the chaplain. In the case of Simon, Richard thought little of the boy's propensity for proper manhood and surrendered him to the priest.

Simon's education about women had therefore come from the opposing schools represented by his brother Roger and the chaplain. Roger was two years older than Simon. He said that young, nubile women could be rated well above mutts and dobbins as entertaining company. They had tits you could squeeze and other attributes that made your pisser stiff. They had wet, hairy holes between their legs that you could put your pisser in to sin. Whatever they said, they always wanted you to fuck them. In any case if you kept to the Dorsay demesne no woman in her right mind would turn you down. Violence was usually optional. Of course fucking was a sin that would have to be confessed sooner or later. The trick was not to die unconfessed or unshriven, or you went to Hell.

Brother Denys strove to instruct Simon that Roger's doctrine was dangerously permissive. He promulgated Augustine's principle: that a lover of God must hate the world and vice versa. Life was an obstacle course full of shafts to Hell, through which one stepped gingerly and queasily towards Heaven. Sex was only permissible as a means of producing further members of the species in accordance with God's purpose. Lechery was a serious sin and pitfall, like any other pleasure – gluttony, for instance – derived from the necessities of phenomenal existence.

Sukie had not brought help when she returned with her dog attendants, sauntering up from the beck with what Simon judged to be insolent sloth. Her legs were now bare to the thigh, since she was carrying something parcelled up in the skirt of her dress. She ignored Simon, going straight to Rabican, who was still a plangent tripod balanced at the edge of the ferns.

'Hee, Dobbin! Squet!' she uttered.

She put one hand to the horse's muzzle and tapped it behind the shoulder with the other. This meant that the contents of her skirt were spilled on to the bracken. There was a damp patch on the wool that fell to conceal her legs.

The horse, as promptly and neatly as its injury would allow, sank on to its knees then collapsed back on to its side. Simon was amazed. Neither his father nor Piers the stableman could have worked that trick with Rabican.

'Gizzun shirt, pretty master,' she said. 'I aren't but got this frock. It all I'm clad in.' She tugged down the neck of her dress, unconstrainedly demonstrating her nakedness beneath it.

Simon just gaped at her, until her eyebrows bunched and impatience made her expression less agreeable. 'Gizzun shirt! Need cloth, see, for pudding.'

Simon took off his fine-wool shirt and handed it to her, resuming his jacket for modesty's sake. She gathered up the drenched vegetation that had dropped from her skirt and twisted it into the shirt, then wrapped and knotted the poultice tight around the horse's fetlock.

The dogs had come up on either side of her and seemed to be

watching attentively, like medical students. Simon asked her, 'What's their names?'

'Yon's Fart.' She pointed at the black wolf, then at the sheepdog. 'An' Snoozer.'

Simon kept his eyes on her instead of glancing towards the dogs. His own voice sounded unnatural to him, a tense whisper. 'How did they come by names like them?'

''Im,' she indicated Snoozer, 'got 'is when 'e were a pup. T'other I bet thoo can guess.'

She gently squeezed the poultice. 'Knit-bone, this.' She turned and knelt facing Simon, her buttocks on her heels, her knees apart. She grinned, revealing an unusually wide gap between her front teeth, then she spoke in a different tone, soft and tense as if she was mimicking him. 'Leave us dobbin, pretty master. I'll mend 'im.'

Simon averted his gaze, pointing across the meadow. 'Is yon the Slatterdale Beck?'

He knew it must be. He had not crossed the beck at any point in his expedition. And if he was still east of the beck he was still on his father's land. Which made it remarkable that this lass seemed not to know who he was.

She shook her head. 'It beck. I don't have no name for it. It only beck hereabouts.'

'My father owns this land.'

She nodded.

'You maybe know my brother Roger,' he went on.

She nodded with less enthusiasm.

'But you don't know me?'

'Aye I do. Thoo's Master Simon.'

'So you know I'm no sprite from Fairyland?'

She grinned again. 'Thoo's bonny enough for a sprite, little master.'

'It's blasphemy believing in fairies. There aren't no spirits on earth except for the angels of the Church and the fiends of Satan.'

He was talking in an attempt to normalize his voice and gain composure. At the same time he was wondering if she was crazy. Her behaviour, which would have been surprising if she had thought him a prince of Fairyland, was astonishing if she knew that he was the son of the lord of the demesne. She wouldn't have treated Roger like this, would she? The whole transaction was much more complex and disconcerting than he had gathered from his brother's anecdotes. The lass acted as if she was completely at ease with him, and now he even saw derision in her gaze.

'That's pig shit is that,' she said. 'There's trolls, oddgobblers, all sorts in Cropton Forest yonder.' She showed him an acorn that hung round her neck on a string. 'It been dunked in church font water, this, way Granny showed us.'

'Was it Granny showed you yon witch-magic?' He made a gesture towards the bandaged horse.

'It aren't magic. Knit-bone pudding. It fix it spreng.' Sukie reached out a hand. 'And sithee, thoo's rent tha jacket.'

She poked her finger into the tear until her fingertip prodded his shirtless rib and downy armpit. Then she lifted her hand towards his face. 'Soft and pink. A weeny soft piggy wi' a busted lip.' She playfully pushed up his nose with her forefinger, making a snout of it.

Simon shook his head free. He grabbed hold of the top of Sukie's dress and tugged it down, ripping the seam apart on her left shoulder. The exposed breast was paler than Sukie's arms and surprisingly large, with a brown nipple.

As she drew her eyebrows into a scowl the flippancy left her features for a moment. It was the moment when Simon felt closest to his brother's agenda. Then she gave her gap-toothed grin and with a kick of a foot and a thrust of a hand she tripped him deftly on to his back.

Snoozer gave a falsetto whine, staring anxiously from Sukie to Simon.

Fart let out a deep, truculent WOOF.

Simon saw that the golden eyes were fixed intently on him and the black fur had risen to a ridge along the animal's spine. Suddenly Fart made a little darting movement with his head and his gums snarled up to show his fangs. Simon made a noise of his own – like the yelp of a lesser and more submissive breed of dog – and cringed into the ferns.

'Hee, Fart!'

As soon as he heard her voice Fart's sable pelt subsided. He swayed his head, licked his chops, wiggled his rump and wagged his tail. He sidled to Sukie and pressed his flank against her, keeping his eyes on Simon none the less.

Simon turned on to his belly and put his face into both his hands, as if he could erase events by shutting out the light. When he felt the girl's hand on his shoulder he writhed in a petulant effort to shrug her off, without taking his face out of his hands. He could hear himself letting out a quiet keening noise, as if somebody was weeping a long way away.

'Oy!' he heard the girl say. 'Shush! See, shush, little master.'

Her fingers came again, wandering over his spine and shoulder blades. 'Sithee,' her voice said. 'Thoo's no more than a pretty weeny poppet. Pink as a piggy and boned like a bird.'

Her hand came beneath his shoulder and she lifted him round. He tried to keep his own hands over his face but she was too strong for him. 'Thoo's not like yon brother o' thine,' she said. 'Nor like my brother Ellis neither.'

She straddled him like a wrestler, pinning his wrists to the ground alongside his head. 'Thoo lie under,' she called down into his face with facetious authority. 'Grass prickles.'

He gazed up into her green eyes, hypnotized by utter humiliation. Among the noise of the insects he could hear the panting of the big black dog.

'Silly piggy,' she said. 'Try this, hm?'

The acorn dangled dancing as she leant her face down in a festoon of brown hair and put her mouth on to his, gently parting his sore lips with her tongue.

Brother Denys Betrays Secrets of the Confessional

BOTH THE CARNAL and spiritual allure of young Simon were all too evident now. The morning sunlight lay glossy on his yellow hair. His straight-backed stance as he knelt beside his confessor seemed both to aspire to purity and to invite chastisement.

' "She undid my points and lowered the front of my breeks," he said.

' "Your member was hard?" I asked him.

' "Afore she touched it, aye," he said.

'Simon was used to being questioned closely by me during confession: I had told him that penance included an unstinting admission of the offence. So Simon would doggedly describe his onanistic sins – even resorting to mime – till it was easy to picture the flushed face of the lad *in flagrante*, the jolting penis and dribbling sperm. Today he had copulation to confess and I, a thirty-six-year-old virgin, listened with unambivalent revulsion.

' "Then she just hitched up her frock," he said. "She weren't wearing pants nor nowt. She slowly sat down on to me, warm and slippy, till I couldn't shift. Then she started shifting, to and fro. She were pinning my arms to the earth, grinning down into my face. It were over in a few moments." '

Brother Denys was unprepossessing: both the events and the conversation he was describing had happened thirty-five years earlier. Since then a skin ailment had reddened his already sanguine features and plucked out his hair, even his eyebrows and eyelashes, giving him the appearance of a skinned rabbit. His nether lip jutted and glistened, his upper lip was puckered inwards as if he was much more ancient than he was. His pale-blue eyes flickered furtively around, never meeting mine. As if to compensate for this he kept a compelling hand on my arm all the time he was talking – though I was firmly seated in my desk in my library niche and rarely showed a sign of wanting to interrupt or terminate the interview.

He sighed, swallowed, continued: 'I spoke with slow calm, as if delivering a dissertation, in an attempt at countering the raw panic of the lad's confession. I told him I was pleased that the act had afforded him little pleasure. It was evidence that he was not destined for a secular life. For the sake of the procreation of the species it is necessary that some men should have carnal traffic with women, but those whom God and nature urge to this necessity are to be pitied rather than emulated. I told him, "Learned authorities – Peter of Spain and Peter of Albano among them – inform us that women, because of their moister natures, are more libidinous and less temperate than men. Thus it is that all women, whatever their protestations to the contrary, crave intercourse, whereas men, being of drier dispositions, can transcend the craving, some more easily than others. It would seem that you, Simon, are fortunate in this respect. Nemesius teaches that the urge to intercourse is the only natural appetite that can be suppressed without ill effect."'

By now I was weary of Denys's narrative manner, embarrassed by the details he cherished, troubled that I was encouraging betrayal of secrets of the confessional. 'Hildegarde of Bingen,' I said, since Denys had paused for longer than usual, 'herself a woman, though one that attained to the ungendered grace of God, admits that men who discharge their seed in lust risk blindness. And Albertus Magnus goes so far as to say that every woman is to be avoided like a poisonous snake or horned devil.'

'Simon was now staring at the floor in the corner of the room, with his lips twisted and his pale face pursed with disgust, as if he could see something repulsive under the ingle bench.

' "I'm mucky," he said. "I'm filthy, Brother Denys. I shannot come with you to the abbey. I aren't good enough."

'The teeth of panic fastened round my heart. "Never despair of yourself, child. Despair is the ultimate and unforgivable sin."

'Simon shook his head. "It's what I went for, Brother Denys. I rode out yonder looking for fornication and mortal sin just the way Roger does. I wished it, for I wished to be a sinner like Roger and have Father belt me."

'Simon wept, his hands to his face, his body heaving. I crept out a hand, an arm and pulled the lad towards me. "Nobody can deny, child, that you made yourself available to temptation and the onslaught of Satan. That was sin and folly. But beyond that . . ."

'Great sobs were rising from Simon's flanks and belly and billowing his rib cage. As my hand traced his shoulder blade and the ridge of his spine I said: "It's clear enough that the forces of darkness were arrayed in strength against you and that you were weak and vulnerable against them. It has been posited, by William of Saliceto and others, that a woman should lie still during intercourse, on her back with her head lowered and her knees raised. That is most conducive to conception and is what the normal woman will naturally do. The fact that the creature that copulated with you lay atop of you in an unnatural position of ascendancy is evidence that it was no mere female depository for male fluid. It was probably a witch." '

For twenty years, since the purge of Byland and the transfer of Brother Simon, Denys had plagued any of us that he could entrap with his embarrassing, vivid confessions: as if he had decided that his penance should be to tell his story until it was as loathsome to the rest of us as to himself. He had grown accustomed to being escaped or evaded even by the most sympathetic brothers or those who felt it their duty to muster a little credit in Heaven by being charitable to the unseemly old bore. Maybe he had even come to welcome the rejection as a punishment which might play its part in his ultimate redemption. When I approached him with a declaration of interest in at least part of his story he seemed nonplussed, like an amorous braggart abashed by a wench suddenly taking him at his word. I had even had to coax him with questions until his narrative achieved its normal impetus.

'At the mention of a witch Simon stopped weeping. He asked, without lifting his face from his hands, so that his voice was muffled, "It weren't a lass then?"

' "Oh yes, a witch is a mortal female. I have warned you sufficiently about women, lad but perhaps insufficiently about witches. All women are more or less in league with the Devil, but a witch is a woman who has progressed to a more intimate relationship with Satan. She has given up her body and soul to him and in return has been accorded access to his magic. The lass you speak of carries all the symptoms of a witch's transaction with the Devil. In the first place there is her bold pride, in the way she addressed you throughout the encounter and in the way she resisted your assumption of dominance which (if for an unworthy purpose) was a right and proper demand against a shepherd girl by the son of the lord of the demesne. Her conduct would be inexplicable in a vulnerable peasant – or in any normal woman confronted by a man – but it is all too usual in those females who have attained impudence by surrendering to Satan's tyranny and protection. Then there are the magical powers she exhibited even in that short encounter – the lore of witching-herbs and the capacity to quell beasts even if they are in agony. Her treatment of the horse –"

'Simon interrupted. "It were 'mazing how she got it to squet. But Piers Stableman scorns her pudding."

' "If the horse mends it will be proof positive of her implication in the black arts, for what can a peasant lass know of horses? Another indication of a witch is the presence of a familiar: that is, a fiend, or even Satan himself, in the guise of . . . you say there was a black dog?"

' "Aye!" he said eagerly. "There were a huge black dog that stared at me all the time, all through the . . . and scared me. A huge black dog with a pink mouth and white teeth and yellow eyes."

'I nodded. "It was undoubtedly the Prince of This World and the witch's master. A lesser fiend would have been more difficult to spot –

disguised as a stool, or a bluebottle . . . Only Satan himself would be so arrogantly blatant"'

Denys was in full flow now, to the extent of using different voices for himself and Simon, like a fairground entertainer. He was moving on remorselessly from the only event that interested me to what he really wanted to talk about – what he always talked about – the fifteen years of his life that were made delicious and terrible by his buggery of Simon Dorsay. I only wanted to know a fragment of the story – an afternoon when Denys himself was not even present – though it was an episode that perhaps had enormous consequences for him and all of us.

'Simon turned his head at last, to gaze at his confessor through long fair lashes that were wet with tears. "She had a way of staring with her eyes into mine that . . . put me in a sort of trance, see?"

' "Witches can do that. Satan gives them the power to enslave our will. You should never look directly into the eyes of a witch."

' "I were bewitched then, Brother Denys? It weren't my fault?"

' "You were guilty of some weakness, child, but I think it no great matter. In the abbey you shall be safe from such onslaughts, with me still beside you to guide and sustain you. We shall eat the simple porridge and pray the two hundred and twenty-two prayers of the routine. We shall walk through the cloisters and the cool gloom of the south shrubbery while I rehearse you in the tenets of the order. Or Brother Sapiens will instruct us both in the library, where are the volumes of the wisdom of the saints and fathers. We shall find grace together."'

Brother Edmund Makes a Report
and Receives a Reprimand

‘IR RICHARD DORSAY, when interviewed by Denys about his son's entry into the abbey, proved less complaisant than anticipated. Denys stressed the baleful influence of the witch, the hapless innocence of Simon, the residual danger to the young man's soul and the urgent need for repair and purification. These arguments only appealed, in the case of Sir Richard, to superficial convention: he nostalgically approved of the predatory lust he chastized in Roger and was secretly pleased that his soppy younger lad had displayed the Dorsay urges. It was actually Rabican who won the argument for Denys: the injury to his favourite horse outraged Sir Richard, reaffirmed his conviction about the uselessness of his youngest son and persuaded him to give the lad to the Church. In any case he was weary of children and wanted rid of them. He wished that he had made more effort to place the boys in noble households. Even as he thrashed Roger he was daunted by the contempt in his son's eyes, the impatience of the young wolf for the death or enfeeblement of the leader of the pack.

'Sir Richard did nothing about the young witch that Denys had reported – having listened to what he considered the rigmarole of his chaplain with the godless scepticism that lurked below his cursory show of piety. To him, neither what had befallen Simon in the summer meadow nor the shepherdess's veterinary skills required a super-natural explanation.'

Abbot Fabian was beside me on the stone bench; not looking at me as I spoke but at the extensive and scrupulously tended herb garden that was one of the two worldly obsessions he permitted himself. The other was of course the library: it was the unjustified supposition of envious spirits at Byland that myself and Brother Vincent the herbalist were great rivals for the Abbot's favour, like the minions of a corrupt king.

'Such moral and spiritual slackness is rife in our era,' the Abbot observed. 'Despite the plagues with which God has warned us and the constant threat of damnation. It is evidenced by the Great Schism in the Church that for forty years confused and distressed the faithful. The very mother of the King of England was recently found to be a sorceress – and here in Yorkshire we have the heavy example of the triumph of Satan that was permitted in Slatterdale fifteen years ago. I hope that the work you are attempting, as well as bringing distinction to the abbey, will play its part in alerting Christendom to the decadence in which it languishes.'

'Indeed, Father. Because of Sir Richard's disbelief the girl Sukie very nearly escaped attention. But Denys mentioned her in a conversation with the parish priest. The success of his own projects made him benevolent: he did not accuse Sukie vehemently, but spoke of her as of one who might be in danger of falling into superstitious error if her wild, lone ways were left unchecked. The parish priest had a word with the reeve of the Dorsay demesne, who disliked the Dobsons because of the surly insolence of Ellis. The reeve spoke to the head of the tithing that included the Dobson family, warning him that all families in the tithing would be held responsible for Sukie's conduct and instructing him to apply pressure on her parents to correct and control her.

'There the matter would have ended, but the head of the tithing was at that time in dispute with Ibbie Dobson over a lame piglet and not disposed to discharge what would otherwise have been a mild and routine mission. He gave his opinion to the reeve that witchcraft was outside the responsibility of a secular tithing. The reeve, who felt that he had already fulfilled his own responsibility in the affair, relayed the opinion of the tithing head to the parish priest, supporting it. He suggested that the priest inform the Archdeacon who was the Archbishop's factor in the North Riding, so that the suspected witch could be investigated properly by ecclesiastics.

'The parish priest was illiterate. To cover himself he sought out Denys, who by now was at the end of his chaplaincy and on the point of departure to the abbey with Simon. The two clerics composed a brief, formal note to the Archdeacon.

'It was only fifteen years later that Denys was able to work out the consequences of this note and associate the story of Sycorax with his own. He knows no details of the arrest, examination and trial: nor do I know how to come by such details, or how to proceed without them.'

The Abbot laid an ancient forefinger on my kneecap, at once a reassuring and reproving gesture. Innocent physical contact was an idiosyncrasy of this devout and ascetic man.

'I anticipated your difficulty in this respect, Brother Edmund, and assumed it to be the cause of what seemed to be a slackening in your labours. I therefore sent to Archdeacon Tertius, requesting permission for you to examine the records of the ecclesiastical court. He has replied to me promptly, graciously and at some length, which is my reason for summoning you to this audience.'

I was surprised. I had thought little of Abbot Fabian's summons – and demand for a progress report – because I had recently been giving him little information (and gathering none). His interest in my penitential task had been more intrusive since the obstructive and censorious attitude of Bernard of Rievaulx had been made clear, but this was the first time that he had gone so far as to take an active part in my investigations, except at my request.

'Unfortunately,' he went on, 'Archdeacon Tertius reports that such records were badly kept under his predecessors. For the decade in question they are only fragmentary, with no mention of Sukie Dobson nor of any investigations into witchcraft.'

I wondered if this was a suspicious circumstance: Satan and Sycorax using their powers to cover their traces. But what I said was, 'Then it is hopeless, Father. For without such information any history I produce will be mere gossip and hearsay.'

He looked directly at me for the first time, quite sharply. My prompt defeatism was probably not his first inkling of what was in my mind. 'Then it is remarkable that you have not yourself suggested that we seek such information, Brother Edmund,' he said drily. 'Fortunately, Archdeacon Tertius not only looks favourably upon my scheme – feeling none of the *jalousie de metier* that informs the attitude of our colleague at Rievaulx – but is of a more sanguine and active frame of mind than you seem to enjoy. He has discovered records in the church archives relating to the attempt to arrest Sukie Trothers, known as the witch Sycorax, fifteen years ago and containing the names of several persons still resident in the region who were officially involved in that event. He has also discovered another person, Simkin by name, who held the post of bailiff to the ecclesiastical court for many years and was actually the arresting officer and present throughout the earlier proceedings against young Sukie Dobson. I therefore propose that you prepare yourself for another sojourn at Kirkholt Grange. You will study the material which the Archdeacon has offered to make available at his Pickering residence, obtain all the information you can from the person Simkin and trace the others mentioned in the records. Then you will return to Nithermoor to interview all informants there rigorously and systematically about the adult life of Sukie Trothers and the reign of Sycorax. Thus in a month at the most you shall gather all the information necessary for the completion of your history. The rest of your penance can then proceed without further delay: the less fraught and queasy business of composing your *oeuvre* in the tranquil security of Byland library.'

He had shifted his position on the bench so that he was observing me steadily as he uttered his last few sentences.

I murmured, 'Father, I wish you would find me another penance, even a heavier one. I do not wish to continue this distasteful history of Sycorax.'

He nodded vigorously, as if I had said exactly what he expected to hear. I knew this mannerism of his and that he was displeased with me. He said, 'It is not for the penitent to choose the penance, Brother Edmund, nor to change it if it proves taxing. Nor is it seemly for the monk to instruct the Abbot. If I am so stubborn in error as to pay no heed to the correction of the great Bernard of Rievaulx, do you think I am likely to submit to the opinion of my librarian? Do you imagine that I am defying the spleen of Satan and his Fiend Sycorax for the sake of mere earthly vainglory, a prestigious book in the library?'

'I am not intending the insolence of instructing or correcting you, Father, but begging you to be merciful to a cowardly sinner.'

I had been suffering from a spate of filthy visions. Clambering and tumbling in hay and silk and breasts and buttocks and hairy filth. Malkin, Nell, Nance, Luce. The taste and stink of simmered lamprey on my lips and my member butting madly in an elusive sheath that was like the flabby bladder of a pig. And there were new dreams, or new components to the only, mortal, ineluctable dream. Alys was in some of them, with her merry eyes and dark laugh.

The extent to which Alys occupied my waking consciousness was even more perturbing than the dreams. As I strolled in the gardens and cloisters or worked in the library, at refectory or at devotion, she would come vividly into my presence with her grey eyes, her smooth cheeks, her slightly parted lips. I would hear her characteristic laugh, then she would take my arm and say, 'Coom, Feyther.' I would feel the soft warmth of her body as she led me again through the dark of Nithermoor. It was more difficult to resist her apparition because it had none of the carnal crudity of other imaginings. I need only ask myself what she might be doing twenty-five miles away at that very moment to summon her with magic clarity: her lissom waist and plump, milky breasts, her calm and nimble poise as she poured drink, mopped the tabletop or lifted her infant towards the ceiling. I could remember every conversation I had held with her and hold it again in my imagination, watching the shifting nuances of her beauty as I doted on every banality uttered in her droll brogue. I made up fresh dialogue as best I could and pictured how the play of her lips and the dancing intelligence in her eyes enhanced the lame lines I had given her to speak. I even managed to take her from the only environment I had for her and introduce her into other scenes: as a lady in a horned hat, side-saddle on a palfrey, her embroidered dress nearly sweeping the earth, or as a shepherdess in a snowy smock on a dale loud with insects in the ferns and sheep among the gorse.

I am all too easy prey for Satan, but not his fool. I was aware that these chaste and doting daydreams were more dangerous to a man of God than the crass allure of Nance, Nell, Luce and Malkin. And when I had confessed all to Abbot Fabian he had agreed with this assessment. Yet he had judged it propitious and to my credit that Satan, frustrated by the inefficacy of his old assaults on me, had been forced to have resource to different and more subtle demons. Such affectionate approval – more reminiscent of my mother than my father – was characteristic of the Abbot's attitude to me and made his present sharpness all the more effective and distressing.

I went on, 'I am too weak and foolish to conduct your investigations out there in Satan's kingdom. I beg you to let me stay within the confines of the abbey as long as I live.'

The Abbot now spoke with the slow emphasis of official pronouncement. 'In this matter, as in all that concerns this abbey, I am uniquely and terribly responsible. In contrast, all that is required of you is obedience. You need to be aware, though, that Satan makes available several forms and levels of disobedience, for which the Church prescribes a corresponding range of penalties. If the spirit is willing but the flesh weak you will be treated mercifully. But if you set yourself up in pride to question my instructions you are engaged in a much graver sort of disobedience, just as I would be if I traduced the rules of the order or refused to accept an edict of the Holy Father in Rome.'

He paused, sighed and placed a hand on his diaphragm. He seemed to be listening to some turmoil of destruction within his own fragile frame. I for my part must have been looking quelled and glum, for he then took hold of my forearm and squeezed it with fond force. 'This is why I have you include an account of your own spiritual experiences in pursuit of the history of Sycorax. It is through your story of penance – the trials you encounter, the truths you discover, the salvation you desire – that an otherwise terrible tale will be rendered pleasing to good Christians and edifying to all.'

The Arrest of the Witch Sukie

HE ARCHDEACON WAS not in residence but a modestly furnished cell had been put at my disposal in his Pickering dwelling, which he shared with his clerk and several other priests. Here I was ministered to by his servants and fed from his kitchen while I carried out my investigations in the town. It was to this base, a grey-stone house that peeped round the church and down the market street, that Simkin was brought.

Simkin was an ancient widower whose children were either dead or gone from Pickering. Many years of service as the Archdeacon's bailiff and summoner had earned him a modest pension, at the discretion of the Archdeacon, which allowed him to lodge with a cooper's family in an alley off the main market street. Shrunk and shrivelled like an old apple, his head encased in a square leather helmet and his frame in smelly fustian, he proved to have a meticulous memory and a sardonic intelligence. His account was nearly as detailed as that of Brother Denys and probably more accurate – narrated in thin, dry tones, clearly and pithily, unprompted and unstumbling. He had spent his childhood as I did in the Vale of York and had stubbornly retained his accent, so that his speech was a welcome relief from the Slatterdale brogue.

He had set out from Pickering on a November morning thirty-five years ago, riding a brown mule and armed with a letter of empowerment from the clerk to the Archdeacon, a summons to the ecclesiastical court and a few oral instructions. Climbing Pickering Beck to the Dorsay demesne he presented himself to the reeve at the manor farm, flourished his documents and demanded that Sukie Dobson might be delivered up to him so that he could take her to Pickering for investigation and trial.

To his annoyance, he found that his instructions were bogus – the girl was neither on the premises nor readily available. The reeve was either unable or unwilling to provide him with a guide across the moorland tops, so he was compelled to go back down to Kirkholt and climb the other fork of the stream, Cropton Beck, via Nithermoor to Beck Gap.

After a four-hour journey on the ambling mule Simkin arrived at Beck Gap in a gloomy frame of mind encouraged by the prospect of not being able to get back to Pickering before nightfall. He was also aware that the denizens of Beck Gap were going to be baffled by his explanations and unimpressed by the documents they could not read. The delivery of a simple summons – never mind the actual arrest and removal of a local lass – could have tricky consequences in an out-of-the-way place like this.

Thirty-five years later, Simkin claimed to have been undaunted by this and every other occupational hazard he encountered in his long career. He proudly asserted that neither fear nor pity had ever interfered with his work – or, indeed, played any part in his dealings with other humans. The most congenial emotion he was prepared to confess to was surly satisfaction at completing a task as well or better than another might have done in his place. I do not know if he included his wife and children in this general misanthropy, for he refused to say anything about his personal affairs.

He had a stroke of luck in that the parish priest, sought in vain in Nithermoor, was actually in Beck Gap, giving unction to a moribund, when Simkin got there. The priest was of course already aware of the Sukie Dobson business, having helped compose the letter to the Archdeacon. It was the priest who introduced Simkin to the Dobson family and explained his mission.

The second fortunate turn of events, from Simkin's point of view, was that the Dobson family offered no resistance, or even resentment, when informed they were responsible for their daughter's conduct, so bound to give Simkin every assistance in delivering her to the authorities. He gathered that Sukie was more or less estranged from her family – spending most of her time on the dale with the sheep – and that her family regarded her weirdness as an embarrassment and liability. Some of them, including her mother, were clearly upset but less at the thought of Sukie being in trouble than from fear of the family being fined or otherwise punished. Others, notably her brother Ellis, a gangling lad with an aggressive face, seemed positively enthusiastic.

'Sukie's a witch an' a sluttock,' he told Simkin. 'Daft, too, scroochin' up trees an' chunnerin'. Best thoo take 'er off an' lock 'er up, for she's loony.'

Ellis volunteered to guide Simkin to Sukie first thing next morning and help with the arrest. Simkin was fed and lodged with the Dobsons, after a brisk but amicable negotiation with Ibbie. He could remember little about the family except that most of them were lanky with sharp noses and thick eyebrows that made them look like angry bitterns. They took this appearance from their mother. Father Tom, who made his drunken appearance when everybody else had eaten, was a podgy, snub-nosed man who looked like none of his children.

As they set out in the early mist Simkin noticed that Ellis was carrying a heavy woodman's axe. When he asked its purpose Ellis smiled, for the first time in Simkin's short acquaintance with him.

'Sukie got this mutt, sod of a black devil-dog four foot high. She's learnt the bugger to kill any fucker she don't like, such as me an' thoo.'

Later Ellis had them take a detour along a ferny ridge then double back down the valley to the hut where Sukie slept. 'For wind is in t'south-east sithee, an' us don't want mutts to snuff us afore we're on 'em.'

A low hut, looking like the remains of a stone wall, was bedded in the grassy valley slope, surrounded by a placid multitude of sheep. To the west the meadow-land rose to become gorse and bracken on the moorland ridge. To the east, across the beck, the forest covered the land. The sheep absolutely ignored the intruders, who had almost reached the hut before the alarum was raised.

A huge black dog with golden eyes came leaping towards them, baying as it came. The alarmed mule almost pitched Simkin to the earth, but Ellis stepped forward to meet the dog as though he had been foreseeing this moment and training for it for years. He swung the axe in a fatal arc that was so deliberate as to be almost serene, splitting the head of the dog like a butcher and dumping the carcass in a twisted heap. Ellis gave a hoarse shout of triumph, a sort of war cry.

There was a sheepdog keeping its distance but yapping urgently. Simkin descended from the mule while keeping his attention on the hut door from which Sukie Dobson was emerging into the November morning. He saw a tall lass who was kept from being pretty by the resemblance she bore to her brother. It was clear she had slept with her socks on, in several layers of woollen smock, this crisp autumn weather. She had been ready for alarms such as carnivores prowling among the muttons and had shoved on her boots and snatched up a cudgel before dashing out to stand bewildered in the chill sunlight.

Her bewilderment lasted only a couple of seconds, then she let out a shrill cry and launched herself at her brother, giving him a couple of solid thwacks with her cudgel before the two men had her down on the earth. Ellis kneed her in the belly and punched her head until she was nearly unconscious.

Simkin restrained him. He had gone along with Ellis's approach so far, on the grounds that the lad probably knew how best to deal with his weird sister, but was averse to unnecessary violence, taking pride in conducting his business with economy of effort and professional phlegm. While he tied the girl's wrists with the mule's tether Ellis gloated into her face from short range.

'Hee, Sukie, fuckin' trollopy! Sithee what's come of tha weird ways! Thissun's Simkin, bishop's constable, off with thoo to Pickering dungeons. An' I've did for yon fuckin' devil-dog an' all!' He laughed, well pleased with events and his role in them, then spat in his sister's face. 'Gizzun now, tha evil squinny!'

Simkin, disdainful of this embarrassing gush of animosity, used the rope to drag the dazed girl to her feet, then to lead her to the mule. Ellis took the axe and made a dash in the direction of the sheepdog, which retreated shamelessly, still yapping.

Sukie was the fourth witch with whom Simkin had been involved and the first for over a decade. The other three cases had all occurred when the clerk to the Archdeacon had been Father Ignatius, a devout man who had been particularly zealous about hunting out cases of sorcery. While Simkin was not susceptible to Sukie's nubility – 'By then I were of t'opinion as shaggin' lasses were a stupid waste o' time' – and took no interest in her as a person, he could not help remarking that she made an unusual and even implausible witch compared to the other three, who had been senile, baffled, inarticulate old hags.

Ellis stayed on the riding to supervise the sheep. Sukie was dragged behind the mule through Beck Gap and Nithermoor, following Slatterdale Beck and the Pickering road out of sheep territory and the fringes of Cropton Forest towards the arable demesnes on the Vale of York.

At first she said nothing, concussed by the suddenness of the arrest, the death of the dog and the beating her brother had given her. Then she shouted up at Simkin, 'Oy! Mister!'

Their passage through Beck Gap was watched discreetly from the shadows of doorways – none of her family in sight. Otherwise wherever they passed folk stopped work in the fields or ran out of buildings. The word 'witch' came readily to the lips of these spectators, even if neither Sukie nor Simkin was known to them: the spectacle of the grim man on the brown mule dragging the battered girl by the wrists was apparently self-explanatory, though it was ten years since a witch had been slain in the North Riding.

'Oy! Mister!'

Simkin observed, in his cynical and caustic manner, that once the witch-word had been pronounced people started to behave as though they had known Sukie and disliked her for a long time. There were some who mouthed and spat at her. A little boy with a black face and a toothless snarl flung a stone that struck her between the shoulder blades. Even sane, ordinary folk – the sort that would claim to be fond parents, generous friends, passionate lovers – lost control, dashing out as if they were welcoming a fair then shrinking back in terror, crossing themselves, as she was dragged by.

'Oy! Mister! Are thoo fuckin' deaf?'

Piqued by this impertinence, Simkin halted the mule and dismounted. Using the tether to pull the girl towards him he cuffed her hard with the flat of his hand.

'Gob it, witch!'

At midday it rained. On the fringe of the autumn forest, Simkin ate boiled rabbit washed down with a skin of wine – provisions purchased from the Dobsons. He gave Sukie nothing to eat – 'They only puke it over you' – but tethered her where she could crouch in the bowl of a tree and avoid some of the downpour. Simkin was protected by his leather cap and jerkin but in any case considered himself impervious to weather. The mule was tethered to another tree, sufficiently far away for its stench and restlessness to be no hazard to Simkin's comfort. It stood uneasily, one long ear laid back, the other rotating slowly on the pivot of its skull.

One of Sukie's eyes had been closed by her brother's beating and her cheek was so swollen that her entire head looked out of shape. After the failure of her attempt to communicate she had withdrawn into the silence of sullen reverie. This did not now suit Simkin, who sometimes, especially when relaxed by wine, liked a bit of social inter-course with his fodder. He therefore passed the time by answering the questions she had not been permitted to ask and amusing himself with her dismay.

'We screws tha. First time, just thumbs wi' t'pilliwinks. Squash thumbs sithee till tha confesses witchery. Then we strips tha stark bare and searches for Satan's titty.'

Sukie lisped from under her bulging lip, 'Ellis is a fucking liar and I aren't no witch. Who witnesses as I'm a witch besides Ellis?'

'It were gentry, sithee, what accused tha. Gentry and clergy. It aren't polite to bother such wi' no witnessing. Once tha confesses and we finds Satan's titty it don't need no witness.'

'I aren't got no Satan's titty on me.'

'Then we'll screw tha proper, wi' t'wooden booties to squash feet, or maybe snap shins wi' t'iron pig. Till tha owns to being shagged by demons, leaping o'er t'moon wi' a broomstick up bum and suchlike. Then tha'll hang, or be let into stocks in Pickering market for two full days, which works the trick, for they're ruffian folk in Pickering Town, and I've never known a witch they didn't finish by busting apart wi' cobblestones.'

'I aren't done nowt.'

This time her protest was a sullen mumble, as if she judged that he might hit her again if she showed too much spirit. Simkin was surprised that she was not more cowed by the events of the day and what he had been telling her.

'Innocent or not is for God to judge, Father Ignatius used to say. It 'appen best I shag tha now lass, afore it all gone to waste.'

He had no inclination or intention to do any such thing but meant the remark as witty and jocular, within his grim range – it still got a chuckle from him thirty-five years later as he repeated it. On top of what she had been experiencing and hearing, it had an interesting effect on Sukie Dobson.

She peered at him through her one eye in awe and terror as if he was a forest ogre. Then slowly the expression in the eye changed, became shrewd and almost gloating, as if she suddenly understood him and found him derisory. Then she shut her eye and starting rocking to and fro, moving her lips.

Thunder growled and the mule shifted fearfully. Cropton Forest was in twilight. Rain came rattling and drumming as if on canvas, or lancing between boles and branches to hiss into the underbrush, smacking into the soil. Lightning caused momentary shadows as if great black hounds were flickering between the trees.

Simkin saw that the girl was clutching something as she rocked and intoned her spell. While he was proud to declare himself the least superstitious fellow in Satan's kingdom, he was always telling himself and others that you can't be too careful these days, so he went across to her, wrenched her fingers apart, plucked the acorn necklace from her and flung it into the forest. She had a sprig of fennel, too, that fell out of her hand. He put his foot on it and ground it into the soil.

Nothing spectacular then happened. The storm did not miraculously abate. Thirty-five years later Simkin gave his dry chuckle. 'But it didn't get no worse, neither.'

The Interrogation and Condemnation of the Witch Sukie

‘EAR NOTHING, CHILD. My name is Father Ambrose. I have been appointed by the Archdeacon to investigate your case. My purpose is to see that you are saved from any sin or error that we find in you and that you are returned to the mercy of God. In the process we shall be as gentle with you as possible.’

Father Ambrose was described by Simkin as ‘a soft old twassock with silky white hair’. Simkin had little imagination and no grasp whatsoever of things of the spirit, so far as I could make out, but he had information from the Archdeacon’s household and the intelligence to be able to speculate plausibly as to how Ambrose found himself with such an unsuitable assignment. Ambrose was not clerk to the Archdeacon – who would be the obvious person to represent authority here – but the Archdeacon’s personal confessor, companion, chess opponent and adversary in theological debate. The debates sometimes became heated and violent, resulting in the two old men breaking off all communication with each other for days. An even more heated debate than usual, in which Ambrose’s views had both offended the Archdeacon and bordered on heresy, was probably the cause of this assignment, intended by the Archdeacon as both a mortifying discipline for his buddy and a corrective exercise in the enforcement of orthodoxy.

The investigation took place in a cell beneath the Devil’s Tower in Pickering Castle. The Archdeacon had signed a respectfully worded request to the steward of the Duchy of Lancaster, the holders of the castle, for loan of the facilities as in previous investigations ten years earlier: the keep was not only equipped with all necessary implements and apparatus but was isolated and insulated to keep the outcry of investigated parties from bothering the general public. Inexperienced in the prosecution of the occult and nervous about the whole business, Ambrose seated himself on a stool across the whitewashed room, leaving the handling of Sukie to the two lay officers of the ecclesiastical court who were present: the bailiff, Simkin, and the town gaoler, Binnock.

Sukie had been stripped, spreadeagled on a trestle table and tied there naked, quivering with cold. The hair had been shaved from her head and body. Simkin, who unlike Father Ambrose considered himself versed in the examination of witches, cast off his usual taciturnity to explain procedure to the priest.

'We screws her now, Father, wi' t'pilliwinks, till she confess. Then we searches her for t'mark o' Satan. That were t'carry-on wi' t'Cropton witches back in Archdeacon Lionel's time.'

Father Ambrose flinched and spoke peevishly. Both he and Simkin were aware, as he spoke, that his protest should be to the Archdeacon rather than to these foot soldiers.

'Where are her accusers? Where are the witnesses? What is the evidence against her? This is not a proper investigation.'

Simkin said patiently, 'It were gentry, Father, sithee, what put this accusation. Gentry an' clergy.'

Father Ambrose nodded his head uncertainly.

Sukie suddenly writhed her body and turned her head, appealing to the priest through chattering teeth, 'I aren't no witch! Give us frock, Feyther! I'm nithered.' She had been paralysed with terror while the officers were shaving her, but the presence of the priest and his sympathetic remarks seemed to have raised her spirits.

Simkin casually leant over and slapped her across the head. 'Gob it, witch.' He took up the pilliwinks, a device for crushing toes and fingers, discovered they were rusty and in poor condition and set about trying to renovate them.

Ambrose opened his mouth to protest. Then he shut it again. He slowly began to nod his head. Then he shook it emphatically. 'No! We must search her first for the Devil's mark. If that is not found then the girl must be declared innocent and no violence offered her.'

Simkin was disgusted. 'We allus tortures first, Father! That were how Father Ignatius laid it down.'

'It was not correct procedure. Make the search for Satan's mark.'

Simkin handled Sukie, he was proud to insist, 'as if she were dead mutton I were searching for taint-worm'. Gaoler Binnock, a fat, wheezy fellow with a wart on his chin, eagerly did the bulk of the handling. If his hands were gentler than the bailiff's they were not more welcome, due to the prurience in his podgy fingers.

Sukie squealed a protest. Ambrose suddenly leapt to his feet and shouted, 'Stop!'

The two lay officials quit their work and stared at him. He was at once embarrassed at his own outburst. 'I mean this will not do. We must proceed with as little brutality and . . . lewdness as possible.'

Simkin permitted himself an impudent snort. He resented this queasy old ignoramus. 'Beg pudden, with respect, Father Wotsit, but we do no more than's . . . looking for Satan's titty like tha said.'

Ambrose approached the table, as if to control the men better from close range. He looked fearfully down at the chill grey flesh that was blatantly outspread. It was probably the first time since his childhood that he had seen a naked woman, even in a dream.

Seeing him above her Sukie bellowed up at him, 'Feyther, I aren't no witch! Make these twats leave us be!'

Simkin moved to hush her again but thought better of it.

Ambrose said, 'It is clear that there are no marks on this . . . surface of the young person. Turn her over.'

'What do tha know, Father?' jeered the irritated Simkin. 'Satan's a crafty one. 'E tucks the titty into 'idey 'oles, sly like, so it aren't that easy to spot.'

Father Ambrose visibly quailed at the distasteful implications of this. He said again, impatiently, 'Turn her over!' It was clear that if the girl was face down she would be less flagrant and appalling to him.

Reversing her was troublesome, involving the unfastening and re-binding of her limbs. Binnock hindered the process: between lecherous absorption and the inhibition of the priest's scrutiny he was reduced to wheezing ineptitude. Fortunately, the less impressionable Simkin kept his wits about him. As Binnock was knotting the ropes Simkin peered, paused, pounced and heaved the girl back on to her side.

'That! Sithee!'

A small pimple nestled among the flossy hair of her armpit that the officers had not bothered to shave. It was a blemish that Simkin had noticed earlier and decided to use if nothing else transpired.

Ambrose curled his lip. 'If this insignificant zit is a teat at which the Devil sucks, which of us is not festooned and stippled with the marks of Satan's . . .?' All the same, he found it hard to resist the notion of his ordeal being over, one way or another. He bent closer and peered at the pimple.

Simkin had proceeded to examine Sukie's body. 'I own it aren't a reet clear un, Father. Maybe 'er arse . . .'

'Take your hands off her!'

The priest's voice was shrill. He collected himself before speaking in a normal voice. 'What we have seen will suffice as the mark of Satan. Untie her and cover her. If the mark we have found is indistinct, it may be a sign that the Devil's power is not fully established in this child.'

Simkin said patiently, 'That'll be best found by t'pilliwinks, eh, Father?'

What next happened was an enduring matter of regret to Simkin, who could not abide to be associated with any sort of professional incompetence.

74

After further examination of the pilliwinks Simkin adjudged them useless. The wooden boot looked in better shape, and it was decided to proceed with this.

At the lightest application of the vice mechanism the frozen and intimidated girl promptly yelled: 'Ow, geroff! I'll say owt!'

Ambrose gestured urgently for the slackening of the boot. Simkin, on the other hand, remembering the counsel of Father Ignatius about the worthlessness of too prompt and painless a confession, signalled to Binnock to tighten the device. Binnock, panicking, happened to obey Simkin. But it transpired that the time and neglect that had rusted the pilliwinks had caused a more serious functional fault in the wooden boot. The mechanism first resisted Binnock, then yielded suddenly as he applied more force and crushed Sukie's foot. She let out a piercing scream. Binnock, muddled, was tightening the device even further when the horrified Ambrose dashed him aside.

'You must confess to me, child, as freely and truly as if I were the priest in church and you were kneeling in the confessional stall seeking absolution. You must first confess that you are a witch.'

Sukie was sitting on a bench with her leg propped. Her foot had been examined, dressed and bound, at the insistence of Father Ambrose, by the vet and doctor who served the castle garrison, but it was causing her much pain. She was hunched forward, hanging her head.

'I reckon us must be,' she said in a croak. 'Granny Sukie were. She learnt it us.'

'She taught you witches' lore?'

'Aye. Grasses an' puddings.'

'I know what you mean. And do you confess to having practised this sorcery against Christian folk?'

'Eh?'

'Have you ever supplied a . . . pudding, to any man or woman, with or without their knowledge?'

She thought. 'I gid a dollop o' summat to Gib Miller, me sweetheart. 'E never knew nowt about it.'

'It was a love potion?'

'Aye, to keep him true an' frisky an' all.'

'And is that all? That can't be all. What about the charms you recite? Do they curse Christ and invoke Satan?'

She shook her head. 'Granny's stuff's nowt about church. It for fairies' luck, sithee, an' agin oddgobblers an' all.'

'Child, the creatures you speak of do not exist. Apart from mortal beasts, only Satan's fiends inhabit the earth. Apart from obedience to God and the Church there is only the lore of Satan. You seek its protection at great risk to your soul. Do you understand me?'

'Aye, Feyther,' she said meekly and winced with pain. She raised her battered face to peer at him confidingly out of her good eye. Father Ambrose dithered his hand down in a sort of benediction on to her shaven skull.

Simkin snorted. It had become clear to him that compared to the Cropton crones of Father Ignatius's day this young witch was going to get off very easily.

In 1414 Simkin was struck down with a fistula that plagued him periodically all his adult life, so was unable to take part in the attempt to arrest Sukie Trothers. Therefore the terrible and amazing aspects of that event had not qualified the complacent shrug with which he viewed all supernatural matters – not disbelief so much as unimpressed acceptance. His vanity made him repeat somebody's suggestion at the time: that his inopportune affliction might have been due to the sorcery of the witch, warned by Satan of the expedition against her and keen that Simkin should form no part of it. It was he, after all, who had arrested Sukie the first time – the only time – in 1394 and he took grim satisfaction from a comparison of the two arrest attempts. While he accepted that the powers of the witch had waxed mightily in the interim, he was confident that this would not have happened if his own approach had been adopted from the first and maintained.

'Witches thrive, sithee, if tha goes along wi' hocus-pocus, saving souls o' t'buggers an' such ket. Best to shut their gobs wi' a bit o' fist.'

He ascribed much of the later trouble to the negligent leniency with which Sukie Dobson was treated: and though I was repulsed by both his cold lack of compunction at human suffering and his inability to see religion in terms other than of brutish superstition, I was compelled to agree with his verdict.

Simkin was present at the ecclesiastical court when Sukie's case was heard but was not asked to testify. Father Ambrose did almost all the talking. He gave an account of the complaint, arrest and investigation, then read out a document containing Sukie's confession that she had practised sorcery as taught her by her grandmother: worn charms, recited spells and administered an aphrodisiac potion to her lover. In answer to the Archdeacon, who was presiding – a chore usually delegated to a subordinate cleric – Ambrose admitted that no attempt had been made to extract confession of more serious offences, such as an infernal pact, copulation with the Devil or practice of malign sorcery against Christians. He gave his opinion that the girl was now contrite and devout, no longer in Satan's power. Her involvement with sorcery had been minimal and had arisen more from ignorance than from a disposition towards evil.

The Archdeacon accepted Father Ambrose's discourse with every sign of satisfaction. In fact his cordial manner towards Ambrose throughout the proceedings made it clear that whatever difference had come between them had been annealed: Ambrose had expiated his offence (if Simkin's hunch was correct) and was restored to full favour.

The Archdeacon then conducted a little investigation of his own. Sukie hobbled forward to stand before the judge's table and was asked if the document just read was an accurate account of her guilt. When Father Ambrose had rephrased the question so that she understood it she assented in a whisper. Further questions prompted her to a formal expression of contrition. She was then instructed to kneel, kiss a crucifix and recite the Lord's Prayer, all of which she performed without significant hesitation or other telltale symptoms. After this the Archdeacon graciously and unreservedly accepted Father Ambrose's recommendation of clemency towards the girl. She was therefore accorded the absolute minimum punishment for witchcraft: a year in prison to be terminated with two days in the Pickering stocks.

The Sojourn of the Witch Sukie in Pickering Gaol

HAT WAS BY no means the limit of Sukie Dobson's good luck and the leniency she enjoyed compared to other convicted witches. The steward to the Duchy of Lancaster, though he had been willing to accommodate Sukie for the weeks leading to the trial, was not prepared to have his dungeon used for the sentence.

The town gaol in Pickering was a modest two-room structure adjoining a pound for strayed animals. One room was a small cell in which tools and implements were stored and which was used as temporary prison accommodation for drunks or suspects soon to come to trial. The larger, whitewashed room served as a courtroom if there was legal business in Pickering, otherwise it was where Binnock the gaoler spent most of his time, slumped at the trestle table, sleeping on a mattress or cooking for himself at the little fireplace in the corner. The gaol was not equipped for long-term prisoners, nor does the criminal code in the Riding encourage them. Most small crimes done by those without the means to pay fines are answered by beating and maiming; anything serious – both secular offences and heresy or sorcery – meets with death by hanging. Anybody likely to spend more than a few days in prison is transferred to York unless the castle is prepared to house them.

It was decided that Sukie should be kept at Pickering. There was very little accommodation at York for women prisoners, and it hazily seemed to Ambrose, on behalf of the Archdeacon, that the girl would be more physically and morally vulnerable in a regular gaol. The smaller room at Pickering was therefore slightly modified to become her residence, and Binnock was informed that he would have to share the other room with more casual detainees. She was fettered by the ankle to a stake that had been driven between the stonework: not from any punitive principle but out of the need for security, since the gaol had neither locks nor doors substantial enough to prevent escape.

Her luck in receiving such relatively luxurious accommodation was to some extent counterbalanced by another circumstance. Since the judicial system does not encourage long-term imprisonment there is no official provision for the sustenance of prisoners. They have to have food brought in for them by their family, or to be able to pay the gaoler for their keep, if they are not to starve. Sukie's family were impoverished both by the terms of their villeinage and by Tom Dobson's alcoholism – in addition to which, they were twelve miles away and ill-disposed towards her.

Father Ambrose, once he had made the impracticable arrangements, never went to investigate Sukie's plight or made any enquiry about it so far as we know. Presumably he told himself that he had obtained maximum clemency for the lass and he wanted to obliterate the whole distressing incident from his mind.

Even if Simkin had felt any need to do the same he would have found it difficult. As summoner and bailiff to the ecclesiastical court he was responsible for seeing that the lay authorities carried out the sentence of the clerics. He also had contact with Binnock, with whom he drank fairly regularly and who confided much when drinking. Simkin was therefore able to give me a lot of information about the year spent by Sukie Dobson in Pickering.

While not subscribing to the retrospective hysteria that sees Sycorax lurking in every lineament of Sukie Dobson, Simkin scoffed at Father Ambrose's picture of her as a devout and contrite child. Simkin saw her as confidently and impudently scheming from the first to thwart the attentions of the court and avoid as much of her punishment as possible. She showed no compunction in exploiting her youth and sex for this purpose and was aided by another remarkable piece of good fortune (or contrivance of the Devil) in that she had the impressionable and pliant Binnock for a gaoler rather than the remorseless integrity of a Simkin.

Binnock was unlovely, fat and forty-five. He had not been happy in love and was of the opinion that the world – particularly the female part of it – was treating him ill. Though he sometimes spoke sentimentally of his sister, who died young, he was a rueful misogynist who spent the bulk of his time in male company, bragging and grumbling about women. He exuded lecherous ambitions beyond the scope of both his circumstances and his sexual capacity, but this was a social pose for the benefit of his buddies rather than a physiological drive. His intellectual and communicative faculties were heavily hindered by his obsession with the sexual implications of anything that anybody said. 'It were all arse end wi' 'im,' Simkin summarized.

Binnock's wife had taken a lout for a paramour who would beat up Binnock at her bidding or sometimes for his own amusement and exercise. As a result of this Binnock had been driven from home and taken up residence, semi-officially, in the large room at the gaol – which was convenient for the secure care of the permanent prisoner now in residence.

Every town has many denizens nastier than Binnock. In the circumstances that had been presented to him he behaved, within his limitations, generously, and in Simkin's opinion like a tender-hearted fool. There was no need for him to use his own resources to prevent Sukie starving to death: if uncomplicated lechery had been his purpose, he was in a position to satisfy himself by force or the threat of it without stooping to make any sort of deal with the girl. Whereas he was so ungaoler-like – so chivalrous, diffident and apologetic – when he broached the question on the second night of her sentence, that she did not fathom what he was driving at and he retreated baffled.

Such was his sheepish delicacy that it was midnight on the third night before he entered her cell resolutely and made the terms of the arrangement clear, outlining the privileges which he felt were his entitlement. When at last she understood what the fat ugly fellow was proposing she rejected him emphatically.

He permitted this insolent rebuff, preferring to have his way in the long run by patience and reasonableness. In case these qualities were slow to turn the trick, he took the additional measure of not feeding her for two days. In response to her complaints he explained again, more calmly and objectively than he had managed in the midnight darkness, that her feeding was not his responsibility and that anything he gave her would be out of affection and gratitude.

At last he had made the situation coherent. They both understood that an acceptance of food by Sukie would be an acceptance of the other clauses of the arrangement. She did not keep Binnock waiting long after that, or test if he was bluffing. She was without any concept of chastity and saw no point in going hungry.

But she did not surrender wholeheartedly or unconditionally. Binnock had physiological problems, to supplement his lamentable personality, which meant that his sexual partner had to be both patient and unfastidious if he was to get any fulfilment. Sukie was not temperamentally equipped to provide this service: it seems that while she could copulate with Satan without disgust, she had her own, arbitrary code of what was distasteful in human intercourse. She vehemently expressed her opinion that she was doing enough by passively and conventionally giving access to her body in return for the food.

Once Binnock had tolerated her refusal to 'suck 'is floppy sausage' (Simkin) or engage in novelties he figured might inspire his lust, he had more or less lost control of the arrangement he had just negotiated. It is therefore further to the credit of this gentle sinner that even then – when he was committing himself to considerable expense for a grudged and unsatisfactory return – it did not occur to him either to resort to violence or let the ungrateful girl starve. But his discontent with his share of the bargain which circumstances had forced on the pair of them brought him to look for other means by which he might profit from his charge.

One notion he had was that Sukie, instead of languishing in solitary inertia when she was not making her desultory attempts at gratifying Binnock, might be employed in useful labour. She was first given cooking and cleaning tasks, supervised on the end of a rope; then, as Binnock became confident that she would not make an escape bid or otherwise endanger his peace, she was set increasingly at liberty and assigned to such work as there was, in the upkeep and conduct of the gaol and animal pound, for which Binnock drew his derisory salary from the burghers of Pickering.

She enjoyed this aspect of the arrangement and put herself energetically to the work, though her practical skills in housecraft and cookery were no greater than Binnock's, so neither his diet nor the premises were much the better for her zest. But such animals as spent time in the Pickering pound benefited from her care and veterinary skills, as did several cats she adopted and the occasional prisoner that inhabited her cell – she now shared Binnock's mattress in the big room.

One evening, when drinking and bragging, Binnock hit on the idea that Sukie could be a source of income as well as a slave and concubine. He took up the practice of inviting acquaintances back to the gaol in return for money or drinks. He found for Sukie a scarlet cape that she fashioned into a frock and he encouraged her to clean her face and wear a scarf over her scrubby hair. She acquiesced with seeming indifference to the drunks he brought her, only demanding that they were reasonably behaved and that Binnock understood that their satisfaction was instead of his own.

The clientele consisted of anybody who had funds enough and had drunk enough at the market street ale house Binnock somewhat furtively frequented, nervous of his wife's lover. In practice this usually meant either Hugh the wagoner, wit and thief who was invariably drunk but only spasmodically solvent, or Adam the host, who always had the money or drink available but was quite often too sober to be tempted to pay.

Whereas Binnock's sexual demands could always be mitigated and sometimes refused entirely, these paying buddies of his had none of his hesitation about insisting on a full return for financial outlay – with violence if necessary. But Sukie learnt how to handle them. Hugh's appetites were unhindered by morality, compassion or self-respect – on the other hand, he was a drunkard of the inert, sleepy sort and Sukie soon became expert in lulling him into unconsciousness with as little inconvenience to herself as possible. Adam would have been a seeker after brutal power if he had not been a social coward terrified of scandal; as it was she could control him directly, without resource to the dithering Binnock, by threatening what an outcry she would make if his conduct was immoderate.

Binnock eventually proposed to let Sukie wander the town at liberty, find herself customers and take on herself the bother of the negotiations. She refused to do this. Whether he would have insisted – and prevailed – remains hypothetical, since one night Binnock was drunk enough to confide his new scheme to Simkin.

Simkin was one drinking buddy of Binnock's who had disdained all proposals regarding Sukie, as he claimed to have disdained every woman he had ever seen (apart from his wife, presumably) and every proposal that the likes of Binnock had ever put to him. He had no objection to the abuse and exploitation of prisoners but was horrified at Binnock's intention to let Sukie loose to wander Pickering at will. It offended not only his professional ethics but his sense of order and logic: a prisoner, by any definition that made sense to him, was somebody incarcerated and deprived of liberty. He told Binnock that his prostitution racket, if it trespassed beyond the bounds of a private arrangement between friends, was likely to land the gaoler in trouble with both his employers, the burghers of Pickering and the ecclesiastical authorities who had put the girl in his care.

Binnock liked to drink with Simkin, despite the latter's occasional, inconvenient officiousness. The bailiff's person and reputation gave the gaoler temporary protection from Hick Gaunt, his wife's hulking and merciless lover, who was always likely to pounce out of the ale house shadows and either threaten Binnock humiliatingly or actually knock him to the floor. Often Simkin was too bored and disgusted with Binnock to respond to his confidences, but sometimes, when his taciturn humour was relaxed by alcohol, he would give the gaoler impatient and uncompromising advice. He told him that as Sukie's gaoler his only responsibility was to prevent her escape and produce her, if she had not starved or otherwise perished, for the pillory at the end of her sentence. Otherwise he had absolute suzerainty over her person and was perfectly entitled to use her for his own pleasure and profit and for that of his friends. Even if he was too squeamish to assert his rights with violence against her, as her only source of food he was empowered and entitled to dictate whatever terms he liked. Instead of which he was not only letting the young sorceress have a say in the arrangements but had become humbly subject to her moods: craving her affection, fearful of her displeasure. By which he was bringing himself to shame and ridicule, betraying his responsibilities as a gaoler and compromising the dignity of the entire legal system of which Simkin counted himself a part.

When he was sober Simkin saw with a shrug that all advice and exhortation was wasted. Binnock was of such a helpless disposition that he was even incapable of defending himself – by legal redress or any other means – against the spite of his wife and the bullying of Hick Gaunt. This passive fatalism was aggravated in the gaoler's dealings with Sukie by the fact that he was besotted by her, if not bewitched.

There can be little doubt that Sukie was still being abetted and protected by Satan and was still nurturing magic powers – secretly, so as not to bring herself to further attention and punishment. Once, when she was furious with Binnock about something, she let her discreet mask slip, hinting that she had special means of making him regret what he did amiss or failed to do to her satisfaction. Binnock told Simkin about this, and Simkin contemplated having it reported to the Archdeacon but decided not to bother. He was pretty confident that the two-day stint in the pillory at the end of her sentence would put paid both to the girl's waxing arrogance and any pretensions to sorcery she retained.

Meanwhile, in Simkin's judgement, Sukie Dobson had become the delinquent queen of Pickering gaol and Binnock her emotional prisoner. Yet Simkin, drunk or sober, hesitated to interfere directly – even though he had some authority, some responsibility – in case it seemed to express a need or anxiety in himself. In any case nothing was happening that bothered him much. He did not like Sukie being freed from the wall, allowed to work outside and wander about unsupervised, but his unease was for reasons of principle mentioned above. He did not think that Sukie would risk the lethal penalties of an attempt to escape. She could not get very fast or far with her lame foot and he was confident that such a peasant lass would assume the all-powerful ubiquity of the forces that held her and be able to conjecture no refuge, once the sprites and hobgoblins of her dale had failed to protect her.

All the same, Simkin, a careful man, when a month of Sukie's sentence remained, approached Binnock and insisted she be securely chained to the wall for the rest of her time. It had occurred to him that the approaching prospect of two days in Pickering pillory might begin to seem more immediately drastic to her than the death she would suffer if she fled and was recaptured. Binnock begged Simkin to come to the gaol and effect the chaining in person, so that Sukie would not blame Binnock for the development. Simkin had already decided to do this since he had no faith in Binnock, particularly where Sukie was concerned. The visit he made to the gaol for this purpose confirmed the impressions he had been gathering from Binnock's boozy outpourings.

Sukie was in the pound, untethered, in her scarlet dress which by this time had become a bit bedraggled. She was sitting expertly astride an upturned sheep that was the only occupant of the pound and either removing a stone or effecting some other improvement on the hoof of the beast. Simkin, who had not set eyes on Sukie for several months, observed that she was plumper and her hair was long enough to cover her ears. As he passed by her, carrying her new chain and fetter concealed in a sack, she suspended the surgery to follow him with a glower of suspicion and animosity. When she was summoned to come indoors by Binnock she ignored the command for a while, then limped in with impertinent sloth, her eyes contemptuous and her chin tilted provocatively.

She submitted to the fettering in disdainful silence. Simkin flattered himself at first that this lack of resistance or protest was because she was in awe of his imperturbable phlegm and wary of his ready fist. Then it occurred to him that she wasn't bothered about being chained because she had no concept of the implications. Even at the beginning of her sentence Binnock had found it convenient to loose her regularly so that she could excrete or urinate in the midden adjoining the pound. Now that she had such an ascendancy over him she was confident that she could get him to free her as soon as the bailiff's back was turned.

Interested in confirming these deductions, Simkin bent over her and held the key to her fetter before her face, then let her watch him pop it into the leather pouch he used.

It took Sukie a couple of seconds to appreciate the significance of the bailiff's mime, then the effect on her was dramatic. Her eyes narrowed to slits of detestation and her lips curled back to reveal the gapped incisors of a goblin and the long canines of a carnivore. Snarling, spitting, hurling straw and filth, she lunged like a yard dog to the end of her chain in an attempt to reach Simkin. Since he had thwarted this by stepping back out of range, she flung obscene insults and preposterous threats at him in a screech that rendered most of it unintelligible. Her features were contorted into the lineaments of a fiend, and her green eyes taunted him to go close enough to slap or otherwise discipline her as he had done in the past. Even Simkin, a fellow it was difficult to impress, could still shake his head ruefully at the memory forty years later.

'It were fair capping to witness. Tha could see for certain what manner of creature she were, under all that poor daft lass cow shit what melted the 'earts of them soft twats at trial.'

Binnock was making small gibbering noises, devastated at the removal of her mask, her transformation into a savage creature of Satan, half brute, half demon. But Simkin was able to countenance the histrionics with a show of equanimity. He did not accept her challenge to battle because, as stated above, he was a man who eschewed redundant violence. In this case the only purpose of violence – to end the nuisance of her abusive racket – was as easily and conveniently achieved by his removing himself from the premises. Which he did, after emphasizing to Binnock that she must be kept secure and ready for the stocks at the end of the month.

He went away in a high good humour that was actually enhanced by the unnerving display he had witnessed. It told him that he had acted shrewdly and in good time. Her fury, born of bitter disappointment and despair, was clearly because her plans had been suddenly dashed. Whatever the penalties of an unsuccessful attempt to escape, she had never had any intention of staying in gaol until the end of her sentence and dying in the Pickering stocks, the way Simkin had foretold to her while they sheltered from the storm in Cropton Forest. She had intended to flee back to the wilds, to the dale-head moors and the forest depths that she knew better than anybody, where she might live as an outlaw, snare and fish, eat fruit and roots and fungi, never let herself be surprised and captured again. She had wanted her foot to get better before she escaped, for she would stand a better chance of avoiding recapture if she was not a cripple and she was well aware of the plight of lame things in the wild. So she had kept postponing her escape attempt, enduring the disgusting attentions of Binnock and his cronies, consoling herself with her cats and beasts and phantoms. Until suddenly she had left it too late and all was lost. Hence her candid, reckless fury – and Simkin's tendency to smirk and gloat.

His satisfaction was tempered at the end of the month, when he was briefed by the clerk to the Archdeacon.

There were vagrants in Pickering – sturdy beggars, as well as the legally maimed – who hung around the market street and set the tone for ragamuffin children. It was traditional that transgressors in the stocks were badly used in Pickering, unless they had friends or hirelings to protect them. If they had enemies more powerful or persistent than their friends they were lucky if they escaped serious injury.

Recently, in the adjoining hamlet of Thornham, a drunkard in the stocks, fortuitously the cousin of a Pickering burgher, had had his head split by the missile of a vindictive neighbour. This had resulted in some anxiety that punishments should be more carefully supervised and the civic or playful brutality of the populace kept below the level of outrage. Official thugs were hired to do sentry shifts by the market street stocks from sunrise to sundown.

Simkin, who had no responsibility for the town stocks, knew vaguely of this development and that in practice the thugs interfered very little with the pleasure of the citizens and the suffering of the criminal. He assumed that in the case of a witch even this trivial impediment to the self-expression of the public would be removed. He remembered fondly and proudly his involvement, under the instruction of Father Ignatius, with the Cropton witches in 1383. Two of these had been hung, the third (Granny Pringle) gaoled for a year in York then brought home to Pickering stocks and battered to pulp with cobblestones. He also remembered having helped another crone suffer Granny Pringle's fate when he was a lad in York Vale, just before his family came to Pickering. Throughout the Sukie Dobson business he had taken grim satisfaction from the thought that any displeasing irregularities of procedure would be corrected at the ineluctable denouement.

But the clerk to the Archdeacon informed the bailiff that there were going to be different arrangements made for Sukie Dobson, based on different principles. The two days chosen for her ordeal were Monday and Tuesday, deliberately avoiding both the Sunday holiday and the Thursday market. An officer of the court was to be present throughout and responsible for the witch's welfare. The often theoretical rules for the protection of the criminal were to be strictly enforced: only soft, harmless rubbish like dung and putrid fruit was to be used for missiles, and nobody was to approach within four yards of the stocks. It was the duty of the officer of the court not merely to make these rules clear to the public but to apprehend anybody who infringed the rules and place them for an hour beside the prisoner in the stocks. The Archdeacon's clerk had already arranged that two men-at-arms, borrowed from the castle garrison, would be put at the disposal of the court's officer to assist him in the discharge of these responsibilities. The Archdeacon's clerk concluded by making it clear to Simkin that the Archdeacon was particularly concerned that this girl should come to no harm – and Simkin, therewith appointed to overall control of the event, would be held responsible if she did.

'I were gobsmacked. Fair clettered. Couldn't for t'life of us work out how t'fuckin' witch wangled it.'

Later, he did arrive at a hypothesis, based on information he came by as well as his own shrewd, profane reasoning. The Archdeacon was fulfilling a promise to Father Ambrose, who had died recently after a series of seizures. During his last rites, conducted by his old friend and chess adversary, some residue of conscience about his involvement with the young witch had presumably surfaced.

It is of course clear to anyone who has had experience of the workings of Satan that the Fiend had devised a means for the survival of his instrument. This is not to deny the validity of Simkin's deductions but to give the events a proper significance beyond the scope of his stinted awareness.

The Ordeal of the Witch Sukie in Pickering Stocks

 OT THAT ALL Satan's contrivances for the safety of Sukie were successful. On the first day of her appearance in the Pickering stocks she had one or two pieces of what the profane Simkin would describe as bad luck.

The use of men-at-arms from the castle proved to be a mistake. The castle garrison in general despised the town, behaved very badly there and were unlikely to be enthusiastic about their duties under the command of a townsman. Simkin and Binnock would have been better served by the usual thugs employed by the town council. This was not a serious problem while Simkin was present: both his bleak air of authority and his trenchant instructions compelled their compliance. But the second mistake – the second of Sukie's misfortunes – was that Simkin had arranged to leave Binnock in charge for hour-long spells at midday and in the early evening, so that Simkin himself could eat, rest and attend to other personal matters. The men-at-arms might be wary of defying Simkin to his face, but as soon as he was absent they disobeyed his instructions, ignored Binnock and went together to the ale house down the street where they judged it would be a simple matter to fetch them in case of trouble.

The third problem was perhaps the gravest from Sukie's point of view. She had been an unspectacular occupant of the town gaol, generally accepted as not a witch but a country lass who was unlucky. When she came into contact with townsfolk she deliberately cultivated this low profile, not responding to the taunts of urchins and being as agreeable and ordinary as she could manage. This had combined with the discretion engineered from afar by the Archdeacon to prevent the finale of Sukie's punishment from attracting unwelcome attention – with one telling exception.

Binnock's patronage had made her unpopular with certain townswomen who had got wind of her forthcoming appearance in the stocks and been pleasantly anticipating it. This coterie was led by Binnock's wife, Thomasin. Hick Gaunt, the lout she had preferred to Binnock, now having left her for somebody he preferred, Thomasin was impoverished enough to feel resentful about the loss of Binnock's paltry income and vegetable broth. She had a revised version of her domestic history which she had recently told so often to cronies that she believed it herself.

'Thon's yonder!' she squealed as she lugged her basket into the market-place. She must have been lurking in ambush up some alley, or maybe behind the church, until Simkin and the soldiers had moved off and Binnock was in sole charge. Her basket contained a number of items that had suggested themselves to her: among the mouldy fruit and cattle droppings there lurked a switch of thorns, a length of chain, a pointed stick and some rocks.

'Thon's yonder trull as witched me feller.'

She pointed. A tall, bony woman of statuesque proportions, the dramatic dignity of her appearance was only diminished by the loss of most of her mossy teeth, the absence of which had collapsed her chops and made her jawline less formidable. Fat Floss, Thomasin's best friend, let out a support squawk of outrage. She had not brought a basket, thinking to borrow from Thomasin's resources or find implements and missiles to hand in the square. A couple of other women had come along with no precise intentions except to witness proceedings and approve of them.

One aspect of the Archdeacon's scheme (if it *was* his scheme) was functioning well: there was hardly anybody on the street. A saturnine yobbo in a buckram doublet was lounging by the drinking trough, fondling a smiling hound. He was not the sort to pelt a girl in the stocks, though he might have amused himself by offering her sexual harassment if Binnock had not been there. Two shaggy children of indeterminate sex were wrestling in the gutter. Along with other children, they had begun by enthusiastically hurling stuff at Sukie, but they had been fazed by the men-at-arms and not scored many hits, from the four-yard mark that Simkin had assigned them, before they ran out of permissible ammunition. Some of them had gone off to fetch more rubbish to pelt the witch but seemed to have found something more exciting to do and not returned. The two survivors now gave up their grapple and attached themselves to Thomasin's entourage.

They were leg-stocks at Pickering. Sukie was sitting bolt upright, her long neck giving her that look she sometimes had, of a nesting river bird about to take flight. She had adjudged her scarlet frock unsuitable for this public punishment and was clad in the only alternative item in her wardrobe, a shift of drab from which her calves and forearms protruded in sunless pallor. She was hungry, since she was not permitted to eat until released at sundown, but Binnock had supplied her with wine that had put hectic spots on her cheeks and made her feel better. She bore the marks of a few soft missiles that had landed on her but was doubtless congratulating herself that the first half-day was safely over when she saw the women. They had struck and spat at her once in the street and had recently taken to shouting gloating threats as they passed the gaol.

Thomasin was advancing purposefully towards the stocks when she was brought to a halt by her husband moving sheepishly to intercept her.

Binnock had been dreading this. While he was determined to do all he could to defend Sukie he also wished to offend Thomasin as little as possible, being in awe of her in any case, with or without her lout of a lover. The only approach available to the coward was diplomacy. 'Tommy!' he said, in a tone of pleasant surprise which (he later admitted to Simkin) was entirely fatuous in the circumstances. It was also entirely the wrong approach to take with Thomasin, because it was what he used to call her when they were younger and fonder. Her grief and just fury at once swelled out of all control, at the sight of her husband defending the trollop for whom he had forsaken her.

Simkin heard of all this later, from Binnock. The bailiff arrived to interrupt a loud affray, in which Binnock was leaping to and fro in a distressed condition while several woman and children were thwacking him with rocks or prodding him with sticks. One of the men-at-arms had emerged from the ale house down the street to see what the racket was about but was standing laughing helplessly at the spectacle.

The civic mutiny was instantly dispersed by the arrival of Simkin, though he was unarmed. In his youth he had built a reputation in Pickering for the headlong mayhem which could erupt from his callous phlegm. On this occasion the prompt flight of the insurgents meant that the dignity of his office and person were not challenged and his temper not evoked. He contented himself with declaiming the names of those fleeing women he recognized, bracketing them with obscene threats. He was actually more moved by his own error and Binnock's inadequacy than by the insurrection and cursed himself and jeered at the gaoler for some time. Binnock was too appalled by the nightmare and relieved at rescue from it to make excuses or say anything much. It turned out that he had only suffered surface cuts and abrasions.

When they got round to examining Sukie, they found that the damage done to her was more serious. She was unconscious. Her body had been gouged and pierced in several places, but her head injuries were graver: her mouth was a glistening cave and her hair a mess of blood.

Cloth was a cherished commodity in Pickering, so they trussed Sukie's skull with strips of her own scarlet dress fetched from the gaol. Binnock wanted Simkin to remove Sukie from the stocks, on the grounds that she was damaged and unconscious, and send to the Archdeacon for remission of her sentence, but the bailiff was not prepared to depart from the strict letter of his commission. He could recall how in more stirring times, under the vigilance of Father Ignatius, the corpse of

Granny Pringle had not been removed until sundown, then brought out at sunrise for its second-day stint. After an intermission while Binnock patched and bandaged her as best he could Sukie was replaced in the stocks. Her lack of consciousness meant that she had a tendency to slump prone, but this problem was solved by propping her with a sack of turnips.

Simkin dismissed Binnock from any share of the supervision, having lost what particle of faith he had had in the gaoler as a deputy. 'He were a mard, flabby twat, yon Binnock, as much use as a weasel's fart.' It was quite clear that Binnock was delighted to be relieved of responsibility – he never came near the market street again, either to enquire about the welfare of his slave and concubine or help protect her from abuse. The damage and indignity he had suffered from his wife's faction had severely shaken him, reinforced as it was by the hulking spectre of Hick Gaunt, who as far as Binnock knew was still Thomasin's champion. It was a test which Binnock's fondness for his prisoner could not hope to pass, given the accidental nature of their acquaintance and the lack of reciprocal sentiment in Sukie.

Simkin coldly told the men-at-arms that he would make sure they were punished when he reported the day's events. He saw no point in making more fuss, because he did not intend to leave his post again and give them any scope for disobedience. Paradoxically, his composure, compared with the bullying and blustering they were used to from their superiors, made them wary of him. For the next day and a half they were docile and assiduous: running his errands, fetching him provisions from the ale house and acting as his constables and monitors.

At this stage the 'luck' of the witch held good, when further violence upon her would surely have proved fatal. Thomasin had been as alarmed by Simkin's nonchalant menace as her husband had been terrified by her attack. Not wishing to make an enemy of the formidable bailiff, she let discretion overrule her grievances and made no further appearance. Sukie sat out the rest of her sentence in poor condition, plagued by blustery wind and wintry rain, but almost unassailed by humans. Her head, now in a round casque of scarlet bandage, made a less human, therefore less appealing, target, and her lack of reaction to the hits scored on her was unsatisfying. One exception to the subsequent lack of sporting and punitive zest was a doughty urchin (maybe one of the wrestlers who had been inspired by the previous day's events) who spent most of the second day, with persevering malice, in scuttling past the sentry to fling fragments of dung at her from close range, always with a shrill shout like a sea bird. He mostly missed and she was in any case only intermittently and remotely conscious. It was several weeks before she had any of her wits again, and there is evidence that she never got all of them back.

The clerk to the Archdeacon declared the latter most displeased by Simkin's unflinching report of the events and their consequences to Sukie Dobson. It was normal at the end of prison sentences for survivors to be released to find their own way back to their parish and tithing as best they could, on pain of further punishment if they failed to do so. In Sukie's case this was considered unreasonable, and Simkin was detailed to deliver her personally to her family in Beck Gap.

Her return, in a December twilight garnished with the first few flakes of snow, was therefore in ironic contrast to her departure thirteen months earlier. She was now astride the brown mule, with Simkin leading it, but this was the only improvement in her circumstances. She lolled and swayed perilously on her privileged perch. Her face – what could be seen amid the blood-caked scarlet pudding that swathed her head – showed few signs of consciousness and none of intelligence. Her family – according to sardonic Simkin – were much more appalled at getting her back than they had been at the prospect of losing her.

That was the end of the involvement of Bailiff Simkin with the history of Sycorax. He is, I think, an honest old fellow with an accurate memory: I have rarely altered or questioned the account he gave me but on a number of occasions have accepted his interpretation of events despite my own considerable misgivings. His failings as a witness, made clear by the later history of the witch, are godless ignorance and lack of imagination. This leads him to see the prologue to an amazing story in terms of profane, banal transactions – and despite long service as an officer of the Church to be brutishly oblivious to the strife between God and Satan for human souls which is everywhere in the world around him.

Brother Edmund Is Drawn to the Ale House in Nithermoor

EFORE I LEFT Byland on my mission I was troubled by demoralizing dreams.

I had two dreams in which I was flying, my arms spread and feet together as if I was a crucifix, over the roofs and buttresses of Byland, then over the smoking chimneys of a hamlet, then the shrunken foliage of a million trees. In both dreams I experienced an exhilarating sense of liberty, like a dunce released from school.

In one dream I lost height and drifted earthwards like a leaf until I was supine in long meadowgrass and a female figure loomed over me. It had the soft, pale body of Luce, my old sweetheart whose husband found us in the water meadow, but the head was of a bird, with a quiff of Luce's auburn hair for the bird's crest. It held me down by the shoulders and stared with small, bright eyes into mine as if it was about to peck out my brain. It lowered itself on to me, as if a hungry mouth was closing on to my member and was sucking it for nourishment.

In the other dream, night suddenly fell as I flew. I hung suspended, blind until a light grew towards me, one star in limitless darkness. As it came closer it lit more and more distinctly the form and features of Alys, like a votive candle in Our Lady's shrine. She lifted her skirts and underneath was naked and hairy as Luce in the water meadow or Nance in the shed beyond Four Acre. I fumbled with the difficulty of my clothing, then with the intractability of my member, which was huge and floppy like an uncooked sausage, yet tingling importunately so that I woke to find my fingers foul with my seed.

It added to my torment that I could not confess such dreams to

Abbot Fabian and seek his wisdom to interpret the symbolic code of the Fiend. He was insisting that I undergo the danger and inconvenience of life outside the abbey for a while, and I had made no secret of my reluctance. I feared that he would think I was inventing the dreams, or at least making myself available to them, in order to persuade both him and myself that I was unsuitable for his mission. Therefore I kept them to myself and went without the comfort of absolution.

I had to count this a little victory for Sycorax and her Master. I was becoming convinced that she knew of my project to tell her story, and I felt that she feared and hated me. While I took comfort from the fact that I got little pleasure from the dreams she was sending me, I could see that their purpose was rather to taunt than tempt me – and they were to make me wary of her Master's power and unwilling to venture again into his kingdom. I granted her the little victory of bereaving me of confession and absolution for a while, rather than let her turn me from the task entrusted me by Abbot Fabian which he was confident was both my duty to God – and the Church and the abbey – and my best means of salvation.

Therefore I took the burden of a sin on my soul – that of withholding full confession for a while – in order to have greater benefit from the shedding of responsibility by obedience. I left the abbey much against my inclinations as a cowardly sinner but prepared at my Abbot's behest to venture where I would be vulnerable to Sycorax, in defiance of her warnings. I had to trust that because I was going to do God's work in obedience to the Church I would have protection. Every mile that distanced me from the abbey and took me again into Satan's land of Yorkshire (which I have described above) made me less confident.

When I arrived at Kirkholt my faith started to revive. Kirkholt has managed to survive the effects of depopulation after the great pestilences of the last century, so far having kept a supply of lay brothers to support the grange and avoided leasing to tenants. Prior Jacobus runs a grange of six monks and a dozen lay brothers and labourers, in the true Cistercian tradition, combining commercially viable sheep farming with the tranquil routine and stark fare of a contemplative order. The monks are excused Terce, Sext and Nones – being at work on their flocks during the hours of daylight – and the open air and hard exercise seem to benefit their spirits, making them friendlier towards each other as well as less wrought with inward strife than their brothers in Byland.

I myself, though now geographically closer to the realm of Sycorax, was paradoxically more at ease at Kirkholt than amid the grandeurs and glooms of Byland where the battle between God and the Fiend was a constant, blatant theme. For several days I enjoyed a lull from inner torment: riding five miles to Pickering each morning in all weathers, engrossing myself all day with interviews in the Archdeacon's residence and elsewhere, then returning to Kirkholt before darkness, in time for supper and evensong with my brothers. For several nights I enjoyed dreamless sleep or serene, unremarkable dreams.

I listened in Pickering to Simkin's long description of the arrest and punishment of Sukie Dobson but also to a number of witnesses with amazing and awesome tales to tell of the later career of Sycorax. Perhaps as a result of these accounts, after several nights of respite the demons assaulted my dreams with redoubled malice. Luce, Nance, Nell, Malkin – and others whose names I had either never known or forgotten – posed and flaunted their crass mounds and stinking orifices, grunting and gibbering, drenching me with their filthy juices, draining my seed and spirit.

These were merely the minions of the witch. It was clear now that it was Sycorax who was bewitching me, haunting me, in the shape of the trulls and bumpkins of my youth. But she was capable of more devastating incarnations. Sometimes she took the form of Sukie Dobson, as described to me by Brother Denys and Bailiff Simkin: lean and gap-toothed, stinking of sheep-shit, in a scarlet gown. Once or twice she appallingly impersonated those emblems of womanhood I considered with pure reverence and implicated them in her witchcraft against me: my mother and sister, Rosamund Mowbray, the pregnant Virgin in the blue gown in Byland chapel, were all besmirched by their confusing propinquity with images of lust and shame. Most of all Sycorax employed the lineaments of Alys, making her maintain the lewd poses and perform the shameful stunts of the lesser goblins. I do not remember the details of these fantasies, nor do I wish to try to remember them, but I think that at almost every denouement Sycorax revealed herself, a skeletal crone with ravenous green eyes and consummated the copulatory spasm of despair.

I made full confession of these impurities to Prior Jacobus and was relieved to receive his absolution but somewhat disappointed by his failure to be horrified. Everybody has lewd dreams, he shrugged, though we must, of course, be abashed by them and penitent. He was equally matter of fact about my growing dread of Sycorax. If I was acting in obedience to the authority of the Church as represented by Abbot Fabian, I could be in no spiritual danger according to Jacobus. 'God never forsakes the obedient. It is the disobedient that forsake God.' His simple faith was refreshing enough but hardly conclusive reassurance for one who had both studied and experienced more than he had and was aware of the lethal complexity of everything.

I did not visit the manor of Dorsay because I knew that it was now derelict and that Sukie Trothers had almost certainly never set foot within the parkland pale of the domain. Roger Dorsay's widow had sold the estate to the Duchy after the calamity of 1414: the peasantry had fled to the south and west and the Duchy had never found another tenant.

It was crucial to my mission, though, that I returned to Nithermoor, where the locals I had recently interviewed about the youth of Sukie had precious information on the years following her release from gaol. I set out for the moorland village with my morale low. I remembered nothing of my previous visit with any pleasure except for the person of Alys – and she was now hedged about with guilt and dread, partly because of Abbot Fabian's warnings concerning her, but mostly because of her incorporation into the plot against my soul by the succubi and incubi of the Fiend. As I climbed the curling track I was less looking forward to regreeting Alys than aware that the road I was on ran past Nithermoor through a wasteland of blackened trees to Beck Gap, the outpost of Sycorax and her Master.

This time I journeyed alone, but Colin had gone two days ahead of me to make arrangements. I would have preferred to return each day before nightfall to Kirkholt Grange, but Colin had persuaded me that it was inconveniently far and that many of the witnesses I wished to interview would not in any case be available until their day's work was finished. I also asked that if possible a point of rendezvous and lodgement other than the ale house should be found for me, but either this proved not feasible or I was not positive enough in my request – lured as I was despite all by the prospect of proximity to Alys – so that Colin felt comfortable about ignoring it. He arranged for me to stay at the ale house for three nights and after scouring the village and neighbourhood for informants had worked out a provisional timetable of interviews, which he promised to be vigilant about implementing or ready to adapt as directed if I found that some informants merited more time and attention than others.

I was deeply relieved, as soon as I set eyes on Alys, at how she presented herself both to my senses and my conscience. The ugly indignities suffered and bestowed by her phantom in my dreams had left no trace on her real person or my response to it. The spectacle of her wholesome loveliness, her modest yet merry deportment, assured me that her role in my filthy fornication with fiends had not been (like Luce, Nance, Nell *et alia*) as a sluttish handmaid of Sycorax but rather as a pure icon (Rosamund Mowbray and the blue Virgin) usurped and despoiled by Sycorax and Satan for my torment. Her hair had grown longer, to cover her ears, since I last saw her, but otherwise her appearance and the chaste warmth of her greeting were entirely faithful to happy memory.

I had been supplied with a purse of silver groats and pennies by Abbot Fabian to pay my expenses while I was exiled from the abbey. So far I had not spent or changed any of them, since my needs had been supplied gratis either by the brothers at Kirkholt Grange or the Archdeacon's household in Pickering. I now gave two of the groats to Alys, telling her that they were to pay for my keep and for the ale with which my informants were to be rewarded if they so chose.

It was a too generous allowance and absurd behaviour. Worldly wisdom does not pay until the service has been received and assessed. At the very most I should have given her one groat on account, reserving the other for my departure. *But a monk who has no possessions is excusably careless with money. And worldly wisdom would be unseemly in one who has renounced the world.* So I hypocritically reasoned with myself in order to justify what was in truth the act of a shifty sinner. I wanted to impress Alys personally with my importance as well as ensure myself a welcome as a generous guest.

From my point of view she took the silver with disappointing nonchalance. I had expected her lovely eyes to widen at the very sight of the coins, since what currency there was at Nithermoor – where much of the traffic was barter – consisted of muddy copper halfpennies and worn farthings. But she gave a small, mysterious smile, just dimpling her cheeks, and said, 'Ee, Feyther! Never buy a pig in a bag.' None the less she did not return the coins to me but dobbed them into the pocket of her apron.

'Do not call me Father, Alys,' I protested gently. 'I am Brother Edmund. I am not old or reverend enough to be Father.'

For two days, determined not to repeat the sinful slackness of my previous visit, I imposed a regime on myself as strict as I followed in the abbey. I did not drink alcohol except for a small mug of ale with midday and evening meals and another, the equivalent of the wine we had in the abbey before Compline, just before I retired to bed, to help me sleep. I had been given exclusive use of the curtained recess in the house next to the ale house and I retreated there during the day – at intervals corresponding, as closely as my business would allow, with Prime, Terce, Nones and Evensong – in order to pray and contemplate before a little shrine I had composed with the cross, beads and candle I had brought from the abbey.

I worked energetically at my questioning of Trissie and others who had known Sukie between 1396 and 1399 – and the larger number who remembered the growth of her legend in the new century – and the majority of the Nithermoor population who had first- or second-hand information about the events of 1414. Experience at interviewing had by now developed skills in me. I was relaxed and sympathetic in manner, encouraging confidences. I knew when to prompt and when to simply listen and was cunning in the use of subsidiary questions to elicit detail or verify accuracy. I had also evolved a code of written symbols which made it possible for me to inscribe a reminder of the salient features of a testimony without interrupting the flow of the witness.

At mealtimes, or in the absence of anybody to interview, I could not resist wooing the attention of Alys. Her child, whom she for some reason called Gog (he was christened John), was now unswaddled and crawling sturdily around the floor of the ale house, meeting many adventures with bench legs, bones, a fat puppy and a brindle cat. I soon discovered that to occupy myself with the child was the surest way to distract the mother from other occupations and get her to talk to me. Therefore I would hold the grubby brat in my arms and let it drool on my shoulder or gouge my neck with its claws, while I was rewarded by Alys seating herself next to me or opposite and describing the prodigious portents of intelligence and courage already manifested by precocious Gog. If I was lucky I could then get her to speak of herself: her decided tastes, limited belief and quiet, stinted history. Meanwhile I could gloat on her intricate eyes and mischievous laugh, her trim figure and flawless complexion.

Mumping Night and the Bewitching
of Brother Edmund

N WEDNESDAY, THE third day, our evening meal was not only considerably earlier than usual but brief and frugal: just crust sops in a little bowl of the turnip soup we had had for lunch. I was wondering if it was consistent with my dignity to complain about this when I was distracted by the fact that even while we were eating the ale house was being patronized by numerous peasants, so that Alys had to keep getting up from the table to serve them. Though Nithermoor folk did not work all the hours of summer daylight, it was early for the field labourers to have finished hoeing and for the herders to have brought their beasts from pasture. I also noticed that these customers were marginally less muddy and ragged than was usual in the locality – and not the usual topers like Gib the miller who spent every evening in the ale house.

I made the mistake of asking Jackin, who was sitting next to me, what was going on. By this time I should have realized that his gentle taciturnity was transformed into bashful panic if he was directly addressed. He looked helplessly across at Alys, who answered for him.

'Mumpin', Feyther. It Mumpin' Night.'

This left me no wiser, except that I remembered having heard the word used several times in mealtime talk during the last couple of days. I had heard it incuriously, as I had learnt to ignore a lot of local jargon that was largely unintelligible to me. When Nithermoor folk spoke to each other in my presence it made me understand that they were largely bilingual and made a special effort in direct dialogue with me.

Thinking back, I was able to associate the word with other snatches of conversation I had heard and other signs that an event was in the offing. Alys and her mother-in-law had been doing a great deal of cooking, all the results of which had by no means yet reached the table. After the midday meal Colin and Jackin had carried all tables and benches out of the ale house on to the patch of flattened mud in front of it which was the closest thing Nithermoor had to a village green and where we were now eating. I had assumed that this was merely to take advantage of the summer weather.

I had preferred them to leave the table where I worked within the privacy of the building. I did not like to be abroad in Nithermoor, a filthy and depressing place, as explained above, with particularly bothersome dogs and urchins. Throughout my stay I had remained deliberately ignorant of my surroundings – either absorbed in my task or taking refuge in devotion – a remoteness only qualified when my attention was occupied by the captivating Alys.

Colin, hearing my question and Alys's reply, looked sheepish and avoided my gaze by taking an interest in his soup. As soon as the cursory snack was over I took the lad aside – before he could sneak away – and demanded a full description of the forthcoming event.

Mumping Night was Midsummer Eve, he told me. There would be strong ale and mutton pasties, music and dancing on the green. When it was dark a bonfire would be lit. A wheel of blazing straw would be rolled from Half Croft Steep. A cow, a sheep and a pig would be driven through the ashes to ensure the protection of Nithermoor beasts from accident and disease for the next twelve months.

I understood then that it was in fact the Eve of the Feast of Saint John, a minor festival which we celebrated in the Vale of York when I was a youngster with dancing, drink and sexual licence but without fires or other superstition. It was not a date of particular significance on our calendar at the abbey, and I knew that several eminent Fathers of the Church looked with disapproval on such pagan, seasonal rituals, esteeming them nothing less than worship of the horned, cloven-hoofed Fiend.

I expressed amazement to Colin that in Nithermoor, which in 1414 barely escaped engulfment by the Fires of Hell – and where folk were still afraid to venture into Slatterdale towards the source of that terror – there should be bonfires blithely lit and fire wheels rolled.

He shrugged. 'I were right young then. I can't recall there never being a Mumpin' Night 'ereabouts. If they stopped it, it soon crep' back.'

Perturbed by his indifference, I said, 'Yet since the events of fifteen years ago this blasphemous feast must have gathered a new and hellish significance, as a propitiation of Sycorax and her Master.'

He nodded respectfully but I could see that he did not take my point or share my views. He looked eager to escape from my company before I turned to more precise matters, but I had no intention of vouchsafing him that relief.

'What is personally galling to me, Brother Colin, is your discourtesy in not informing me of this impious event. Had I known of it a week ago I would have fixed our visit to avoid it. Had I known of it only yesterday, I might have rearranged my schedule to return to Kirkholt Grange this evening.'

Colin's face assumed a penitent expression. 'I never felt as it'd bother thoo none, Feyther. It's nobbut a midsummer frolic.'

I could see that further remonstration would be wasted on the clod. He had clearly attached himself to the abbey grange at Kirkholt from economic rather than spiritual considerations. He missed the muddy profanity of Nithermoor and had been glad to make my mission an excuse for yet another visit there and delighted to be able to wangle it to coincide with Mumping Night.

It was still possible for me to get down to Kirkholt Grange before nightfall and this is what I should have done. But the notion of saddling the stot and setting out was unattractive. In view of my confession to Prior Jacobus, I was loath to give him evidence that I lacked faith in the protection of the Church or courage against superstition. More practically, I would have to be back in Nithermoor in the morning, since there were a number of pertinent questions I still needed to put to Trissie March, one of my most important informants.

I decided that my best plan was to stay remote in the interior of the ale house, interviewing whoever Colin brought me, then retire promptly to my cubicle to spend my time in contemplation and prayer until it was dark enough to try to sleep. I was resigned to the fact that it might be too noisy to sleep until after midnight, when Colin assured me the festivities would cease.

For an hour or so I was busy, my work interrupted by the comings and goings of Alys's parents – who seemed to have taken on the burden of the ale house for the evening – and by the hubbub and music out-doors. Colin brought numerous people to talk to me in an attempt, I suspected, to keep me occupied and forestall any last-minute demand to be escorted to Kirkholt. Most of these 'informants' were lads and lasses of Colin's own age group, some of them having journeyed from outlying huts and hamlets. They claimed to have secondary information culled from relatives but in fact had little of interest to impart. Some of them were plainly fabricating, motivated by the prospect of the free stick of ale which Colin had told them was available.

I had to pass out of the door of the ale house to arrive at the hut where my curtained recess awaited me; but before I set foot out of the door my plans were already modified by the smell of mutton pasties as they were carried from the kiln behind the ale house to the tables on the green. I decided to drink my customary good-night mug of ale at one of the tables where the pasties were generously piled. As I drank I could both assuage my hunger and watch the festivities – which were at first sight innocent enough – and I was confident that I would have retired to prayer and sleep before darkness fell, the fires were lit and the worship of the Fiend began.

I later ascribed to the malice of Sycorax the deliciousness of the pasties, the strength of the ale (a special brew for Mumping Night) and the fact that somebody kept filling my mug as soon as I emptied it. Several other factors conspired with these to bring me to folly and shame. I was sitting among the elderly, the impotent spectators, which gave the festival a patina of harmlessness. Beside me was the parish priest, an illiterate peasant I disdained, yet whose presence was deemed by my hypocrisy to mitigate the situation. His deference flattered me into confidence in my own corrupted judgement, and the fact that he drank more copiously than I did encouraged me to excess.

The muddy green was thronged with two dozen couples who danced to a simple, repetitive pattern produced by the toot of a fife, the thud of a drum, the scrape of a bow. They were not all youngsters: married couples were dancing – some of them middle-aged – and one or two leathery bachelors still languished among the unattached young. It was a progression dance, two rows of partners forming and re-forming, such as I remembered from my youth, with the peculiarity that every so often the music would stop abruptly. The attention of all participants would focus on the couple who found themselves face to face at the end nearest to the musicians. This couple would then either separate – at which everybody jeered and groaned – or take hands, leave the dance and, loudly acclaimed, pursued by urchins, dogs and laughter, move out of sight among the village outbuildings or through the hedge into the fields. Their return to the dance – some after a few minutes, others after considerably longer – was greeted with the same amused applause.

This was the mumping dance, the parson told me. It was a very ancient business and perhaps once an accepted means of courtship or betrothal but nowadays just a source of harmless fun. I was not as confident as he was that the proceedings were innocent – some of the couples seemed to me to return to the dance in a disordered and elated state – but a second potion of ale made me more tolerant of such venial transgressions. A third serving made me positively nostalgic for my sinful youth as I sat in habit and tonsure among the old crones and codgers and watched the dancers. It seems reasonable to assume that some malign influence was at work on me, rather than find it feasible that all my faith and penitence, sixteen years of study and devotion, were flung to smithereens by two mugs of strong ale.

Alys was one of the dancers, and I watched her avidly. The unmarried girls all sported some white item – usually a kerchief or wimple –

among the browns and drabs of their garments, but the older women who were dancing allowed themselves more garish colours. I was shaken at first to see Alys in just such a scarlet frock as Gaoler Binnock (according to Simkin) had provided for Sukie Dobson. She even had a scarlet kerchief of the same material over her hair, as if she was deliberately making reference to the witch's gruesome bandage. But it was difficult to sustain these morbid associations as I watched how the ardent colour offset the delicate complexion of the lass and how the frock draped the plump sleekness of her contours as she stretched and turned in the dance.

I wished I was young and kitted out in a woollen jerkin and muddy boots. I wished that Alys was a white-wimpled maiden bobbing demurely in the dance. Oblivious to the rigmarole we would turn our heads to watch each other, try to maintain eye contact, yearn for the sudden magic silence to trap us together at the end of the row. If I had met her or somebody like her when I was young, I told myself, everything would have been transformed. Even if she was merely a peasant lass my parents scorned, I would have courted her respectfully and steadily, strolling and chatting, Sundays and festivals, proceeding by an orderly escalation of kiss and caress to nuptials, fatherhood – meanwhile never losing that sense of awe at her loveliness that would make me feel like a shepherd of pagan antiquity who was privileged to be visited by a goddess. My carnal experience would not then have been merely a series of queasy tableaux culminating in the retributive club and boots of the husband of Luce. I would not have vowed myself to a life of penitent chastity for which I was entirely unsuited, where the demands on me were impossible and the penalties calamitous. I would not have attracted the attention of Satan and his goblins. I would have been tolerated by God and His Church as a simple clodpoll and been permitted to indulge in continual sweet congress with Alys for the purpose of procreation.

But Alys's comportment, as I sipped my ale and watched her, made it difficult for me to sustain my sentimental reverie. It was as if she had put off reserve with her apron and donned a different personality to match her scarlet caparison. She laughed a good deal, with her teeth and eyes gleaming. Her face was hectically flushed, and I noticed that she twice quaffed from the ale mug of a bystander when there was a pause in the dance.

There was no doubt that she was the darling of the mumping dance and the queen of the festival. The musicians, who could of course halt the dancers when they wished, entered into a ribald conspiracy against her, so that she was three times caught at the end of the row, to the jubilation of the entire gathering. Each time it was with a different partner: first a sallow yokel with a wall eye, then her cousin Colin and at last her husband. Each time she showed not the slightest hesitation in merrily leaving the dance with the partner whom chance or the mischief of the musicians had furnished. Each time she was away from the dance for what seemed to me to be a considerable interval – though her first two absences were briefer than her tryst with Jackin – and each time her re-entry was greeted rapturously by everybody.

Just as I had been uncritical of Alys's comeliness, presented with its contrast to the muddy deformities of Nithermoor, so I had been eager to assume her modesty and virtue because it seemed to permit me to lavish attention on her and even admire her physical qualities. Abbot Fabian – never having seen the wench, but with the wisdom of sanctity and obedience – had concluded at once that it was my guilt, seeking some means of disguising or mitigating my carnal cravings, that had compelled me to my idealization of Alys. My attitude had not arisen from her deserving, any more than the Nithermoor rabble were now making her a special mark for their applause and mirth because they were awed by her beauty and inspired by her virtue.

I saw that her popularity arose naturally and spontaneously from her being the ale wife of the community: a fact that until now I had chosen entirely to discount, for the protection of what my hypocrisy told me was my innocent regard for the girl. I had less excuse than most for this convenient ignorance, since during my brutish youth I had had many dealings with ale wives – both in the city of York and the villages of the vale that surrounds it – and knew them for whores, procuresses, thieves, receivers . . . depending on their age and attributes.

On my last visit to Nithermoor, after I had parted from Alys in my curtained recess, the evocation of Abbot Fabian and his instruction had been sufficient to sober me to repentance. This time his revered memory could make no impact against the ale in my head, the lust and music in the air. So it is in Satan's kingdom. The defeat of the Fiend on one occasion makes the sinner no less vulnerable but only more confident in exposing himself to the next temptation.

A mouthful of ale seemed to temporarily clear my perceptions, and I discovered that the parson, my occasional interlocutor and drinking buddy, was gone from his seat across the table. Another development that had taken place in an interval in my awareness was that night had fallen. A full round moon was bathing the green in gentle light and nobody had bothered to light torches. In any case the dancers and musicians were gone from the green and the tables were deserted apart from myself and a couple of other sots. I could still hear music and a hubbub of voices, but it was coming from behind me at diminished volume. Turning from the moon towards the music I was able to see, above the hovels of Nithermoor, the loom and flicker of a bonfire against the sky.

Alys was moving among the tables, clearing away ale mugs and the remnants of the mounds of mutton pasties. Her husband and parents had presumably gone with the mob to the bonfire celebrations while she was left to serve ale, clear up debris and guard the sleeping child. To protect her finery she had donned her apron which shone – like her hands and face and forearms – milky under the midsummer moon.

I fumbled in my pouch for a silver groat such as I had given her on my arrival at Nithermoor. As she approached my table I held out my hand towards her with the coin in the palm – overturned my hand on to the tabletop – then withdrew it with a flourish to leave the coin exposed there. It was a gesture that had been customary in the ale houses of

York and which I now assumed would be understood by an ale wife or any wench in an ale house. If she pocketed the coin it meant a bargain had been struck. If she picked it up, spat on it and returned it to the table it meant that it was considered insufficient.

But Alys did neither of these things, nor did she respond in the only other manner the convention afforded, by shaking her head in rejection of the proposition. She looked from me to the coin as if she was entirely baffled by the proceeding, then moved aside to salvage any intact pasties from the table and place them in a pannier she was carrying for the purpose. They were clearly going to provide the basis for tomorrow's bill of fare. Crumbs and fragments she swept to the floor, where they were gobbled up by the dogs that were attending her.

I deduced that the codes of the sinners of York were not necessarily understood by the bumpkins of the North Riding. Picking up the coin between my thumb and forefinger, I held it out so that it glinted in the moonlight.

'This is yours, pretty Alys,' I crooned at her, 'if you will guide me to my bed and give me a Mumping Night kiss.'

She silently carried on with her work until the table was clear.

At first I was angry that she was ignoring me, then I decided that such could not be the case, for she had always seemed both a respectful and a good-natured lass. I thought it more likely that she had not heard me distinctly because my voice was blurred by excess of ale.

Some fading flicker of sobriety made me hesitate to repeat my embarrassing speech. I emptied my mug to quell this tiny bashfulness, but before I said anything she had finished her task and was standing opposite me. The pannier was balanced on her left hip, and she had a cluster of ale mugs in her right hand. The moon was behind her, so that her head was a dark outline, her features hidden as she leant forward and spoke quietly.

'Thoo, Feyther, piss off.'

The Homecoming and Wedding
of the Witch Sukie

'THERE'S SUMMAT FRIGGIN' sure,' said Ibbie Dobson. 'I can't be doing wi' yon loony in this 'ut.'

Simkin had unceremoniously lugged Sukie into the house, set her down by the hearth and departed without a word, deeming that events sufficiently explained themselves in this case. She had stared at the fire for a while, but nobody had managed to get any sense out of her before she flopped over sideways and lost consciousness. Ibbie and Trissie had moved her against the wall where she would not be under everybody's feet and where she had now lain for several hours – hardly breathing, her head still swathed in the scarlet rag – while she had become the topic of a lively family conference, many details of which we must imagine for ourselves, since we no longer have any witness as casually graphic as Simkin.

The personnel in the Dobson ménage had changed significantly over the last twelve months. It was good luck for the witch that her brother Ellis had been drafted into the Lancastrian soldiery, his insolence having exasperated the reeve and his family being without resources to pay for commutation. While the loss of the strongest and most active Dobson was an economic blow, it was mitigated both by the likelihood that Ellis would have quit them soon in any case (he was savage with resentment at doing more than his share of the work) and by the immediate absence of the sullen thug. Another departure (of a sort) was Mitch, Sukie's thirteen-year-old brother, who was mostly on the moors and ridings, having inherited his sister's hut and herding duties. On the other hand, Sukie's elder sister Bab, married three years back but now a widow, had returned to the family seat with two toddlers.

With Jeff and Ella, respectively nine and eleven, that meant eight occupants of the house before the readdition of Sukie. It was not the numbers that were worrying Ibbie. She was used to a crowded hovel: everybody sleeping on straw in a tangle or crouched round the frugal hearth in winter, jammed against each other for warmth. But Ibbie had always got on particularly badly with Sukie and had been glad to be rid of her when they put her on the dale with her granny five years ago. Now she had come home not merely as a convicted witch and the shame of the family but as a disconcerting, witless creature who might not be able to work or even look after herself.

'It's us lass though, Ibbie, eh?' said Tom Dobson coaxingly. He was propped in a corner away from the hearth, sharing a bladder of apple wine with his buddy, Watkin Trothers, whom the lure of the wine had brought there to coincidentally partake in the Dobson family conference.

Tom took a swig from the bladder then added, in more negative tones, 'Anyroad there's nowt to be done. She's down to us by law.'

Bab let out a threatening snort. She was physically similar to Sukie and Trissie but more heavily and aggressively featured than either of them. She had the Dobson temper but none of the lone and dreamy nature that had brought Sukie into the clutches of the Fiend.

'They should've hung the bugger if she's a witch,' Bab declared. 'They'd no right bashin' 'er fuckin' brains out an' leavin' 'er for us to nourish.'

Tom said, 'She'll happen get a few wits back, then we could put 'er up dale wi' Mitch.'

'We haven't muttons up dale for one to tend, never mind two,' said Ibbie.

Tom said, 'Aye, but she'd happen feed 'ersen wi' fishin' and trappin' like she used to could and be no cost to us.'

Ibbie shook her head disconsolately. 'She'll not have wits for nowt, by t'look of 'er. An' as soon as she settled Mitch'd be skriking to be back in Beck Gap. He won't fancy stopping out yonder wi' a loony. An' 'e'll ruin us, that sod, wi' t'grub 'e can shove down 'is throat.'

Trissie Dobson remembers that once or twice the debate was interrupted when Sukie suddenly let out a moan and there was a terrified silence. All eyes swivelled towards the still shape in the shadows. Presumably Bab's nameless toddlers, who must surely have been present, were also silent, impressed by the ambience. They probably put their thumbs into their mouths and gazed from face to face of the assembly, trying to work out what the problem was.

At some point Bab shouted, 'It aren't fucking fair! She's no right comin' 'ere where we was promised first and there's no fuckin' room.'

Later Watkin Trothers, after a particularly heavy swig from the wineskin, called out, 'Give me the wench! I'll 'ave 'er if nobody else wants 'er.'

Nobody took him seriously at that time – he was the sort of hapless drunk who had trouble getting himself taken seriously – but everybody later remembered his outburst, because what he proposed came to pass.

'This were Watkin:

'Aye, the nummock. Robin Clegg, the twat. 'Oldin' yon stringy brindle cock on t'palm of 'is fist wi' 'is thumb up it bum to render it lively. "It nobbut three year owd," 'e goes, "an' it worth six ales." An' thoo know me, I just goes, "Oo aye, three year owd?" An' 'e goes, "Aye, that's it, I swear to God." The gobshite. Eyes like a midden rat. But thoo know me. I just goes, "Oo aye? Three year owd?" An' 'e goes, "If thoo buy us four ales that's straight for two I owe thoo an' t'cock's thine." An' I goes, "It fuckin' funny it nobbut three year owd, for I sold thoo that twat three year back and it weren't no fuckin' chicken then. An' another thing," I told 'im straight, the fucking gobshite, "an' another thing, it aren't no fuckin' two ales thoo owes me, it three fuckers." Last time that fat twat tries it on wi' Watkin, eh? By . . . !'

Mat Fettler was an ancient maniac in Nithermoor who had been introduced to me by Colin as a specialist in impersonations. Mat gave me no useful information – indeed, seemed incapable of logical or consecutive thought – but three times, when a name was mentioned to him, he went into a rigmarole like the one above. Two of these were impersonations of Watkin Trothers; the third was of a parish priest of the same epoch, an ornate parody of a sermon that I have not retained.

I do not of course know whether Mat's impersonations were good ones, nor did I remember to ask anybody to vouch for them, but the unpleasant way that Mat twisted his lips and squinted his eyes as he performed the soliloquy told me at least that he had a low opinion of Watkin Trothers. This was an opinion he shared with Trissie Dobson and everybody else who remembered Watkin.

At the time of Sukie's return to Slatterdale Watkin was about thirty-five years old: a drunken curmudgeon who was mostly discounted, except that folk tried to meddle with him for no longer than was strictly necessary. He had a little forge in a shed by West Copse, but his hulks and sulks and the truculent shoddiness of his work meant he offered very little competition to the smith at Nithermoor. Watkin did cut-price work for those in Beck Gap who were unwilling or unable to travel to Nithermoor or who considered the smith too leisurely and costly. He supplemented this income by poaching and hiring himself out as a labourer at harvest time and other seasonal crises.

According to Trissie, Tom Dobson was Watkin's only friend and even he would admit from time to time that he did not like Watkin or get a lot of pleasure from his company. The pair were bound together by addiction to alcohol: a vice which many find less abject and shameful if they can furnish themselves with an accomplice. Beck Gap society could not support many drunken wastrels, nor did the toil and stint give many the leisure or hardihood for alcoholic excess except on feast days. Tom and Watkin were therefore thrown into each other's company: in Mother Jennet's shack, the nearest thing Beck Gap had to an ale house, or in Watkin's shed or the Dobson dwelling where they drank brews they had made themselves or acquired from other home producers. Sometimes, if their funds permitted, they went together to the Nithermoor ale house four miles away. They abetted each other in the embittered or euphoric visions which their boozing brought them, condoled each other against the world that had brought them to this pass and confirmed each other in their self-indulgent acquiescence to defeat.

This makes them sound similar, interchangeable fellows, but several witnesses spoke kindly of Tom: Trissie in particular was eager to contrast the characters of the two drunkards. Tom was consistently mild and easy, flippant and melancholy. Why he needed such dogged consumption of alcohol was a mystery, since it seemed to have no impact on either his mood or his demeanour. But drink strongly affected Watkin, embellishing and exaggerating his state of mind. His high spirits became noisy and indiscriminate mirth; his low moods plunged to maudlin dejection. Either of these conditions could turn ugly if he met with any cross or sometimes if he merely sensed that he was not getting sufficiently enthusiastic applause or sympathy. It was Tom's bland, assenting nature which ensured that there was very little trouble between the two of them even when they were very drunk.

'Meaty and juicy, an' I just wiggles me fingers, sithee, like this, when she lets out a skrike, the fuckin' bitch, an' tries to tug 'er frock down. Thoo knows what they're like. She'd picked on t'wrong un this time, though. "Eh," I goes, just like that, "keep still thoo teasin' fuckin' cowbag, no wench changes 'er mind on Watkin Trothers." Eh? By ... !'

Taken together, Mat's impersonations gave an impression of Watkin's usual discourse while boozing which was confirmed by those others who remembered him. Sometimes he related his dealings with his fellow men, giving gloating accounts of petty triumphs gained by his wit and *savoir faire* against a world that was always out to trick him. Sometimes he bragged about sexual exploits in which women were maltreated with contempt and suspicion. These anecdotes were deemed inventions by all who knew him, particularly the ones about women: for several years, up to the time of Sukie's return, he had been known to do nothing for entertainment but drink. Before that he had been married twice, but both wives had died young, one of a domestic accident, the other in childbirth. No children had survived infancy.

Tom Dobson was not a fastidious fellow and found Watkin an acceptable enough drinking companion, for want of an alternative. On the other hand, the foibles one accepts in a drinking crony may not seem so tolerable in a prospective son-in-law. After the drunkard's intention to marry the mad witch-girl had somehow progressed from joke to accustomed fact in Beck Gap, Tom started noticing perturbing attitudes and opinions in Watkin that had previously seemed merely amusing. Watkin was scornful, for instance, of Tom's lack of domestic assertiveness and the resultant insolence – as Watkin saw it – of the Dobson women and children. Watkin had given Tom a lot of advice about the strict measures needed to ensure that a dominant male got proper respect and had a household that served his requirements. He sometimes accompanied the advice with accounts of drastic but just chastisement which he had administered to his own wives when obedience or enthusiasm failed them. Tom found it difficult not to associate the sentiments emphasized and illustrated by Watkin with the rumour still persisting in Beck Gap that the death of Watkin's first wife may have only been accidental in a technical and qualified sense of the term. Tom began to experience a growing compunction about committing his daughter – even that weird and inconvenient daughter – to the care of his boozing buddy. He went so far as to voice his doubts to Ibbie.

Ibbie's sensitivities were coarsened by the stint and squalor of a life devoted to keeping herself and her dependants above the level of calamity: a drunken husband, fourteen childbirths, seven fractious surviving children, the daylight hours for twenty-five years taken up with domestic duties and spinning wool for a Rievaulx grange. When difficult Sukie had gone, then truculent, ravenous Mitch, then awful Ellis, she had seen like a gleam of dawn on her horizon an emptier and easier house making less demands on her. Just herself and Tom, her ally Trissie and the two younger kids who were relatively cheerful and hard-working so far.

Then Bab had arrived, with her contentious manner, her overbearing demands, her two hungry toddlers. Then Sukie, a demented invalid. Ibbie could see fate regaining force and malice, resuming its pitiless war on her. Ibbie, more than anybody else, had persevered in keeping Watkin to his nonchalant proposition by simply acting as if the matter was settled and ineluctable. She was relieved and delighted at the prospect of Sukie being taken off her hands without any mention of dowry or other terms, by somebody who could provide her with a modest livelihood and accommodation.

Ibbie scoffed at Tom's misgivings. There was no evidence that Watkin had ever been seriously violent to his previous wives. They had occasionally been seen sporting superficial bruises but nothing worthy of remark. Some women provoked and deserved an occasional slap, Ibbie said, either by immodest behaviour or by being so submissive that their husbands came to feel that they could treat them how they liked. The bulk of the testimony about Watkin's brutality came from his own drunken lips and was probably as fanciful as the rest of the gobshite's boasting. Drink was his worst fault as a prospective son-in-law and Tom was hardly well placed to take exception to that since he drank at least as much as Watkin. Moreover, marriage might succeed with Watkin as it had failed with Tom: tempering his drinking by giving him a reason to go to bed relatively sober. Ibbie seemed to remember that Watkin's boozing had much increased since his second widowhood. She also felt that if he did sometimes use his heavy hand on Sukie it might be no bad thing. Ibbie had always blamed Tom's failure to discipline his children for their faults in character and her own sense of inadequacy. What Sukie had needed all her days was a good thrashing, and it was what she would need again if she recovered any semblance of her wits and spirit.

Public opinion at Beck Gap agreed with Ibbie. Sukie was considered very lucky to be alive and as a convicted witch possessed no right to a say in her own destiny, even if she had been in a position to insist on one. It was generally felt that her family had had a raw deal and that to marry her off was the most satisfactory solution for everyone –

including Sukie, so long as she did not expect, with her history and in her condition, to make a brilliant match. Watkin's proposal was deemed generous by some, who were prepared to qualify their dismal opinion of the fellow on the strength of it. When word of the match, together with the notion of its suitability as an end to the Sukie Dobson scandal, reached Richard Dorsay, he not only waived the marriage fine but sent three silver groats via the reeve and the reeve's man to Watkin, both as a reward for his proposal and as a payment that would bind him to it.

The wedding had to wait until Sukie was sufficiently presentable. Her skull healed fairly quickly, and once her hair had grown to cover the scar she bore no sign of physical damage apart from the foot which Simkin and Binnock had crushed in Pickering Castle. This was an injury she would have for the rest of her days. It gave a wince and lunge to her gait that made her unmistakable at any distance.

Her mental condition improved more slowly and less satisfactorily. Trissie proved an expert on this topic, since it was she that mostly had the care of Sukie until the latter's marriage. Sukie quickly recovered the ability to dress, eat and keep herself fairly clean. Soon she could do jobs like chopping wood and tending the fire, if somebody was with her to remind her what to do from time to time and keep her attention on the task. Some complicated operations, like giving first aid to a wounded animal, she could do spontaneously and impressively, but there were other tasks, such as binding straw or slicing turnips, that would either baffle her into lamentation or plunge her into a dream.

She did not seem to understand much of what was said to her. This often seemed to be the result of inattentiveness, as if other voices were calling more urgently within her and blotting out what external folk were trying to communicate. But at other times she seemed to concentrate very hard on what was being said – her eyes brilliant with hope then sullen with disappointment – as if she found herself among strangers whose jargon would from time to time contain an accidental phrase in her own tongue. She recovered her powers of speech very slowly, instead using a variety of dog-like keening noises which seemed less an attempt to communicate than to express and relieve her own feelings.

The parish priest of the epoch was a meek little peasant, who was in accordance with public opinion on the need to domesticate the mad witch and submit her to the care and discipline of a husband. With this in view, he was grateful that Watkin was sober enough on the day to cooperate in the ceremony – and saw no problem in either patiently prompting a response out of Sukie or in accepting any noise she then made as a token of assent. A sheep that Mitch had driven down from the dale was slaughtered and roasted: a sick, lame sheep that none the less gave style and prestige to the event. The population of Beck Gap, invited to partake in the mutton, brought bride-ale of their own and there was music, dancing, drinking, dispute and fornication such as would bedizen any feast day or normal wedding.

Sukie wore the family bridal gown which her grandmother, mother and sister Bab had been married in and which later was rescued from Watkin's shed, repaired and stored to be used by Trissie and Ella in their turn. But Sukie showed awareness neither of the sacred and traditional aspect of proceedings, nor of their significance to her own person. She ate and drank, when it was offered her, with an appetite that had recently started to dismay economy-conscious Ibbie, but she did not go in search of nourishment or do anything that required initiative. She sat in what seemed almost total incomprehension of her surroundings until she was escorted by her staggering father and equally staggering husband to Watkin's shed by West Copse. There we lose sight of her, but she presumably waited to pay the marriage debt at the back of the shed in the filthy straw (hard to imagine that Watkin had bothered to clean out the nuptial chamber) when her husband and father had finished whatever booze they had brought with them from the feast or found on the premises.

The Comportment and Gruesome Death of Watkin Trothers

FTER HIS MARRIAGE, Watkin Trothers stopped drinking alcohol in his own shed or inviting his buddy there. If he ever gave a reason for this it has not been remembered. The only other observed alteration to his routine or bearing was that late at night, on his way home from Mother Jennet's or wherever he had been drinking, he formed the habit of singing an impudent little ditty full of sexual imagery and *double entendres*.

This musical development was regarded optimistically – as an indication that marriage might have alleviated the morose aspect of Watkin's sottishness – until it came to be known that he had also taken to beating his new bride, to an extent that surprised many of the inhabitants of Beck Gap. Despite the old rumours about the death of his first wife, Watkin had no general reputation for thuggery. Though he was often bitter and brutal in speech, he was never known to be physically violent to anybody except his wives – and to Sukie, for some reason, much more than her predecessors. While he sometimes beat her during the day, if she annoyed him or he was in a bad mood anyway, most of her beatings took place at night – when he was drunk – and expressed a range of whims and tempers: ferocious wrath, amorous cruelty or even knockabout humour.

The shed at West Copse was well within hearing-range of other dwellings and neighbours came to attach new importance to the late-night song of Watkin Trothers, greeting it with groans, as the prelude to the racket of Watkin beating his wife that was going to keep them from their sleep. We can assume that the singing had an even more unwelcome significance for Sukie, crouched in the shed. If he was not singing she would be able to hope. At least once a week, if he was sober enough, he tended his poacher's snares in the Dorsay woods. On other occasions, for no discernible reason, he went home silent and relatively sober, with no fracas following his arrival. Or there were times when he was too drunk to sing and fell into unconsciousness as soon as his willpower had staggered him home. Or there were times when he was too drunk to get home at all. But as soon as she heard the singing hope was lost.

Trissie March was of the opinion that Watkin sang specifically for Sukie, because it amused him that she should savour her ordeal in advance, knowing he was on his way to her. Trissie shrugged when I asked her why she thought her sister had submitted to this rather than take flight into the darkness. ''Appen Sukie'd tried that once and got brayed worse for it. Anyroad, Sukie were stupid daft.'

The Dobsons were out of range of the doings at West Copse, but they got reports from those who lay awake and winced or chuckled depending on their natures. Apparently the noise, apart from some percussive effects, all came from Watkin. Sometimes it was furious bellowing, but often enough it was full-throated, open-hearted laughter, as if some irresistibly hilarious jest was in progress. Sometimes the vocal efforts were more subtly disruptive of the neighbours' sleep: whimsical, wheedling, sniggering, with just an occasional catch of breath or irregularity of pitch indicating some physical effort at variance with the monologue.

Nobody ever heard a sound from the girl, not even the whining noises that she made in normal circumstances. It was only when she appeared in daylight – bruised or limping more than usual or otherwise damaged – that her contribution to Watkin's evening and the damage she had shipped could be assessed.

Once or twice she suffered more serious injury and failed to emerge at all the next day. Trissie once ventured over to West Copse and found her sister with her legs so bruised that she was unable to walk. Another time Watkin, who was without medical expertise, claimed that she had fallen and called in a neighbour to snap her dislocated shoulder back. Another time she miscarried after a beating when she was several months pregnant. When she became pregnant again it was widely assumed that the same thing would happen, but amazingly she escaped decisive injury until after a girl child had been born. Anybody who thought that this event indicated some relenting in Watkin was soon disillusioned: Sukie had nursed her daughter for only a couple of months when after a particularly noisy night at West Copse the child's skull was fatally fractured. Watkin said Sukie had dropped her on to the forge anvil.

None of the neighbours ever rose from their pallets to interrupt the events of West Copse, nor did they protest to Watkin about his treatment of Sukie. Among the riff-raff of the North Riding, even more than in other districts and echelons, the right of a man to do what he wishes within the confines of his home and treat his dependants as suits his humour is a principle jealously guarded and universally respected. It is essential to the self-respect of those who are otherwise the prospectless dregs of society that they should have the powers of a despot over their women and children. Fellows like Tom Dobson and Gaoler Binnock, ruled and flouted by their wives, are objects of contemptuous disapproval, while there is general consensus that heavy-handed husbands like Watkin Trothers at least have their hearts in the right place and are upholding proper principles. The leathery peasants of Beck Gap maintained – and their bruised wives agreed with them – that Watkin had more reason than most to lose patience with a practically deaf and dumb wife who could not cook or clean for him or do anything to help him scratch a living.

Even with the weight of such opinion against him, Tom Dobson found it difficult to support what was happening to his daughter. He blamed himself for having succumbed to Ibbie's arguments and suppressed his doubts before the marriage. He felt strongly enough about it to shift from his boozy lethargy and struggle with his own temperament and conditioning. Despite his habitual avoidance of any sort of

125

critical or contentious stance – and the horror of embarrassment that clutched him at the remotest threat that such a stance was needed – he brought himself to complain to his son-in-law about Sukie's treatment. At first his complaint was so tactfully insinuated that Watkin either missed the point or ignored it. Then Tom complained directly, though mildly, as one good fellow to another. Watkin, caught in a tranquil mood, had the grace to be sheepish and apologetic – 'Supped a drop too much, sithee' – but made no subsequent effort to forego any of his evening entertainment. Tom, heroically, persevered with ever more emphatic complaints until Watkin told him roundly to mind his own business, at which each spoke bitterly and menacingly to the other, but a resort to violence was precluded by the feeble physique of Tom and the diffidence of Watkin regarding extramarital fisticuffs.

After that Tom no longer went to Mother Jennet's to drink with Watkin, nor was Watkin welcome to drink with Tom in the Dobson cupboard corner. While Tom felt content with himself for having acted on principle, he could see that he had not actually achieved a lot on Sukie's behalf. Therefore he gallantly broached the matter with Ibbie: in some ways, from his point of view, a much more serious step than confronting Watkin. He suggested that they should formally complain to the authorities – either the Lord of Dorsay or the Archdeacon – about Sukie's treatment, or that they should even take matters into their own hands, reclaiming their daughter and spiriting her off to Mitch in Slatterdale, where Watkin would surely never be organized enough to find her.

Ibbie was furious. Her own conscience had been troubling her. Her preferred solution was to confess her worries to the bland and non-committal priest and otherwise be as deaf and blind as possible. In pursuit of this she had shunned Sukie after the marriage and later was to show no interest whatsoever in her granddaughter's brief career. Now she resented Tom speaking out because it sabotaged her own stance, as well as putting her husband in a position of moral ascendancy.

She managed to speak calmly, with cold finality, to the following effect: Tom was a nincompoop. Any complaint would have to be made via Dodge Ingram, the tithing head, who was in cahoots with the reeve of Dorsay. The Dobsons and the Ingrams were still feuding, whereas Watkin Trothers was strangely in favour with the Lord of Dorsay who had sent him three silver groats. The less they had to do with the Ecclesiastical Court the better, in view of Sukie's previous experience there. Sukie was now, thank mercy, Watkin's property and a loony for whom nothing could be done. An abduction, even if Mitch would cooperate, would be bound to land the whole family in serious trouble. Tom's proposals were foolish and his interference futile unless his real plan was to upset his long-suffering wife, in which case he had done well.

It is to Tom's credit that after this rebuff he still timidly grumbled from time to time, so that there was an additional note of discord in the Dobson household. Trissie, who provided me with much of this information, was torn by the contention. She generally preferred her mother's flinty, joyless efforts at raising seven children to the affable, beery uselessness of her father, but in this specific case she felt a sympathy for Sukie that tempted her towards her father's faction.

'Sukie treated me fair enough, though we were never friends, afore she went off to be a witch. It were shameful 'ow Watkin brayed 'er. Mam could of stopped that. Mam could do owt if she put 'er mind at it. But she were worn down by then.'

At this point Trissie broke off to make an observation about her sister: 'Watkin were a shitbag, but there were summat in Sukie what made folk bash 'er. She were the most provoking lass. I know missen, when we was younger, she'd make me fists fair itch to bash and throttle the bitch, way she'd perch 'er 'ead on one side and sniff like a queen. As if it were shit she were looking at. Even after she'd lost her wits she'd still some of that look. There were summat inside of 'er. Happen it were t'witch in 'er.'

I thought these last remarks of Trissie March perceptive within her limitations and still find them interesting, since they point to the dichotomy which has constantly faced me in dealing with what is in effect a hybrid creature composed of the mortal Sukie Trothers and the Fiend Sycorax that infested her. You will have observed that in this chapter my intention to record faithfully and factually has been hindered here and there by compassion for Sukie Trothers and indignation at the brutish yokels of Beck Gap whose malice, cowardice and ignorance conspired to furnish a living Hell for the silly lass. This is error.

I need to continually remind my readers (and myself) that it is the story of the Fiend Sycorax that I am recording, without which the story of the peasant wench Sukie would have neither purpose nor interest. Once this is understood it also becomes clear that pity and compunction only serve the interests of Satan.

Throughout the period I am describing the Fiend Sycorax was resident in the shell of Sukie Trothers. The blows of Watkin only bothered the Fiend in so far as they threatened the health of the human body which it had chosen as a vehicle and somehow managed to preserve from the proper course of justice in Pickering. And Sycorax was working, while lurking and biding time. Sycorax was rendering the body it inhabited suitable for the Fiend's next instar: rendering it into a hapless, pitiful, unmenacing victim that nobody would think worth bothering about or guarding against until it was too late.

It is sentimental weakness, or some failing even more congenial to Satan, if I and my readers feel pity for Sukie Trothers. If Sukie Dobson existed at all by the time of her marriage, it was in such close proximity to Sycorax that they were indistinguishable. If the girl Sukie had still been present as an independent awareness she would have welcomed any punishment, whether it was visited on her by the Holy Church or the fists and boots of Watkin, that might have embodied her true penitence, rid her of Sycorax and saved her from an eternity of Hell. The worst betrayal of Christ's sacrifice that we commit and the greatest service we perform for Satan is when we are tender with the body at the expense of the soul. The folk of Beck Gap did well not to succour the witch. It might even be that Watkin was not the bestial creature I have presented but was reacting from an incoherent but nevertheless God-given impulse, out of commendable hatred of the Fiend he sensed inside his witless young wife.

Trissie had some sense of the possession of her sister but no grasp of principles, therefore her perceptions, though not unintelligent, were oblique and profitless:

'I were round wi' Sukie a lot of t'time after she 'ad babby, for I were capped wi' babbies them days. And when she were nursing yon babby I'll swear she were right as rain. She'd know what I said and say English words at me, slow but sure, and tended babby as well or better nor any mam I ever seen.'

While one has no reason to doubt the accuracy of this testimony, it leaves one entirely unenlightened. We cannot tell whether we are glimpsing a remnant of the real Sukie (not, by all accounts, a maternal creature), or if it is the guile of Sycorax pretending maternal love to confound discovery, then and now.

One night, about a month after the death of Sukie's daughter, the Cleggs, who were the closest neighbours to the Trothers shed at West Copse, were interrupted in their attempt to sleep by Watkin Trothers returning home singing.

It was the song he usually sang on his way from an evening's tippling to home, wife and evening meal. Because Sukie was incompetent the meal would be something he had prepared himself and left her to try to remember to warm for his return. The song was of his invention, in that he had adapted the lyrics from dirty jokes and feast-day ballads that took his fancy.

After each ragged verse of a quatrain ballad Watkin, a talented but untutored musician, would whistle a verse, but his whistle was a husky sigh of air through his front teeth that did not carry like his full-throated baritone through the darkness. It reached the Cleggs as considerable silences between the verses, so that each time one might think that the song had mercifully ceased. They knew better than to build up hopes of this, having lived alongside Watkin Trothers for the two years since his marriage. It was Alan Clegg who had fixed Sukie's dislocated shoulder, and Joan had gone with Sukie and Trissie into the copse to bury the unchristened child.

Alan said, 'Jesus! Yon twat's back on form, and we shan't sleep yet a bit.'

He sounded more resigned than angry and his voice was already thick with slumber. He and Joan had spent a long day hoeing and were exhausted.

The singing reached full volume as Watkin passed the Cleggs then dwindled as he went down the track to his shed.

Alan said, 'Let's 'ope 'e soon 'as the fuckin' witch knocked out so we can all get a night's kip.'

Joan did not answer because she was already asleep, having learnt to ignore the neighbours in a way that Alan never quite had. She later claimed that a wafting sensation was troubling her sleep, as if she was being bothered by the wings of a giant bird that was flapping in the darkness. She was snug enough, though, to be furious when Alan woke her a little later.

'Listen!' he hissed at her.

She heard the bullying rant of Watkin Trothers, punctuated with percussive sounds as he emphasized his utterances.

'Shit! Why should I listen to that what I've 'eard 'underds o' times? For Christ's sake, let us sleep!'

'No, Joan, listen! It's summat . . . it's daft . . .'

Then she heard what Alan meant. There was another voice in the hubbub of the shed at West Copse. It was as if a gruff stranger was intruding on Watkin's soliloquy. At first it sounded like a mere offspring of Watkin's voice, an echo, then it became a bass accompaniment that took on a life of its own, like a dog barking in tune and cadence with its master's bellows.

As they continued to listen a weird and terrible thing happened.

Watkin's voice faltered, let out a couple of last, spiteful phrases and was gone. The other voice went on, thickening as it raved until it had lost all semblance of Watkin. It swelled to become the baying of a massive hound, the roar of a dragon, the baleful triumph of a demon, something trumpeting sodden with blood, unimaginable.

Then there was total silence. Joan nudged Alan.

'What the fuck were that?'

He clutched her arm. They lay for a long time listening to the silence.

As soon as there was clear daylight Alan collected several neighbours together. The troop went gingerly down the track and through the open door into the Trothers shed.

Watkin was stark naked in the forge annexe, half upright against the anvil where Sycorax had jammed him. Both his hands were fixed with bloody fingernails into his belly, which had ballooned like the distended bladder of a pig. His face was purple and swollen, his eyes bulged with terrible astonishment, his mouth was so wide aghast that the other features were distorted. His tongue was dark blue, stiff as a phallus and jutting out a remarkable distance between his teeth and lips. The anvil that was acting as a plinth stood in a pond comprised of sticky blood and the contents of his bowels and stomach.

Sukie was not on the premises.

The Comportment and Gruesome Death
of Abbot Fabian

 BBOT FABIAN SEEMED smaller and frailer, his manner vaguer and more subdued than I had pictured him in my absence. His complexion was all phlegm and black bile. His pallid skin seemed stretched on to his skull by suction from within: there could be little doubt that he was ill. It was rumoured among the monks that he was also depressed by disputes with Abbot Bernard of our sister and rival abbey at Rievaulx.

At my first confession after my return to Byland I told him everything that I had told to Prior Jacobus and also such matters as I had deemed beyond the Prior's scope. I told him of my dreams, the incubi and succubi with which Sycorax had been tormenting me and how I had withheld these things from my confessions before I left Byland for Kirkholt Grange. Then I told him of my trip to Nithermoor, my flirtation with Satan, my rejected overtures to Alys.

He said gravely that it was risky to withhold confession, even of what seemed trivial matters. It was not for the individual conscience to judge what was trivial in the eyes of God. Happenstance or the malice of the Fiend could take away a sinner's life in an instant and to die with any sin unabsolved could be a very serious business. Exhorting me to be more circumspect in future, he proposed four dozen Hail Marys, to be recited between Evensong and sleep, for the sin of withholding confession. He regretted that I still seemed helpless to quell the imp of lust that had driven me into the abbey in the first place – and prescribed another dozen Hail Marys for the sins of lewd fantasy and proposed lechery.

Abbot Fabian and I were together later in the day, taking a syllabub with gooseberry wine in the herb garden that was his favourite spot in the world. While we watched Brother Vincent fussing among the panoply of herbs that Brother Sapiens had promulgated, I broached the topic that was devouring me. We had a habit of discussing my confessions informally after the event, rather as two old peasants will recapitulate a bear-baiting or other sporting occasion as they drink their ale.

'Father, is my history of Sycorax to proceed?'

I was perturbed by the leniency of the penances he had given for transgressions that had been lacerating my conscience. My interpretation was that he was weary of me and had given up hope of bringing me to greater worthiness.

Abbot Fabian raised his hoary eyebrows and regarded me calmly. I knew that his bland, worldly air did not do him justice. It was needed to deal with a multitude of folk at various levels and registers, in order to pursue his vocation and maintain the interests of the abbey. But within he submitted assiduously to God and the Holy Church, including them at all points in his deliberations and giving them absolute surveillance of his temporal negotiations.

'Proceed? Is there any question of it not proceeding?'

'I feel a profound sense of unworthiness for the task.'

I felt a twinge of apprehension as I uttered the words, for I remembered the stern response a similar speech had aroused in him during an earlier interview. But his voice was now avuncular with mild reproof as he said, 'You have spoken of this before, and I have answered you.'

'And I strove to follow your direction, Father, and be obedient and worthy, as long as my weakness permitted. But since then I have gathered further, convincing evidence of my unworthiness. I have transgressed again and betrayed the work entrusted to me.'

'You have confessed your transgressions and I have absolved them. Perform your penance, continue to strive to obey and do not insult the mercy of God by lack of trust in it.'

I nodded and lowered my eyes in submission. His reassurance was presumably the sort of thing for which I had been angling. That would have been the end of the topic – at least for the time being – but I could not help saying, as we basked in the sunlit silence of the garden, 'I am amazed and relieved, Father, at the lenient view you have taken of my lewd and even blasphemous dreams – and the sinful speculations culminating in my vile proposal to the woman Alys . . .'

The Abbot took a slow sip of gooseberry wine. I had presented him with the sort of opportunity for exposition and instruction which I knew he relished. I flattered myself that he had missed me, as a companion and audience, during my expedition into the Riding.

'Brother Edmund, I have been aware of your weaknesses for sixteen years. I was aware of them when I chose you for the Sycorax mission. It is I who must answer to God for your transgressions. It is my scheme that Sycorax detests and it is with me that she is at war. The assault upon you is a trifle, a speck of marginalia, compared to how I am harassed and beleaguered by the Fiend.'

I looked at him in surprise. His words indicated an inner strife which he had never complained of before and which I had never suspected in this serene and saintly man. Brother William, devout but stupid, was the Abbot's confessor: I had always assumed, if I thought about it at all, that these confessions would be brief and routine matters. Certainly Brother William, even when vested with the authority of the Holy Church, would lack the wit or erudition to give the Abbot counsel or contribute anything other than by ceremonial rote. I suddenly felt pity for Abbot Fabian, who did not have the resource of a confessor he revered and trusted but was more or less responsible for his own conscience and liable to the terrible consequences of error.

He went on: 'Bernard of Rievaulx, a contentious meddler, has made a complaint against me to a higher authority – the superintendent of the founding French branch of our order – who has sent me a missive decreeing the inadvisability of the history of Sycorax as the topic for a Byland library manuscript.'

I decided that I had misconstrued his previous speech. He had been reckoning the malice of Sycorax, in his case, more in terms of doctrinal politics than lascivious demons.

He went on: 'It is known that the Fiend can find lodgement in those most exalted in power and supposedly sanctified in spirit. He skulks concealed in the vestments of great cardinals in Rome and we have seen in our own lifetime that he can even claim the office of Holy Father. But if I am to resist the spleen of Sycorax and Satan against me, as manifest in the machinations of Bernard of Rievaulx and his ancient French dupe, I must solicit distinguished opinion in the Church, looking as far as Rome for friendly authority if need be. As a first measure I have canvassed the opinion of my friend the Archdeacon of this diocese. He is enthusiastic about my project regarding Sycorax, which coincides with an initiative of his own, and is confident he can enlist the support of the Archbishop of York.'

I was listening respectfully but somewhat absently, feeling such doctrinal and diplomatic manoeuvres beyond my scope, though I felt honoured that he was confiding them to me.

He said, 'The Archdeacon recently sent his newly appointed clerk to confer with me, an active and zealous Dominican, Friar Gervase. This personable young man has a vision of a mighty campaign, such as the Inquisition employed against the great heresies in centuries past, to eradicate the witchcraft and Devil worship that is rife throughout Christendom. He is convinced that our history of Sycorax, coupled with an energetic prosecution of abuses in this region, can bring us glory in God's cause as standard-bearers of the crusade. Friar Gervase will be interested to hear of the woman Alys.'

A mistle thrush was on the wall above the herb garden. Brother Vincent was pottering around so peacefully that he had not frightened it away. Its song was the only noise disturbing the sunny summer afternoon.

I carefully placed my glass on the bench beside me. With his last sentence Abbot Fabian had suddenly claimed my full, appalled intention.

'Why would he be interested in Alys, Father?'

'You tell me that the woman Alys has been used as an intermediary by Sycorax in her practices against you. Friar Gervase is keen to examine all such cases.'

'It's my fault, Father, that I thought lecherously of her and let her infest my dreams.'

He put his ancient hand lightly on my knee, a warning gesture I remembered from our previous interview. 'Beware, my son, how much guilt you take upon yourself. Remember that we are dealing with Satan. It is a very grave matter to assert that you welcomed him willingly and of your own accord.'

I did not at once notice the threat implicit in his kindly advice. I said, 'The girl isn't guilty of anything, Father. You cannot give her to examination.'

'The innocent have nothing to fear.'

'None of us mortals is innocent, Father. You've often told me so. In any case, you can't break the secrets of the confessional by reporting what I have told you about Alys.'

He removed his hand from my knee. 'You are impertinent. As your confessor and as your abbot I have the right to insist, on pain of ex-communication, that you bear full and frank witness to Satan's abominations as they afflict you. As it happens, I do not need to enforce your cooperation, since you have spoken just now in this garden of the role played by the woman Alys in your bewitching. It is therefore no longer a secret of the confessional.'

I rose from my seat and stood trembling on the gravel path, shouting down at the venerable old man who was my spiritual mentor, 'Father, I cannot understand why Alys should be arrested, forced into an admission of guilt and destroyed as a result of my dreams. I can see no God or Devil in this, nor in the history of Sukie Trothers that I have been gathering. I can comprehend no great witch Sycorax and her magic but only a foolish lass who was abused by bullies. I think Satan exists only in the credulity and cruelty of man.'

My raised voice had scared away the mistle thrush, so that there was a profounder silence when I paused. I had caused the retreat of Brother Vincent, too: he had deemed it discreet to withdraw, though he went slowly, turning his gaze and pricked ears back towards the intemperate rating of the Abbot by Satan through the lips of Brother Edmund.

Abbot Fabian said nothing until Brother Vincent was out of earshot. Then his voice was old and faint and dry as if he was very weary of the world and his responsibilities in it. Yet there was a measured cadence to his words that intimidated me with its suggestion of remorseless certainty and purpose, in contrast to my blustering petulance.

'To deny Satan is to deny God. It is to say that the Church and Saints, the Mother of God and Christ Himself are liars. It is what Satan most rejoices to hear you say. Aquinas has said, *"All the changes capable of occurring naturally and by way of genius, these the Devil can imitate."* Satan hides in mundane phenomena in order to gull us into the blasphemous despair that makes us irrecoverably his. Before you contemplate such despair, Brother Edmund, make sure that you are proud and bold enough in evil to be able to stare unblinking at Hell.'

That was enough for me. I let out a contrite groan and fell on to my knees on the gravel path. It was my father confessor, my friend and spiritual guide for sixteen years, who was pronouncing this awful doom. His wrath was terrible to me, for it had been his love and patience, in comparison to the brutal fury of my earthly father, that had won me for Byland and God. Nor was it his anger that annihilated my defiance so much as the terror he communicated on my behalf with his thin, remorseless drone. My crouch of supplication was almost between his bony knees, but he did not place a hand on my cranium as I hoped he would.

'Nor is Hell the only peril you face, my son. You need to understand that I cannot commit the woman Alys for examination without mentioning you, the complainer against her. Given the clear and commendable zeal of young Friar Gervase, you will probably be examined for witchcraft.'

'Father, my outburst was put into my mouth by Satan! Sycorax was speaking from my lips. It was never in my heart. Tell me what I must do.'

At last he put his hand on to my head, but rather more gingerly than on previous occasions, as though he had discovered that my skull contained distasteful matter. 'You must cooperate fully with Friar Gervase and testify at the trial of the woman. Then you must complete the task I have set you. *The History of the Witch Sycorax* must contain no hint of the atheistic despair that I have heard with horror today. It must not be a history of ignorant atrocities in Yorkshire but an account of the war between God and Satan that will strike terror and salvation into the souls of its readers. It is more important than ever that the book should include an account of the writer's unworthiness, doubts, spiritual torment and eventual arrival at a state of relative grace. I therefore insist that you include, for instance, every word that you can remember of the crucial conversation we have just had. In case your memory or judgement fail you, I shall be glad to edit and extrapolate your account.'

He rose to his feet by placing his hand on my shoulder and leaning against me. 'You have failed in obedience and now obedience has become more difficult, for there is ground to be recaptured from the Fiend. But all the same it is easier for you than I. You have only to obey me and your sin, in a sense, becomes mine. That is my burden as Abbot. I have carried it for two decades of Yorkshire sinners, refugees from Satan's empire, younger sons who were an embarrassment on the smallholding . . .'

He set off along the path towards his quarters, but when he had gone two or three paces turned, surprised me with a grunt and grimace, almost a giggle, and said, 'My burden has been hellish since I discovered Sycorax and earned her hatred. The witch goes to preposterous extremes in her attempts to befoul the soul and break the resolve of a feeble old man.'

I gazed at him with awe and wonder as he turned away again and walked painfully off, his gaunt shoulders hunched and his frail cranium glistening in the sun. It was the second time during the interview – and they were the only two occasions ever in our relationship – that he had complained of the persecution visited on him by Sycorax. It was clear now that he was speaking of his own spiritual torments rather than political nuisances arising from his rivalry with Bernard of Rievaulx. I understood that he knew the witch as I did: not as an edifying historical topic, nor as a vague sub-department of Satan's malice, but as a vivid and intimate personification of evil.

Abbot Fabian never supervised and edited this manuscript as he proposed.

He was ill. Though he persisted in attending all the offices of the horarium, he took to his bed for much of his spare time, or was treated by Brother William in the infirmary. He still heard my confessions and once a week summoned me to the herb garden to report on my work and read extracts to him, but his response was then listless and vague: he would soon move the conversation to impersonal matters of Church doctrine. He never spoke of his own plight and made it clear that enquiries on the topic displeased him.

Neither in conversation nor in the confessional did he mention Alys: and I was careful not to do so, for I was hoping desperately that sickness and responsibilities had made him overlook the matter. My reviving it, seeking to have my fears dispersed or confirmed, might have fatal results for both the woman and myself. I occupied my mind as best I could by writing this chronicle, my anxiety diminishing as summer passed and I heard nothing more of Friar Gervase.

At the end of September, three months after our conversation in the herb garden, Fabian did not appear for Matins and Lauds.

The Cistercian horarium observed at Byland is more suitable for Mediterranean summers than wintry Yorkshire. We sleep at sunset, until roused just after midnight by the dormitory bell. After Matins and Lauds we go back to bed until daybreak, when the bell summons us to Prime and Mass. We mostly reach the church for Matins in a chill and somnolent daze.

Since the Abbot normally played no part in the service of Matins it passed without his absence being noticed. When it came time for Lauds we waited, bemused. Fabian invariably led the singing of the three psalms of praise by performing alternate verses solo in his reedy tenor. After a desultory discussion Brother Clarence took the part of the Abbot, his gruff baritone sounding weird to us in the unaccustomed office.

I assume it was because I was famous as the Abbot's favourite that Brother Clarence approached me after the service and suggested that we went together to see what ailed Fabian. Brother Clarence, a natural leader and taker of initiatives, was so detested by Abbot Fabian that the latter preferred to do without a Prior and deputy rather than appoint the obvious candidate. The two men had as little to do with each other as possible.

While the other monks herded back thankfully into the dormitory, Brother Clarence and I each carried a lanthorn past the penitentiary cells to the Abbot's room that was the least comfortable cell in Byland. We found his door flung wide and the room in as much turmoil as the sparse furnishings allowed. The pallet was stripped, the blanket flung like a mangled snake into the room's corner, as if extreme heat had made it intolerable. The stool and table were overturned, the missal and crucifix spilled on to the floor.

By candlelight, Brother Clarence and I gazed at each other questioningly. I said, 'He has been ill for some time.'

'But he has never missed Lauds. Where is he now?'

'Perhaps he has gone outside for fresh air. Or perhaps he is in the infirmary, being bled and medicined.'

'Hush!' He hissed this so urgently that I thought I had offended him with my speculations. Then, seeing that he was listening intently, I did the same.

We could hear the baying of a great hound, a fair way off, beyond the abbey walls.

'Have you ever heard that before?' Brother Clarence's voice was a tense whisper. I shook my head. I could think of nothing that I wanted to say.

Before we went to the dormitory we looked in the infirmary, in vain. Then we looked in the latrines, though we did not expect to find Fabian there. As Abbot, he had his own receptacle for nocturnal excreta, a clay pot which he kept outside his door and which was the only undisturbed item in his habitation.

When the bell rang for daybreak and my brothers trooped off to the lavatories to wash before Prime and Mass, I went off alone: crossing the cloister garth and taking the path that wound behind the chapter house and the reclusive cells. In four sleepless hours I had had leisure to think where Abbot Fabian would go, if not into the church, to seek refuge.

I found him in the herb garden, close to the bench where he had quelled my mutiny and spoken to me of the war waged by Sycorax against him. An unusual frost that grey September dawn had combined with rigor mortis to stiffen the corpse into almost a sitting posture, with knees and elbows bent. The old man was naked and looked like a plucked, starved bird. His fists were clenched tight, in terrible resistance to the assaults he had undergone.

Apart from the fact that there was no sign of blood or other bodily fluids, I could not help but be struck by the similarity with the death of Watkin Trothers as it had been reported to me. Abbot Fabian's face was flushed dark with blood and black bile. His tongue jutted purple and swollen between his gaping gums and his eyes were wide and amazed.

The Flight of the Witch Sukie and the Advent of the Fiend Sycorax

ATAN'S SUBTLE CONTRIVANCES were assisted, as they very often are, by the underestimated, deadly sin of sloth: the death of Watkin Trothers was never properly investigated. The supernatural horror of the event which had struck all witnesses was brought tardily and inefficiently to the notice of the spiritual authorities, then discounted by the Archdeacon and his advisers.

The Archdeacon, though his role in proceedings had been remote, had been unpleasantly affected by the Sukie Dobson business – the only witchcraft investigation during his tenure – particularly since it had coincided with the death of his old friend Father Ambrose. The Archdeacon was frail and venerable and wanted no further nastiness of the sort. The involvement of Sukie herself in Watkin's death made it paradoxically even less likely that the Archdeacon would countenance the suggestion of diabolic intervention, since he had previously been much criticized in some quarters for his leniency in letting the young witch survive.

Deciding on the matter three weeks after the event and twelve miles from the scene of it, it was easy for the clerics to find naturalistic explanations for the startling phenomena: the awesome barking of the Fiend, for example, was attributed either to a coincidentally passing dog or to bellows of agony coming from the moribund. It seemed both logical and convenient, from the reported evidence, that Watkin had died of some intestinal malady brought on by the vast quantity of alcohol he had consumed over the years. Tom Dobson and others had borne witness that Watkin had for some months before his death been subject to vomiting and stomach pain, though whether such testimony was known to the clerics is uncertain.

The secular authorities were less decisively inactive but no more effectual. That part of the North Riding that falls into the area of the Pickering Forest is subject to a mish-mash of government. Theoretically, the entire vast triangle between Pickering, Whitby and Scarborough is royal hunting forest, preserved and administered by the Duchy of Lancaster from Pickering Castle. In practice much of the unforested land in the region is farmed and grazed and the administrative control is shared *ad hoc* with boroughs, abbeys and manorial lords. Normally the Duchy restricts its policing to the forest laws against poaching, the erecting of enclosures and the removal of timber. It expects local land-holders to deal with other infractions and only involve the castle in cases of particular difficulty or gravity.

The death of a drunken peasant, however spectacular in detail, was not considered an important item on the agenda of the Lord of Dorsay. The reeve of the manor did not go in person to enquire into Trothers's death but sent Vince Emblin, his yeoman. Vince was steady and shrewd, but another quality that made the reeve fond of employing Vince as a deputy was that Vince would not zealously uncover abuses and cause a furore if things could be peacefully, politically and profitably left alone. This characteristic was welcomed and conspired with by the folk of Beck Gap and particularly by the tithing that included Watkin and Sukie Trothers, who were indisposed either to waste time looking for Sukie or be held responsible for her disappearance.

It was resolved, to the satisfaction of all parties, that Watkin had most likely poisoned himself by his drinking habits. Sukie, though she was known to have once possessed skill in herbs and veterinary medi-cines, was adjudged to be too mentally damaged to have poisoned her husband, being capable of only the most basic culinary efforts. Her dis-appearance was admitted to be suspicious but could be ascribed to terror at her husband's loud and ugly death, compounded with insanity that prevented her from retracing her steps once she had fled. On the morning after Watkin's death Beck Gap had taken a day's rest from labour and raised a hue and cry in search of Sukie, in vain. It was agreed by Vince Emblin – and later by the reeve – that that was sufficient for now. It was thought advisable that if and when she turned up she should be examined at a session of the manorial court, but nobody sensed any urgency in this, since nobody had high hopes of getting much sense out of Sukie even if she could be found.

She was not found. It may well be that her fiend and familiar, once it had horribly destroyed Watkin Trothers at her bidding, had welcomed her astride its furry back, as she had dreamt in her youth and as was to happen on future occasions. In an instant she had flown on her Master through the secret night air to some forest depth far from Beck Gap. But even if she was not yet so adept in magic or subject to Satan, she had only to limp off into the darkness, chance or instinct pointing her in the right direction, to arrive before daybreak in the wilds of Slatterdale on the forest rim, where the only risk of human contact was the occasional shepherd or forester.

However she escaped from Beck Gap, Sukie Trothers disappeared for eight years into the vast wilderness of the forest that stretches east as far as Scarborough, north to Whitby. The upland regions of the forest are chiefly open moorland, but the slopes and dales are thickly wooded. It is only significantly inhabited as one approaches its boundaries: the Esk to the north, the Derwent to the south and the eastern coast.

Where she went and how she survived can only be conjectured. There are outlaw bands close to the high roads throughout the forest. She may have found acceptance with these for a while, for women of any sort are rare and prized among them. She may have lived with a shepherd or coppicer on the outskirts of some community at a far edge of the forest. She may have kept away from men, after her experience with Watkin, and always lived alone, as she did later: on fruit and roots and berries, by fishing and snaring, even gardening, only approaching the human race in the throes of a remorseless winter to trade with them or steal from them. Throughout this time she was progressing in her transformation from Sukie into Sycorax: the more she became Sycorax, the less she had to concern herself with phenomenal sustenance and the less we need concern ourselves with how she scraped a living and survived winter. We can assume that her Master was not only providing for her but copulating with her and entertaining her with small foretastes of the power that was going to be hers for a while in exchange for her filthy soul for ever.

During those eight years, 1399–1407, her family did their best to forget her. Tom Dobson died of a constriction of the heart. Trissie married Peter March and moved into the March household, a similarly overpopulated hovel twenty yards from the Dobsons'. She had three children, two of which died. The five remaining children of Ibbie and Bab grew up truculent and turbulent in the Dobson tradition. Folk in Beck Gap still spoke scandalously of the murder of Watkin Trothers, but only with the same knowing relish that they had previously employed on the death of Watkin's first wife. The spectacular and supernatural aspects of his death seem to have lost a degree of credit, until years later when the burgeoning of Sycorax made such events lurid with hindsight.

After eight years – either trusting that the passage of time would have obliterated the circumstances of her departure or because her turgid wits had actually forgotten those circumstances during that time – trusting in any case in the protection of her Master, Sukie returned to the Slatterdale area. She was spotted now and then at fairs and markets in Pickering, selling medicinal herbs and lucky trinkets. Her appearance had so changed – grey, haggard, weathered and wrinkled – that though she was not yet thirty years old she was taking on the aspect of an old crone: yet she was recognizable enough by her limp, her long neck and her peremptory green eyes. Her powers of speech had been restored to her by her Master's art, sufficiently for her to ply her trade by declaring the purpose and price of her products, but she spoke with difficulty, in a whining voice like a foreigner, and seemed unused to the local dialect. It is also evident that her intelligence was more or less mended, for it is not feasible that the half-witted drudge of Watkin Trothers could have collected and prepared medicines or engaged in financial transactions.

In time she increased her appearances and activities in the area: keeping clear of Beck Gap – which indicates that she had not totally lost her memory – but visiting Nithermoor and other settlements about once a month. She went as discreetly as she could from door to door, plagued by dogs and urchins, trying to interest housewives in her wares. Or she would take up her post, like a tinker, near the church or ale house at times when they might provide her with custom.

Few people liked to be seen buying from her openly, but all the same she built up a trade of sorts. She would frankly describe her wares as well as she was able, to instil some confidence into prospective buyers, and many of the potions she touted are remembered vividly to this day. Some of them were straightforward medicines which are still used by Pickering and Slatterdale folk: gentian for the digestion, coltsfoot for coughs, sorrel for catarrh, theriac of snake venom against the pestilence . . . Others had more interesting and dubious functions: violets to control menstruation, mint to prevent premature ejaculation, Belladonna for livelier dancing at feasts . . . Still others, mostly aphrodisiacs, were compounds of many plants – she would proudly falter out a long, exotic list: sanicle, spindleberry, melick, butterwort, cranesbill . . . The rest of her goods were items such as: charms resembling saints' knucklebones but crudely carved from thornwood, pagan rosaries of threaded acorns . . .

It became known that she was living in a forested ravine to the north-east of Slatterdale, in a foresters' shelter. She must have given this information of her own accord to somebody, and it turned out to be a good business move. There were folk in Nithermoor who would not have accosted her in the street or opened their doors to her but felt prepared to make the discreet three-hour journey to the witch's shack; and the reports of those who went to this trouble were impressive regarding both the results and the ambience. Over the years her reputation as wise woman grew, helped by the utter absence of competition in Slatterdale: the nearest doctors were in Pickering Town, their treatments regarded with scorn and their prices with awe by the country yokels.

Trissie March became my best eyewitness to this epoch when she went to visit her sister in 1409, ten years after Sukie's flight from Beck Gap and two years after her return to the area, in which time she had not been seen once in her native village.

'I went wi' Cat Ruddock, as wanted summat to fettle 'er owd Ned. She begged us to go wi' 'er, for she were frit o' witchery. I were curious to see Sukie, for I'd 'eard of 'er time and oft but never clapped eyes on 'er since she come back into Slatterdale.'

The two women chose a Tuesday, when it was known that Sukie would be in to callers – later in the week and at weekends she did her circuit that took her as far as Pickering and must have involved her spending a night sleeping rough somewhere. Trissie and Cat set off as soon as Cat's husband Ned had gone to work – from his point of view it was to be a secret mission – and walked for two hours, climbing Slatterdale to the valley head then crossing the ridge and dipping down forested slopes to the little ravine that was the lair of the witch. They had muffins and apples in their shoulder bags and refreshed themselves once or twice from the beck. It was a mild and balmy September morning.

'I were capped to be walking along in t'sun, free and easy, when I were supposed to be pulling drasty cabbages. I were sick to wangs o' that. Granny March were tending t'bairns.'

The mood of the women sobered as they entered the witch's ravine. 'It were a black, damp spot what chilled brawns. Too little sun got at it.'

147

Cropton Beck ran slow and dark past a slab of rock shaped like a clenched fist. This was how they knew they were in the right place. As they climbed a narrow track through birch, pine and tangled underbrush the baying of a huge hound confirmed their arrival.

Sukie did not emerge from her dwelling to greet them. Nor could they approach the shelter, because they were intimidated by the huge, black, noisy dog that was tethered to the door post. 'Very spit of t'owd Fart she used to have on t'ridings.' Cat Ruddock wanted to set out at once on the long trip home, her enthusiasm for the errand having entirely evaporated. Trissie persuaded her to wait awhile, reasoning that the dog would perform the function of a summoning bell as well as an alarm and that Sukie would be somewhere in the vicinity and come to investigate. Sure enough, before long the dog gave up baying and took to whimpering and writhing, licking its chops and threshing its tail with delight. Sukie Trothers, the witch Sycorax, emerged from the cover of an elderberry thicket and crossed the gloamy little glade that fronted the shelter.

'I reckon she'd had a good squint at us first, to see we was no menace.'

The witch ignored the waiting women and entered the dwelling: the dog following her in joyfully, which his tether permitted, and now paying no more attention to the intruders than his mistress did. Trissie led the way to the doorway and called out, 'Sukie!' There was silence from inside except for the heavy panting of the dog.

Trissie looked inside. The shelter had been solidly built with logs and waterproofed with mud from the beck. It was windowless, and there was no hearth. It was lit only from the doorway, so that Trissie had to step aside before she could make out the scene in the interior.

'There were a fair ram o' shit and other mullock and manishment. Though it were swept clean and there were nowt in it, nobbut. It were t'mutt and t'witch what stunk.'

The witch crouched at the far perimeter of the square that was the living area. She was propped on the dog, which she used as a sort of couch or cushion. On the other side of her was a pallet of straw, obviously her bed, now occupied by a dozing brindle cat.

A Pickering woman (not an eyewitness) told me that the witch was supposed to have a deformed child, an ugly thing that crawled on the floor of the hut. Trissie saw no sign of this, nor is the idea supported by anybody else I have spoken to. The rumour may have arisen from the error of a short-sighted customer in the gloom of the hut, but it is known that the familiars of a witch can change shape as they wish or appear differently to different witnesses at the same moment.

In front of the witch, between her and the door, was the only real furniture in the house: a low, wide construction that could be used either as a bench or a table. Behind her the roof sloped away to ground level to form a triangular annexe or storeroom. The floor of this area was thronged with items that could not at first be identified by Trissie from her viewpoint.

The women were motioned inside, then by means of another gesture invited to sit aside so as not to block the doorway light.

'I said, Sukie, our lass, it's me, Trissie, tha sib. She never said nowt. She gawked at us as if she were deaf and we'd fell from t'moon.'

Trissie had been prepared for her sister's memory being as fragile as her wits. All the same, she was dashed by the total lack of recognition. 'Nobbut ten year after she seen me last, how would she not remember me or even speak? I were 'er good sib even when she were mostly daft. It were me she'd talk to when she were nursin' 'er babby. It were me as 'elped 'er bury 'er misborn babby in West Copse, when she wouldna give it to t'mutts.'

Cat Ruddock (up to this point a cipher in Trissie's narrative) seems to have asserted herself at this stage, suddenly becoming composed and businesslike: explaining slowly and loudly what she wanted (a miracle, given Ned's chronic inertia) and what she was prepared to pay for it (not much). The witch still said nothing, but commenced taking from the annexe behind her a selection of several small parcels, plus two or three little clay pots such as a child might make, placing them all on the bench that was her shop counter. While she was doing this Trissie was able to observe her carefully and come to a dramatic conclusion.

'All on a sudden I started to reckon it weren't Sukie. It were an owd bag twice us age. 'Er chops was wrinkled like they'd been in vinegar an' 'er lips was sunk where 'er teeth was buggered. It were an owd hag witch what were fetching to look like Sukie, wi' Dobson eyes and a crooked foot and a dog like Fart.'

Meanwhile the witch had taken a floppy wild rhubarb leaf from a pile in the annexe behind her. She shook powders and fragments on to the spread leaf from the items on the bench, intoning the contents of each carefully unfolded package or tilted pot:

'Baneberry. Ransom. Buckler. Cow wheat. Winterbane . . .'

Her voice had a whine in it that was reminiscent of the loony whines of Sukie Trothers. Otherwise it was the composed and intelligent voice of a foreign woman who was having difficulty with English pronunciation.

She carefully folded the rhubarb leaf into a square parcel and proffered it to Cat. 'Stir it in soup and warm it up good, but it mun't boil.' With her other hand she performed a flippant arabesque that ended palm up awaiting payment. It was a gesture that Trissie remembered as characteristic of Sukie when they were children.

When Cat had paid and they were departing Trissie had one last try:

'Don't thoo know me, Sukie? Don't thoo remember nowt?'

The witch gazed at her blankly and said nothing. Trissie thought later that Sycorax had been wary of saying much to Sukie's sister and betraying her disguise. On the other hand, it may merely be that Sycorax did not spend more words on humans than was absolutely necessary for her purposes. Just at that moment the dog lifted its adoring head towards her and licked her in the ear, which made a sucking noise.

On an inspiration, Trissie said, 'Yon's like t'other bugger. Mutt thoo had on t'Ridings.'

Slowly the witch smiled, showing mostly gums. 'Fart,' she said.

('She reckoned she had me there, but I weren't fooled,' Trissie told me. ('A witch what could take on Sukie's look and limpy leg could learn the name of a fuckin' mutt. Still, I'd getten 'er to open 'er gob.')

'Thissun called Fart an' all?' Trissie asked.

The witch pushed away the dog's visage then tickled him behind his ears, making him grin.

'Satan,' she said, grinning back at him.

Mayhem Is Wrought by the Fiend Sycorax in Pickering

HAT WAS THE last sighting of Sukie Trothers. Trissie March's perception of her sister's transformation into Sycorax was probably exaggerated by hindsight – she still sometimes referred to the witch as Sukie in her accounts of later events – but Trissie is now emphatic that she came away from that encounter convinced that the sister she had known was irrecoverably dead and determined to have no further dealings with the witch.

The electrifying effect of the potion on Ned was offset by a second dose killing him. This can be seen as a microcosm of the rise of the witch in Slatterdale and beyond. Her magic became darker and more baneful as her fame grew.

Her remedies gained much acclaim within the region, until people were prepared to travel the long day's journey from Pickering to consult her in her lair. It is possible that the occasional lethal slip such as in Ned's case brought her more benefit from publicity than she lost by the disaffection of wary customers. She started to demand her price in advance, rather than take what the buyer chose to give her; and she eschewed bargaining, adopting a haughty, take-it-or-leave-it approach that increased the prestige of her products.

Gradually her doctoring broadened its scope and became much more ambitious. She used not just herbs but sorcery to cure the sick who came to her. Nor did she restrict herself, as sceptics claimed at first, to mental and imaginary afflictions. She could ease a muscular strain or a bellyache, help bones knit, cure sterility and strangury, make boils and goitres vanish, by laying a hand on the injured or diseased part while she chanted the names of several hundred fiends.

She could also work magic for the bereaved. She gave them potions that sent them into a trance and by flinging powders on to flames could make the faces of their dead loom amid coloured smoke and a stench like brimstone. Sometimes it was herself that she put in a trance and the voices of the dead came out of her lips, exactly as they were remembered by their relatives, mentioning secrets that only members of the family could possibly know.

If Sycorax had restricted her magic to healing and comforting it would have been impious enough and evidence of the strong power of Satan invested in her. But she also used sorcery against people specified by her clients or sold folk the means to work their own devilry. Much of this mischief consisted of spells demanded by the besotted to bewitch and enslave the objects of their passions, but some of it served hatred, being intended to destroy the health or luck of an enemy or rival. A number of witnesses have testified to me of the success of these charms and practices, but I shall not serve and glorify Satan by further describing them here.

Over the course of several years the witch's habits and comportment changed, as her pride grew with her reputation and her malice with her power. She only practised her healing and other magic arts for those who visited her forest lair and these learnt to take quite substantial gifts such as a red grouse, a hare or a knitted muffler. When she descended from Slatterdale she no longer carried merchandise but came entirely and simply as a beggar, silently accosting those she met with an outstretched palm, or standing at doorways attracting attention with a peremptory cough.

She started to include Beck Gap in her journeys, which she had not done for some years after her return, though it was conveniently on her route to Nithermoor and Pickering. These visitations were a source of acute distress to Ibbie, who was terrified of this phantom of her daughter that looked like a cartoon personifying retribution, but in fact Sycorax's visits to Beck Gap did not differ from her visits to other hamlets and Nithermoor village. She did not avoid the family hovel in her door-to-door circuit of cursory extortion, but neither did she linger longer there than anywhere else or show any sign of recognition when a relative (never Ibbie) thrust a coin or scrap of food through the sacking that the Dobsons used as a door.

At Beck Gap and elsewhere, she accepted whatever was given her without either thanks or complaint. If she specifically asked for anything, as she sometimes did, she paid for it with coins out of the pouch she wore round her stomach. The payment was offered without negotiation or scrutiny, so that some folk found themselves disproportionately enriched while others were left feeling robbed.

It was very rare for anybody to contest these random payments, offer her abuse or defiance, refuse her requests or ignore her outstretched hand. It became universally known that it was foolhardy to cross the Slatterdale witch and evoke her curse. Some she cursed were almost immediately gored by their own pitchfork, snared by a collapsing barn or decapitated implausibly by the blade of the flax trunnion. Others developed unsightly chancres or excruciating gallstones. Others found a sodden sort of marsh scab was slaughtering their upland sheep in dry weather.

The memorable spectacle of the witch delivering a curse was evoked for me by an eyewitness. She would raise herself almost on tiptoe, her wrinkled visage thrust forward on her long neck like a lanthorn being held towards the object of her animosity. Squinting along her outstretched thumb like an archer taking a sighting, she would intone a threatening gobbledegook, full of fricatives and sibilants, which has been described to me more than once as 'saying the names of fiends'. It may have been in imitation of these noises she uttered that the name *Sycorax* was first applied to the witch, though it is as likely to be a derivative of *Sukie* formed by somebody with a smattering of Latin.

The success of her curses allied to her increasingly formidable demeanour put folk in great awe of Sycorax. There was no longer any question of urchins insulting or stoning her – they would scamper for cover as soon as she limped into sight. This went for adults, too: her approach was usually saluted by an emptying of roads and shutting of doors. In Pickering Town on market day her progress up the street would be discernible by a space moving through the crowd as folk shrank away as from a leper or rabid dog. The stallholders held their ground and answered her requests politely but with as brief and little contact as possible. The town constables – two had been appointed on full-time pay since the sojourn of Sukie in the stocks – kept clear of her. Even the dogs had got wind of something and were wary. Simkin claims boldly that he was the exception – 'I weren't afeared o' yon daft bitch, sithee, for I knew her and she knew me' – but according to other witnesses the bailiff behaved like everybody else and kept a low profile when Sycorax was in town.

The two representatives of the medical profession in Pickering campaigned for years against Sycorax, both because of the trade she took from them and out of general hostility to unqualified health care. There was an ordinance in force in Pickering against women practising any medicine but midwifery, but there was some doubt as to whether this applied to the sale of herbs, and by the time the borough council had decided against the witch on this point she had stopped bringing produce to Pickering and only tended patients in her Slatterdale lair far from the jurisdiction of the borough.

Even when the witch was more or less terrorizing the peasantry she avoided contact with the authorities. Her begging rounds kept well clear of the church, the castle, the abbey granges, the Dorsay manor and home farm. It was observed that she shrank from any contact with local nobility, and if she passed prosperous burghers or their wives in the street she would not put out her hand. The temporal powers of the region, if they noticed Sycorax at all, were amused by the terror she inspired in the rabble and regarded her as a matter for the Church to investigate.

The two Pickering doctors therefore applied to the Church, citing

Sycorax as a witch, then canvassed around Pickering, without success, to find somebody of substantial reputation who was prepared to claim that she had bewitched them. By this time the North Riding had a new Archdeacon (even more frail and doddering than the one that died in 1399) who left everything to his clerk. The current clerk was a social charmer and political scoundrel devoid of any religious belief or interest in spiritual matters. He was disinclined to bestir himself so long as Sycorax was restricting her activities to the lower classes and not causing scandal (or criticism of the clerk to the Archdeacon) among people that mattered. Since he did not include the two Pickering doctors among people that mattered, he advised them to approach the borough council and evoke the ordinance against women practising medicine.

It may be that further perseverance by the doctors would have persuaded either the secular or spiritual power to take some action against the witch, but at this juncture the more vocal and energetic doctor died of a particularly unpleasant bladder infection. His timider colleague and competitor could not help feeling that this was due to retaliation by Sycorax, and he was encouraged in this by local opinion, which took a gloomy view of his own prospects. At the same time he inherited a lot of the business of the deceased, so no longer felt economically threatened by loss of trade to the witch. He gave up all action against her and even grew cautious of speaking ill of her to his patients.

Just as Sycorax seemed relieved of the chief threat of harassment, there came the sort of happenstance against which even Satan seems unable to provide. A group of sturdy beggars invaded Pickering and made a nuisance of themselves. This led to the borough council reviving a neglected order against begging and instructing their constables to enforce it. The offenders promptly left Pickering, and the incident seemed closed to the constables until they were admonished to enforce the rule rigorously in future and realized to their horror that they would be expected to do something about Sycorax when she next appeared.

As it happened, she did not appear for several weeks, which allowed the public to inform each other about the situation and build up a sense of pleasant anticipation, as for a forthcoming football match or hanging. It also allowed apprehension to fester in the constables: two brothers, Dodge and Billy Gaunt, whose uncle featured earlier in this history. They were strapping lads who wrestled drunks and cudgelled dogs with insouciant *élan*, but they publicly admitted themselves fazed by the Sycorax assignment which they felt was beyond the scope of their thews and weaponry. What they said to each other in private is not known, but they probably agreed that they feared the witch's curse and would avoid it at all costs, even to the neglect of their duty. It would be clear to them, though, that both the borough council and public interest were not going to let them ignore or avoid Sycorax. They must have also agreed that they wanted to keep their jobs which gave them both prestige and an enviable income.

Whatever their deliberations, the result was that the Gaunt brothers stuck close together on market days and carried heavy bludgeons. It is not known whether their plan was to dash out the witch's brains without negotiation or whether one of them was going to arrest her (or order her out of town) while the other stood ready to cudgel her at the first sign of her launching into her curse. Circumstances prevented both these stratagems.

Sycorax was spotted coming down past the castle on the road from the dale: an unmistakable figure with her mane of iron-grey hair like a thistle blossom and her hobble seemingly emphasized by the stick she had taken to using. Sukie Trothers was thirty-four years old, an age at which peasant women are reckoned elderly in the North Riding. All the same, there was something incongruous about the tentative limp and stoop of the witch, as though a younger woman was learning to act the part of a crone.

News of her arrival caused a scampering frenzy in Pickering Town. By the time she turned into the market street the stalls at that end of the street had been abandoned even by their owners. Halfway up the street, advancing towards the witch, were the Gaunt brothers, thrust along and encouraged by an excited mob. Many of the mob had armed themselves with cobbles and a few had managed to snatch up more sophisticated weapons. Whatever the Gaunt brothers had planned, it was evident that once they had confronted the witch she would be very lucky to get out of town alive or even reach the qualified security of the gaol.

Sycorax came to a stop and drew herself up from her crouch over the stick. It was a critical moment. To an ignorant stranger it would have looked as if a crippled woman was confronting an armed crowd of townsfolk, but of course that is not how it was. Sycorax's Master's magic was arrayed to protect her. Yet it needed to be properly directed by her and not too vigorously opposed by faith in God, profane violence and sheer chance, if she was to survive. If she had done what was expected of her – squinted along her thumb and begun to curse – she would surely have been hushed by a hail of cobbles and clubbed to death.

She gazed at the oncoming mob as though it was exactly what she had expected to see when she turned the corner. Seeming to understand at once that nobody else was going to do anything, or throw anything, until the Gaunt brothers were close enough to confront her, she serenely let them approach until the constables were ten paces from her. Then she suddenly raised her stick like a marshalling baton; then pointed it as a death-wand, adjusting it so that it trained along the front rank of the advancing mob, choosing its victim.

'Thoo could tell as she weren't frit,' one onlooker told me. 'She squinnied down yon stick like a fowler picking out a pigeon – all the fuckin' time in the world.'

The constables halted, the mob with them, five paces from her.

There were a few moments of stillness and silence, the sort of pause that could only possibly last for a few moments. The witch would be pounded to death the instant she started to curse or made any gesture other than the slow, hovering, hypnotizing movement with the stick. In any case the pause was just because nobody wanted to be the first to attract her attention, for she would surely only have time to destroy one person with her evil eye. The impasse would be solved in an instant and all would be over for the witch, when somebody relatively safe, in the third or fourth rank of the mob, hurled a cobble or shouted defiance.

Billy Gaunt raised his bludgeon, stepped forward a couple of paces, let out a whimper and plunged to the earth as if a giant, invisible hand had felled him.

This had a paralysing rather than galvanizing effect. The townsfolk watched Billy with horrified fascination as he squirmed supine, his limbs twitched, his body arched and jerked. He then put his hands to his throat and threshed and kicked with his legs while letting out a series of hoarse, strangled barks like a dog choking on a trapped bone.

They never lost awareness of the witch, who stood utterly composed, not even glancing down at the dying man. Her green eyes, the eyes of a predatory animal or fiend, roamed across the front row of faces before her – none of whom met her gaze. She slowly adjusted her outstretched stick until the point was aimed directly at Dodge Gaunt. Her voice seemed to spring suddenly out of her, very loud and harsh, enunciating the outlandish, terrible syllables of her curse, that a witness suddenly and vividly evoked for me fifteen years later:

'Sceaboles! Harchiel! Cheros! Elgemith! Herenobulcule! Timayule! Stuff like that. It were mullock, but it put shits up us just then.'

It seemed as though she knew exactly what she was supposed to do – when it would be fatal for her to curse – when it would be fatal not to curse – as though she had rehearsed the scene many times, or as if she was an exactly tuned instrument being played by the prescient Fiend.

Dodge Gaunt dropped his club, groaned and turned in flight, blundering against those behind him. It was the signal for a panic-stricken stampede: folk bucketing into each other, tripping each other, tumbling over the fallen, scrambling desperately up and away, all the while yelling and screaming like scared children at Hallowe'en.

Several seconds later the street was deserted except for Sycorax standing over the inert body of Billy Gaunt. Once they were sheltered behind buildings or in doorways some folk were brave enough to peep out and watch her, but nobody considered throwing or firing missiles at her or doing anything that might attract her attention. Pickering High Street had been seized by the witch.

As soon as the street was clear she ended her recitation, leaving one last wailing syllable to echo in the air. She lowered her stick to the ground and leant on it as usual. Only then did she allow herself to gaze down at the purple-faced corpse of the constable (who had choked on his swallowed tongue), which she subjected to a leisurely but incurious scrutiny. Next she ambled across to a vegetable stall and carefully selected several items which she placed in the shoulder bag of sacking she wore. From her pouch she took as usual a random coin and placed it on the edge of the stall. Taking a last look up the empty street she turned back the way she had come: never looking round or betraying any sign of haste or nervousness.

'Dipping and bobbing wi' t'weird gait she 'ad. Left at crossroads an' off up Nithermoor road. Nobody went after 'er. It were a few minutes afore anybody'd cross street to where Billy lay dead.'

Brother Edmund at the Trial
of the Witch Alys

EFORE I SET out for Pickering to attend the trial of Alys, Prior Jocelyn was kind enough to summon me to his quarters. These were the cell and study that Abbot Fabian had used, with an adjoining room now utilized as a reception and hospitality area, quite luxuriously furnished with woollen and sheepskin rugs that Jocelyn had brought from Rievaulx.

Jocelyn had been Claustral Prior of Rievaulx, Abbot Bernard's deputy, for several years, but was now in temporary charge of Byland and a candidate for the abbacy. This sudden development, supposedly in response to the needs of Byland, was in fact the consequence of Abbot Bernard's headlong diplomacy and a triumph for Rievaulx, in the long rivalry between the abbeys, which it would have distressed Abbot Fabian to have foreseen. Jocelyn's candidature had powerful sponsors, and he had so far impressed the Byland monks as the sort to bring order and prosperity to the abbey: it was evident that he would be elected unopposed.

Prior Jocelyn was a tall, commanding man, big-nosed and keen-eyed, with sarcastically mirthful lips. (He still possesses all these features, but I use the past tense for the convenience of my narrative.) He was drinking what looked like expensive Gascon wine but offered me none, nor did he invite me to sit down, so that I stood submissively just within the doorway of the room throughout the interview.

'A fine mess your precious Abbot has landed you in, Brother Edmund!' he greeted me cheerily.

Prior Jocelyn had a poor opinion of Abbot Fabian, whose reputation had also sunk very low among my fellow monks. The godless indignity and demoniac ugliness of his death had been particularly damaging to his esteem. I had defended his memory as best I dared: asserting, as I truly believed, that Abbot Fabian had been slain by demons he valiantly resisted and defied to the last. But I had soon become aware that as a favourite of the old Abbot I was to some extent sharing his eclipse. In particular, Prior Jocelyn had not taken on the role of my personal confessor but had given me to Brother Decimus, a geriatric without prestige in the abbey. In my spiritual strife with Sycorax I was left to my own resources, plus the recollected wisdom and sanctity of my lamented spiritual father.

'I am glad to testify at the trial of the witch,' I muttered, 'in obedience to God – and to the late Abbot – and to you, Father . . .'

Prior Jocelyn smiled. 'Don't go blaming me for your problems, Brother Edmund! It was Fabian told the Archdeacon's clerk you were bewitched.'

'It was for my sake, Father. I'm grateful for his care.'

I think my loyalty to Abbot Fabian was irritating to the Prior. All the same, he chuckled. He was a resolutely jolly man.

'Are you? Then you're a ninny. For you also will be on trial in Pickering and should not forget for one instant that your comportment is being judged. The bewitched may be an accomplice of the witch. The victim of sorcery, having proved accessible to Satan, can be justly and logically suspected of sharing a pact with him.'

He was only telling me what I knew. I was deeply anxious as to how much Abbot Fabian had told the Archdeacon's clerk regarding my blasphemies in the herb garden. I was also terrified that Alys, when tortured for the names of her confederates, would have taken the obvious, reciprocal step of proclaiming me as an accomplice rather than her victim. My discomfiture clearly showed on my countenance, and it put Prior Jocelyn in a better humour with me. He smiled again.

'All the same, glad and grateful, jolly good, that's the right idea! Grateful for your plight, glad to atone, submissive to the Church. That's the way you've got to seem to be in Pickering, if your soul and body are to survive. Above all I advise you to watch out for Friar Gervase, for that young fellow combines zeal with ambition to a degree that I find intimidating.'

It was amazing evidence of the mercy of God and the wisdom of the True Church that, since my full and crucial confession to Abbot Fabian at the end of June, Alys had not featured in my foul dreams. Nor, for that matter, had I had blasphemous congress with the cynosures of womanhood that I revered. I was only plagued by Malkin, Luce and the other persevering ghosts of my youth – except that these lecherous reveries were still prone to switch to outright nightmare: the grizzled mop and gummy grin of Sycorax surfacing like a drowned trull through the features of my foolish wenches from the Vale of York.

Despite this alleviation my morale was low. I was aware that I was in acute peril from two formidable sources and could see no satisfactory means of defence against either. On the one hand, I had absolutely no confidence that I would be able to survive the spleen of Sycorax when she chose to direct it fully against me: for she had destroyed Abbot Fabian, my guide, mentor and confessor, many times stronger, purer and more devout than I. On the other hand, I was vulnerable to the punitive might of the Holy Church, being under strong suspicion of collusion with the forces of evil.

It was the Church that presented the most immediate threat to my physical well-being, and it was the Church that I must urgently propitiate for the sake of my soul. I understood that my only hope of salvation – both spiritual and physical – lay in my testifying fully and gladly before the court, enthusiastically assisting in the doom of the sorceress Alys that had bewitched me and satisfying the scrutiny of the formidable Friar Gervase by any other means that proved necessary. But I did not relish these tasks as an innocent victim, or a truly repentant sinner, would have relished them.

In fact I did not relish the idea of leaving Byland again – ever again, in my whole life. I came here in the first place somewhat reluctantly, under pressure from my mortified father and the threat of further vengeance by Luce's husband, and did not unreservedly and gratefully take my vows. Yet I now deduced, from my recent experiences, that any venture outside the walls and rules of the abbey might well be calamitous to my susceptible spirit.

On the other hand, the fate of Abbot Fabian had shown me that the security of my Byland haven was an illusion. I was nowhere safe from the wrath of the Powers of Light and Darkness, nor was there any hope of respite from the dichotomies that were gates to damnation.

'Poor Abbot Fabian talked to me at length about you, Brother Edmund. You are already much more to me than a witness against a witch or a sinner eager to atone. I want you as an ally, a chronicler of the work which is my destiny and privilege. The Archdeacon regrets that he cannot be your host this evening but sends you his cordial regards.'

I suspected that at that moment the Archdeacon was dining in some more splendid room in the house, hardly aware of my existence, but all the same I was flattered by the welcome Friar Gervase was giving me. He had done me the honour of having a pallet prepared for me in the cubicle next to his own in the Archdeacon's residence. Having taken the Holy Sacrament together at the hands of the parish priest we were now dining on trout simmered in milk, clearly an item from the Archdeacon's table, and I was drinking white Bordeaux wine, though Gervase drank only water.

'To my delight, the Archdeacon has agreed to preside in court tomorrow. It will give a weight to the persecution of witchcraft which is sadly deficient both in Yorkshire and throughout Christendom. If witches are brought to justice at all, it is on a random and *ad hoc* basis that has no proper consequence. There is sore need for a written compendium, a procedural guide such as the Penitentiaries for confessors. Or even a Directory of Sorcery, like the Directories against Heresies issued by the Holy Inquisition. Abbot Fabian spoke highly of your literary powers. Perhaps you will consider undertaking such a work when your *History of Sycorax* is complete.'

Friar Gervase was tall, lean and comely. The humours were harmoniously blended in his complexion, betokening an auspicious conjunction of planets at his birth. His tender brown eyes seemed to caress what they saw. The set of his lips in repose imparted a good-natured expression to his countenance. Venial vanity was betrayed by his facial hair, which was clipped and shaved as scrupulously as his tonsure to create a narrow, uniform band along his jaw and upper lip.

He went on, in phrases that seemed as precisely clipped as his beard, 'The examination of the witch Alys has been a case in point. Anything that I have not supervised personally has been neglected or fudged. Whereas the forces against us are organized and resolute. The ignorance of my assistants has been compounded by the remarkable stubbornness of the witch. It is with great difficulty, after long and bothersome travail, that we have obtained a confession. If there had been an habitual procedure or a Directory to guide us –'

I broke in to verify what he had said. 'Alys has confessed to witchcraft?'

Friar Gervase placed his spoon on the remnant of fish in the bowl and closed his eyes and moved his lips silently. He kept me waiting for his response to my outburst while he thus thanked God for what he had just eaten. He had performed the same personal observance at the beginning of the meal, in addition to the Latin grace he had recited for both of us.

At length he slowly crossed himself, dabbed his beard with the sleeve of his habit, gazed at me with his soft brown eyes and sighed.

'You are hoping that your testimony will not be required. But your testimony is essential, Brother Edmund. We need it to justify the drastic action we have taken against the girl. And it is as essential for you as for us. You have an urgent need to demonstrate your allegiance.'

'It would be a great disappointment to me,' I managed to say, 'if I was not called to testify.'

*

Gervase kept me awake long after Evensong. He set out to relate to me something of his life history, but did so in such loving detail that on this occasion he only got as far as his actual birth. He told me much about his parents and grandparents, all of whom seem to have been individually remarkable and brought together by specially meaningful circumstances. He also went into great detail about the astrological coincidences that accompanied his birth and the various prodigies that contributed to the event. I suspected that he was disappointed that I did not note down the information he gave me.

The Archdeacon's court was held as was customary in the priest's chamber above the chantry chapel in Pickering church. Proceedings were not open to the public, which was just as well, for the room was not spacious.

Neither was it imposingly furnished. A trestle table, decked with a red cloth and a rosewood crucifix, confronted an assembly of stools and benches that were intended as seating for witnesses, court officials and a number of clerics whose functions were mysterious to me. There was a stool for the accused immediately in front of the table and to the right, and there was a bench far to the left where the prosecutor sat, though he rose whenever he addressed the court. Witnesses were expected to stand to the front and left, facing both the judge's table and the accused.

There were two chairs and a stool behind the table. The more pompous of the chairs was occupied by Archdeacon Tertius, a fleshy, sanguine, middle-aged man considerably more robust than any of his recent predecessors. On the other chair was a thin little fellow in the cap and cravat of a civil lawyer: Master Bennet, the Clerk to the Duchy of Lancaster. On this occasion the Archdeacon had asked the Duchy to constitute the Temporal Power, rather than the town council. A Cistercian monk not known to me, probably borrowed from Rievaulx, was perched on the stool and acting as scribe.

The scribe's task was made easier by the fact that the case had become a formality as a result of the witch's confession. Most of the material – the indictment of the witch, the testimony against her, the account of her examination, her confession – had already been committed to writing, which gave an air of recital to proceedings and meant that the scribe would be able to translate the documents into Latin at leisure when the case was concluded. In this, as in many other features of the trial of the witch Alys, it was evident that sorcery proceedings under Friar Gervase were very different from the slack and benign business that had permitted the survival of Sukie Dobson and the creation of Sycorax.

The accused had presumably been brought in a cart from her dungeon in the castle. She was carried into court by two castle soldiers, each holding her by an arm and a thigh. When they had propped her on the stool one of the soldiers drew another stool alongside and kept her upright by wrapping his fist in the dusty grey rags that clothed her like the cerements of an ancient corpse.

I did not recognize her. Her head had been shaved and was now covered with bristly stubble. She held herself very still, humped like a bird on the stool in her grey rags, or moved with extreme sloth and caution like an ancient arthritic. When she was carried in her head had lolled so that her face was not visible to me, nor could I see it from where I was sitting, nor had I any wish to do so.

Friar Gervase was the prosecutor, now that he had persuaded the Archdeacon to replace him as judge, but the indictment was read by another cleric in the Archdeacon's retinue. It was quite a long indictment, having been extended to include everything the prisoner had confessed since her arrest. In brief, she had made a pact with Satan, copulated with Satan, performed unnatural acts with him and kissed his anus in adoration. She had flown by sorcery to Black Sabbaths and there eaten hashed children and corpses out of graves. She had used sorcery to injure Christians, at the bidding of both her Master and the great witch Sycorax who was Satan's regent in Yorkshire.

As soon as the indictment had been read Friar Gervase rose to his feet and smiled at me. I was seized with a faint, ridiculous hope that he would request my signed testimony to be read, or even read it himself, without troubling me. But of course he called me forward to testify. This meant in practice that I had to stand and confront the court while my deposition was read: describing the work I was engaged on that had aroused the enmity of Sycorax, the subsequent excessive plaguing of me in dreams by demons and the role played by Alys in this persecution.

During all this I tried to stare steadfastly at the fat red features of Archdeacon Tertius, who appeared very much as though his mind was entirely elsewhere, deliberating some more congenial topic. But every so often my gaze was dragged by unwilling fascination over to the stool of the accused, and for one horrible instant she looked up and across at me, her eyes meeting mine. Those grey eyes were unmistakably the eyes of Alys, but at the same time they looked utterly alien: as cold and remote as the eyes of a reptile or a dead wolf. I glanced immediately away, giving such effort and attention to not looking at her again that I badly fumbled my confirmation of the deposition, compelling Friar Gervase to repeat his question and clarify what I had said.

The only other material witness was the arresting officer, the Archdeacon's bailiff. He had of course made no written deposition but testified by answering a series of questions put to him by Friar Gervase. At the friar's instruction he had searched the ale house and adjoining dwelling house at Nithermoor before making the arrest. He had found a number of hairs of various colours in the comb of the accused. Also a number of items under a straw pallet that suspiciously resembled finger-nail parings. Also a misshapen candle, a rope plaited widdershins and a knotted cord.

Friar Gervase then read to the bailiff an account of the examination of the accused – a repetitive tally of tortures applied sporadically and unimaginatively over a period of several days: the thumbscrews, the boot, the rack, the gag of gauze down the throat, the rope round the temples, the hot iron, the weights to crush the knees and shins. These technical details were interspersed with the questions repeatedly put to the witch and her spirited, obscene retorts. Eventually she had broken down and confessed, but when taken to another cell and required to repeat her confession untortured and unthreatened – as Friar Gervase deemed essential for a valid confession – she had promptly resorted to her earlier defiance, so that hours of further drastic measures were required to achieve her permanent surrender.

I looked at the witch again – now that I was safely behind her and out of range of her eyes – amazed by what I heard of her resistance, but her head was stupidly drooped between her shoulders and she seemed insensible. Whatever strength Satan and Sycorax had given this profane, ignorant woman, to enable her to defy the might and wisdom of the Church, seemed now to have entirely deserted her.

The bailiff assented that the account read to him had been a true account of the examination proceedings and their outcome. He agreed that he had been present throughout the examination. Friar Gervase went on to read the confession of the witch.

This elaborated considerably on each of the points of the indictment, the accused having been assiduously questioned for convincing details that would verify her confession. Sometimes Satan came to her as a black dog, sometimes as a goat, sometimes as a large black man with red eyes. He was the weight of a sack of malt; his member was enormous, his semen copious but very cold. She had flown to the Witches' Sabbath astride a black dog sent by Sycorax to fetch her. As well as human flesh she had eaten toads, biting and chewing them raw while they sang canticles. (Sycorax had been on a great throne and Satan, in the shape of a giant goat, on another.) She had danced through a bonfire while the blazing arms of unbaptized infants were used for torches. She had practised against the lives of neighbours by burning candles shaped to represent them or by sticking pins in effigies. She had knotted cords to curse men with impotence. She had used the hairs and fingernails of a virtuous old woman in Nithermoor, an enemy of both Sycorax and the ale house, to give her stomach cramps and a wart on her nose.

The witch gave no response when asked if she assented to this confession. She was roused by the soldier next to her, and her head was lifted towards the prosecutor, who repeated the question. When she still failed to answer, Friar Gervase rephrased the question:

'Do you deny, then, that this is your true confession, made without compulsion and signed with your mark?'

When she again said nothing the friar proposed to the court that her lack of denial should be taken as assent.

Apparently the Archdeacon had some scruples about this logic. He commanded that the prisoner be raised from her stool by the soldiers and held upright while the friar repeated the second version of the question. Alys made a noise in her throat, and her head wobbled slightly. Archdeacon Tertius then told her loudly that if she wished to retract any part of her confession she must speak at once. She said nothing, and the Archdeacon instructed the soldiers to replace her on the stool.

Friar Gervase then addressed the court, requesting as prosecutor that the court formally convict the woman Alys of witchcraft and sentence her to death by hanging. The Archdeacon, after brief consultation with the temporal power, acceded to these requests, and the remainder of the business was restricted to practical arrangements such as the setting of the date for the execution.

Master Bennet, on behalf of the Duchy of Lancaster, asked that it should take place as soon as possible, since the castle had already suffered considerable inconvenience in housing, feeding and supervising the prisoner.

Friar Gervase accepted this but pointed out that it was important, now that the witch was convicted, that she should be interrogated more rigorously and thoroughly than before, in order to ensure that she had not withheld anything crucial from her confession, such as the names of accomplices or the identities of any witches she had seen and recognized at the Sabbath. Such information was essential for the finding and prosecution of other agents of Satan. Eliciting it might take some time, since the present frail condition of the prisoner would preclude too boisterous an approach. Then a period should be allowed for the prisoner to recover sufficiently so that the hanging was not made unseemly or ridiculous by her condition. He estimated that a month would be the minimum delay required.

Master Bennet retorted that in a month it would be winter, when events would be liable to postponement owing to heavy weather. Since the burden of carrying out the arrangement would fall on the Temporal Power, he felt it only fair that the Temporal Power should have the decisive say in such arrangements. He proposed a fortnight.

Archdeacon Tertius adjudicated a compromise of three weeks; positing that the hanging should take place on a Sunday, when the populace were free to be entertained and instructed by the event.

'You must not leave yet, Brother Edmund!'

My mule was saddled and I was securing my little bundle of possessions when Friar Gervase appeared in the stable yard, having obviously hurried to catch me before my departure.

'You must not sneak away like this!'

I was afraid of him. But he was smiling, shielding his eyes with one hand from the autumn sun, almost playfully blocking my mule's exit from the yard. His robe and sandals, clipped hair and smooth, sallow skin rendered him as a composition in different shades of brown, the only exceptions to this monochrome effect being the whites of his tender brown eyes and his fine teeth that his smile showed to advantage.

For all his handsome affability I was not happy that he had intercepted me as if I was an absconding patient from a bedlam. I opened my mouth to speak with what dignity I could muster.

Before I could utter anything he observed, accurately, 'You are about to say that you must return to Byland, to your work. That the witch is condemned and there is nothing more for you to do here.' He shook his head chidingly. 'On the contrary, there is still much to be done. For the moment there is the further interrogation of the witch.'

'I would be of absolutely no help to you in that work.'

'I wish you to witness it and later record it. It is a battle in the war against Satan and Sycorax. I would expect, too, that you are happy to do so, as the bewitched party.'

'You must not judge me by your own standards or I will disappoint you greatly. I entered Byland because I am not capable of conducting the fight against Satan as you are. I must strive to obey and adore God within the safety of the abbey and its rule. I bring only shame on myself and discredit to any cause I serve if more is asked of me.'

His smile had vanished some time ago. At this point he pursed his eyebrows into a frown. 'Brother Edmund, you are making a mistake. To join forces with me in this instance and gladly do God's work, though it is unpleasant to you, would remove a residue of suspicion from your predicament.'

I understood that he was not motivated by malice towards me. Far from setting a trap for me, he was giving me a chance to get out of a trap that I was already in. He not only wished me well but saw my value as a chronicler of vital matters, including his own exploits against Satan. All the same, I was incapable of accompanying him to the interrogation of Alys even if it would save my soul and body to do so.

'I cannot do what you ask. Apart from that I will do everything that I can and as my Abbot instructs me. I will joyfully attend the hanging of the witch and glory at the destruction of the evil agent of Sycorax even as I pray for the soul of Alys.'

He nodded compassionately, but I could tell that he was not satisfied. 'The burning of witches, such as is practised in France and Germany, seems more appropriate than hanging. I am encouraged that Lollard heretics have been burnt, in the Midlands and South, in recent times. Fire is both a purifying element and a symbol of eternal punishment – a small part of my divine mission will be to introduce its use in such cases. But the hanging, *faute de mieux*, will doubtless edify your soul and relieve your spiritual plight. Further succour will be available when you identify for me the other incubi and succubi which Abbot Fabian mentioned as having afflicted you.'

I saw with horror that another unpleasant test was being applied to me. 'Those are merely sinful memories that have plagued me for years. Feckless lasses of York Vale in my distant youth.'

'If you supply me with their names and last known whereabouts I will have them found. It will do no harm to examine them, since they have tormented you for so long.'

'It is my lechery that has tormented me. And recently Sycorax has turned my lecherous weakness into atrocious blasphemy. It is Sycorax we need to hunt out and destroy.'

At this he approached and laid a hand on my arm. A golden light seemed to gleam in his brown eyes as if my words were a source of great delight to him. 'What you say is very close to my heart, Brother Edmund. I am not as other men. I have sacred purposes bestowed on me by God. It is a scandal against God and the Church that the defiance of Sycorax has been left to triumph. My mission here in the North Riding is to avenge that sacrilegious triumph. I will destroy Sycorax and restore the Cross. Satan shall be found and exorcized wherever he lurks, in whatever heart he hides. And you shall chronicle this. Your history shall end gloriously with the triumph of the True Church.'

I admired and envied his confident strength. Yet I confess with shame and guilt that something in his enthusiasm, or in the confident intimacy of his approach, repelled me. The mule shifted sideways and away from him as if it shared my reaction, but for my part I did not dare remove my arm from the pressure of the friar's hand. I said, 'I was using Sycorax as a metaphor for Satan's evil in general. It seems to me that Satan is never happier than when Christians destroy each other because of his mischief.'

Fortunately, he chose to ignore my last point, since his mind was occupied with something important he was about to tell me. 'Sycorax is no mere metaphor, Brother Edmund. She still lives in the forests beyond Slatterdale.'

'She has not been seen for fifteen years.'

'She has not been seen because nobody has wanted to see her. That is often how Satan's evil survives. But it is something I will not permit.' His hand tightened commandingly on my arm. 'Before you go, Brother, you will give me the names of those witches in the Vale of York.'

The Expedition Against the Fiend Sycorax, 1414

HE EARLY CHAPTERS in this history of Sycorax were compiled from the testimony of only a handful of witnesses: on some of whom (Brother Denys, Simkin, Trissie March) I had to rely exclusively for many items of information. By comparison, my accounts of Sukie Trothers's return to Slatterdale and the slaying of Billy Gaunt by Sycorax in Pickering were taken from a number of sources, among whom there was agreement except over minor details.

The following is an account of the 28th August 1414, an infamous day in this region. Many people in Pickering and Slatterdale were eye-witnesses to the events of that day and there is nobody in the North Riding who does not have knowledge of the subject culled indirectly by word of mouth. Therefore I am presented with an overwhelming body of information: some of it contradictory and some of it clearly spurious in that it derives from old legends and superstitions rather than real happenings. It is very difficult for me to pass judgement on this material – and decide between conflicting accounts – because of the astounding, miraculous nature of almost everything that has been imparted to me.

If what follows strains the credulity of those who read it, I can only assert that I have rarely reported items that have not been vouched for by at least two informants and have suppressed a good deal of matter that I consider to be sensational and dubious.

In the summer months that passed after the attempt to arrest Sycorax and the death of Billy Gaunt the witch never went back to Pickering, nor did she beg in Slatterdale. It is also hard to imagine that anybody was foolhardy enough to travel to consult her in her lair, unless they were themselves in pact with Satan: if anybody did, no knowledge of it has reached me. In that time she took vengeance for the abortive assault upon her and put the whole region in terror.

No rain fell on Slatterdale during June, July and August of 1414. The sun was high and white in the sky. The hot, heavy air lay like butter on fields, forest and moorland. Trees and plants seemed to crackle with thirst. The dust on the high road smouldered. No birds sang. Both Pickering Beck and Slatterdale Beck ran dry and several wells emptied so that folk had to journey for hours lugging water for themselves and their beasts.

A plague bore off two score inhabitants of the region: exploding them into vomit and excrement, swelling their glands and turning their faces black. At the same time there was a terrible murrain that afflicted cattle and sheep alike. Living beasts seemed to rot in the heat, lame in the hoof and drooling from ulcerated mouths.

In Pickering the witch aimed her malice more precisely and settled scores. A fire destroyed the gaolhouse where Sukie Dobson had languished and several other buildings in the quarter. Dodge Gaunt was crippled by a donkey's kick. Binnock and his wife Thomasin were found mysteriously dead, untouched by plague, as if they had been gently smothered in their sleep. Simkin was immobilized by a virulent fistula, aggravated by the remedies of the town doctor.

These calamities were accompanied everywhere by prodigies and portents. An apple tree ran blood. In Nithermoor a horse ate a piglet. In Beck Gap twin boys were born each with three sets of teeth and four thumbs. A dog on the Dorsay estate spoke Latin from its kennel on a night of full moon. Sycorax appeared in dreams to countless inhabitants of the region, gloating at them with pointed fangs and robbing them of further sleep. She was also spotted naked astride the spire of Pickering Church and riding her black dog Satan through the night air above Nithermoor.

It took a while for the terror to percolate through to those echelons of society that had effective power. First Pickering Borough Council met to discuss the elimination of both their constables and Sycorax's resistance to arrest. It was considered unlikely that there would be a rush of applicants for the post of constable, given the possibility of Sycorax's return at any time. Therefore a fund was started among leading tradesmen and a prime of silver pennies offered those who were selected as special constables, with no duties other than to guard against Sycorax and effect the arrest of the witch if she reappeared. A force of a dozen desperate and indigent men came into being, but nobody was confident that these would deal with Sycorax any better than the Gaunts had done. At length the Mayor and council overcame their political reluctance to defer to the castle and requested a troop of soldiers to patrol the town on market day when the threat of the witch was most rife.

Relations between the Duchy of Lancaster and the burghers were poor at that time, so it came as no surprise when the Steward of the Duchy at first refused the town's request. Then drought, plague and other distress caused by the witch in the Duchy's territory in Slatterdale brought the Steward to give the matter more attention, relent and grant an audience to the Mayor of Pickering.

The two men agreed to combine resources and arrest the witch as soon as she made an appearance in the town. They also agreed that it was looking increasingly likely that Sycorax would keep out of Pickering in future, while continuing to afflict the whole district from her forest lair. It was therefore necessary to consider sending a force up Slatterdale to arrest her on a charge of vagrancy and the murder of Billy Gaunt.

But the third point on which the Mayor and Steward agreed was that this was no mere legal or military matter. A secular force would be inappropriate against the witch and might prove as powerless as the Gaunt brothers and the Pickering mob, with even more disastrous consequences. If Sycorax had the terrifying powers now being attributed to her, her magic could only be countered by the Church. In the first instance, the order for her arrest must come from the Archdeacon, so that the Temporal Power could act with the full support and protection of the Spiritual Power.

By this time the murder of Billy Gaunt and the reign of terror conducted by the witch in the Riding was spreading through the Christian world: the Abbots and Abbess of Byland, Rievaulx and Rosedale had all made representations to the Archdeacon. For the protection of Sycorax Satan had infected Archdeacon Damian with senile debility and his clerk with a scepticism remarkable in a man of God: for the clerk continued to contend, in the face of all evidence, that the witch was a mad woman, Billy Gaunt's death the result of mere terror, the heatwave a coincidence and the plagues a consequence of the heat. The Archdeacon ordered the arrest of the witch, on suspicion of murder and devastation by satanic arts, only after receiving an appalled and peremptory communication from the Archbishop of York.

Understandably, after the weeks of drought and plague, terror and rumour, the expedition to arrest Sycorax aroused violent interest as news of it raced through the district in the week before the event. The throng outside Pickering Church on the morning of the 27th of August 1414 was full of a crusading fervour that was already mixed with a sense of joy and deliverance.

Most of the crowd was gathered just to see the expedition depart and wish it well, but a considerable number of brave spirits had come actually to join the crusade. They were apprentices that had been released by their masters for the weekend, labourers excused from work on the granges, peasants prepared to neglect their fields and stock or leave them in the care of their families. Some were bearing billhooks or axes, as if there was a battle in the offing. Many had protected themselves with crucifixes and rosaries, while some were doubtless concealing sprigs of fennel, verveine and other pagan charms against evil. They attached themselves loosely to the official military forces which were distinguished by uniforms: the dozen castle archers in their hauberks, the twelve special constables of the borough in light-brown caps and jerkins that had been devised for the occasion.

Others had been attracted to the event for less heroic reasons. A fiddler, a bagpipe player and a drummer performed around the crowd, while a young woman collected coins on their behalf. Barley sugar vendors and other opportunist hawkers carried their wares on trays or in pouches of sacking. There were jugglers, contortionists, a fire-eater and other paraphernalia of the feast and the fair. A good deal of alcohol was being consumed, though it was not yet noon.

Twelve clerics – monks, priests and friars (nuns were deemed unsuitable for the project) – had been selected and gathered by Father Norbert, then Pickering parish priest, to represent the churches, abbeys and priories of the Riding. Other clerics had obtained dispensation from superiors or come on their own initiative to add spiritual weight to the crusade. Every cleric who undertook the expedition was to carry a holy object – a cross, a missal, the bone of a saint or other potent relic – and was committed to prayer or sacred song for the whole twelve miles to Beck Gap. The incidence of the number twelve was considered particularly auspicious for the expedition: it being the number of Christ's disciples – or rather, the number made up by the eleven virtuous disciples and the Master Himself.

The castle had provided an ox-cart loaded with bread, wine, salted fish and blood pudding. The town council's contribution was a second cart bearing the tents and pavilions that were usually saved for May Day and other such festivals but were now going to provide accommodation for the night's bivouac at Beck Gap. The Mayor and council were also offering a silver penny to every townsman present at the actual capture of the witch.

The church was packed when the Archdeacon in person administered the Sacrament, not merely to the twelve archers, twelve constables and twelve priests who were his official agents for the arrest of the witch but to all who were prepared to offer themselves to the cause and accompany the posse. Anybody who wanted one was given a small cross of twigs and twine that had been made by the catechism class at Pickering Church and blessed in bulk by the Archdeacon. Everybody was also blessed directly, not only by the Archdeacon but by several other ecclesiastical dignitaries who were assembled there, though the assertion made by some that the Archbishop of York was there in person is almost certainly inaccurate.

There were speeches. The Archdeacon, doubtless feeling that he had done his stint in church, contented himself with beaming and blessing and spreading great confidence and contentment. The Mayor of Pickering made a long speech which was entirely inaudible owing to the boisterous morale of the non-clerical section of the populace. The Steward of the Duchy of Lancaster got a better hearing, for he was on horseback, gorgeously caparisoned and accompanied by several squires who were almost as splendid. Moreover, he was rarely seen in Pickering, whereas the townsfolk were all too accustomed to occasions being protracted by the drivelling of the Mayor. But the speech of the Steward was dry, concerned mostly with the fealty and gratitude which the town owed to the castle, and seemed largely inappropriate to the event. He had the good sense to shut up when it became apparent that he was being ignored.

The waving, cheering, tipsy mob threw barley for luck and with music, laughter, prayers and oaths, hoorays and goodbyes, somersaulting urchins and barking dogs the parade left Pickering for Nithermoor, the gateway to Slatterdale. They set about the eight-mile uphill trek in the heat of the day, the heat of the drought, the heat of the summer of the terror of Sycorax.

Over a hundred left Pickering, among whom not a dozen were women. The way was led by the only person on a horse, Sergeant Garth of the castle archers, who was in charge of all temporal aspects of the expedition. He went at walking pace so that his men could keep up with him easily, plodding along sweatily in their hauberks of boiled leather, carrying their unstrung longbows like lances. The sergeant had a crossbow and quiver of bolts slung at his saddle. They were followed by the clerics, led on foot by Father Norbert: likewise suffering in their habits in the heat but otherwise absorbed in learning to chant and sing together under the direction of a short, fat curate who was choirmaster at Pickering Church. The twelve Pickering constables were not as discernibly aligned as their military and clerical counterparts, being caught up in the accompanying rabble that was the great bulk of the expedition: capering and dawdling, gossiping and disputing, singing and dancing to the primitive little orchestra that was still with them and drowning out the more discreet and melodious efforts of the clergy. The ox-carts trundled behind, falling back several hundred yards in the course of the journey.

At Nithermoor they were met by more music – flutes, timbrels and a mandolin – while they were refreshed with ale and lard cakes on the village green. The population of the village had clearly given up the notion of work for the day and declared it a holiday in anticipation of the coming of the Pickering host.

When they set off for Beck Gap their numbers had been considerably swelled by the men, women and children of Nithermoor, who had heard rumours of an even more exciting junketing at Beck Gap. There, where the troop arrived in the early evening, the factors of the reeve of the Dorsay demesne had organized a major display of hospitality: mutton was roasting over open fires on the common. There was brief consternation when a hundred and sixty folk, instead of the estimated three score, turned up to join the hundred Dorsay retainers and peasants who had already gathered, but the provision had been generous and the ox-cart of the castle trundled up with supplementary provisions.

The pavilions were erected in a parched meadow that bordered the common. Inevitably a bonfire was lit, then eating and drinking, music and dancing went on into the night, under brilliant stars and a round moon. Eventually folk slept in the pavilions or on the straw of the hovels of Beck Gap or simply stretched out in the meadow or amid the gorse and heather of the common: snug and stifling in the warm, heavy air. The clergy, all sharing one large pavilion, were unanimous in keeping themselves focused on the spiritual issues. They interrupted their observances only briefly for supper, then retired to bed earlier than everybody else, though in the circumstances it was not easy to sleep.

What Befell the Expedition at the Lair of the Fiend

HE MORNING OF Sunday the 28th August 1414 brought an eastern sky the colour of blood that some secretly considered an evil omen. It accorded with the hungover eyes of others who awoke to a more sober awareness of the business in hand.

The clerics rose at dawn (as some of the previous night's revellers were retiring to sleep), prayed together then heard each other's confessions. A bell roused the archers, the constables and anybody else eager or conscientious enough to heed it: all of whom were shriven before the Holy Sacrament was administered in the parched meadow amid a dusty, cloying morning haze. Breakfast of bread, cheese and watered wine was then taken.

A council of war between Father Norbert, Sergeant Garth and Alan Babbs, who was captain of the town constables, decided that the host at Beck Gap was too unwieldy, undisciplined and noisy for the next stage of the mission, the march through Slatterdale to the witch's stronghold. Twelve likely lads were selected from the volunteers to supplement the twelve archers, twelve constables and twelve priests. This trimmed force was augmented by half-a-dozen foresters with hunting dogs who had been summoned to rendezvous at Beck Gap by the Duchy Steward and two bloodhounds with their handler, specially borrowed by the Steward from the King's Sheriff in York. Some of the rest of the mob returned to Nithermoor or Pickering, but the majority settled down at Beck Gap with the Dorsay peasants to pick at the remnants of the feast while awaiting the return of the expedition and the captive witch.

Just before the expedition set out they received an unexpected and less welcome addition to their numbers when a large hunting party of gentry arrived from Dorsay Manor. This was headed by Sir Roger Dorsay, the brother of the monk Simon of Rievaulx, and now Lord of Dorsay, famous in the Riding for the profligacy of his hospitality, among other, less attractive characteristics. A profoundly godless man, he regarded Satan and Sycorax, drought and plague as matters best dealt with by increased self-indulgence in flippant company.

Within the territory of the Royal Forest, the manorial rights of Dorsay extended over part of Slatterdale, and the inhabitants of Beck Gap were technically Dorsay villeins. Demarcation with the jurisdiction and administration of the Duchy of Lancaster was blurred and sometimes problematical. Therefore the Steward of the Duchy had thought it politic to consult Sir Roger about the arrangements for the arrest of the witch – and Roger had seen it, as he tried to see almost everything, as an occasion for wassail and amusement. The roast sheep provided for the posse and the Dorsay peasantry at Beck Gap was only part of the entertainment that had been arranged – the part designed for the lower orders and not even attended by the gentry. At Dorsay Manor the same evening there had been a much more ornate and exotic meal of chicken, suckling pig, wild boar and wastel bread, to which relatives and like-minded acquaintances had travelled from all over the shire. Several such feasts were on the social agenda, to be interspersed with healthy exercise such as would be provided by today's entertainment, which had brought the Dorsays and their guests well clear of the manorial parkland where they normally hunted and hawked.

They had come to hunt the witch: or, more precisely, were interrupting a hunting foray to combine it with an amusing novelty. They intended to accompany the expedition that morning and witness its progress, then picnic in the forest before traversing Slatterdale back to the manorial park.

Sir Roger announced all this affably enough but in a tone that made it clear he did not consider it negotiable. He was a heavy, blue-jowled man clad in a hunting outfit of green linen to counter the heat and astride a prestigious black stallion. Eleven men and seven women formed the Dorsay hunting party: all clad in cool, expensive linen like Sir Roger, but brightly and variously coloured. The women wore sumptuous long gowns that flowed from their side-saddles almost to the floor and had the headgear fashionable at that epoch, resembling small tents thrown over satanic horns or antlers. With the party were over a score of grooms, huntsmen, falconers, musicians, bearers and attendants; also greyhounds, mastiffs, pack horses, falcons and even a lap dog transported in a wicker cage by an attendant whose only function was its care.

Sergeant Garth was clearly horrified by these recruits, who seemed at least as big a potential nuisance to him as the rabble from Pickering and Nithermoor that he had just managed to jettison. If the Steward of the Duchy of Lancaster had been there he might have resisted the incursion, but as a knight and nobleman Sir Roger easily outranked anybody who was actually on the expedition and a sergeant of archers was helpless against him.

Father Norbert was particularly distressed because of the known profanity of Sir Roger and several of his guests that might counter all the priest's attempts to give a spiritual ambience to the expedition. But he was even more powerless than Sergeant Garth, who was after all in charge of the Temporal Power responsible for the arrest. It would have needed the Archdeacon in person, rather than his clerk, to wield any authority against the Lord of Dorsay, even if Sir Roger would let himself be influenced by any cleric.

Father Norbert was brave enough to insist that since the expedition was on behalf of God's Church, at the behest of the Archdeacon and aimed against the evil powers of Satan, all who took part in it or accompanied it should take part in an *ora pro nobis in tenebris* prior to departure. Rather to his surprise neither Sir Roger nor any of his party raised an objection; dismounting and kneeling with automatic carelessness as they regularly did, between orgies and atrocities, for their parish priests or the Dorsay chaplain. Norbert rather wished that he had insisted on them all being shriven like the archers and constables. He compensated by delivering a homily in English about the sacred gravity of the mission before launching into the Latin text. It was a chant that the priests had been practising during the previous day's journey: under their leadership the calls and responses sounded particularly impressive in the warm morning meadow outside Beck Gap, not far from the hut at West Copse where Watkin Trothers was slain.

The first of the awful and amazing events of the day happened next. As the last notes of the last response died, as Father Norbert was raising his hand to administer a concluding blessing, a faint breeze stirred the meadowgrass and caressed the faces of the worshippers. It was subtle enough not to be much noticed at first. It persevered, became slightly more pronounced, until it was impossible to ignore that air was moving in the meadow which had been windless throughout the summer.

This put the gathering in very good heart – must have impressed even the most feckless sceptic in the hunting party. The priests were unanimous in hailing it as a sign from God in answer to the prayers. The huntsmen, foresters and Sergeant Garth were the more inclined to accept this interpretation because the breeze was from the north-east and so entirely favourable to their cause. The lair of Sycorax being to the north-east, the breeze would muffle their approach and prevent their scent from reaching the nostrils of the witch's dogs.

The breeze was in the faces of the expedition as it climbed into Slatterdale beside the dry beck. The music for this day's march was provided by the jingling little bells on the bridles of the cavaliers. The number of horses present was a nuisance to those on foot and the behaviour of the hunting party – or at least its noble components – was bothersome to Sergeant Garth. Some of them carried wineskins at their saddles, from which they refreshed themselves and others of their group as they travelled. It led to one of them, more efficiently refreshed than the rest, amusing himself by continually blowing his hunting horn as loudly as he was able.

Sergeant Garth protested to Sir Roger Dorsay that such a racket might easily warn the witch of their approach. Dorsay merely shrugged.

'Why not give the old bat a sporting chance?'

This appalled Father Norbert, who was strongly suspicious that the hunting party from Dorsay was a device of Satan's to sabotage the expedition. He was a little comforted when Sir Roger had a laughing word with the horn blower, who desisted after a few more defiant blasts.

The hunting party were also generally troublesome because of their urge to blow their horns, fly their hawks, loose their dogs or set off in pursuit if anything living crossed the path.

Fortunately, it was only rarely that anything worthy of pursuit appeared in the scorched dale. The Ridings were parched and the heat seemed to be frying the grass; the sheep had been taken over the ridge and closer to what was left of Cropton Beck. The gorse and heather seemed dusty and brittle. The feet of men and horses kicked up a sort of smoke that floated on the slow breeze and was slow to settle after they had passed. Bordering the track to the east were the outskirts of the great forest: oaks, chestnuts, birches, occasionally pines, stricken with heat so that their leaves looked like metal and their trunks crackled. There were no birds singing. The route was lined with the crisp corpses of frogs. Twice they passed the bones and ravaged carcass of a sheep, from one of which a couple of crows flopped heavily away.

As they approached the valley head one of the constables – a lad who had been particularly festive in Beck Gap and particularly slow and ginger that morning – suddenly swerved aside and collapsed in the heather by the track. He lay on his side with his arms wrapped round his belly and his knees almost touching his chin, like a foetus in the womb. A thick brown vomit like mutton broth gushed out of his throat and lay on the ashen heather immediately alongside his flushed and swollen face. Another constable was detailed to stay with him and his condition fairly confidently ascribed to the previous evening's excess, but all the same the event had a damaging effect on the spirits of some of the company.

At the valley head the breeze was more robust and actually served to mitigate the heat. One of the foresters pointed north-east across the pelt of the outspread forest to the far horizon where a low grey rampart seemed to divide earth from sky.

'Rain, sithee!'

People crossed themselves and one or two of the priests launched into prayers of thanksgiving. Father Norbert called out: 'Praise God that it is almost the end of the reign of Sycorax in Slatterdale and the suffering she has brought to the people of Yorkshire.' A ragged cheer greeted this and the fool with the hunting horn raised it to his lips and let out a little bleep.

Sergeant Garth gestured frantically for silence. His voice did not have the commanding resonance of Norbert's: everybody had to strain their ears to hear him over the snuffling and shifting of the horses and the whimpering of the dogs as he appealed, somewhat querulously, for discretion and order, now that they were close to their quarry.

Sir Roger proposed that the mounted hunters should descend from the valley head, negotiate the slopes of Misperdale and cross the eastern summits to enter the forest north of Sycorax's hut and cut off her retreat.

Sergeant Garth, dismayed, objected that this might well alert the witch to danger, since the cavalry (as well as making a predictable fuss and racket) would be windward of her dogs. They would also complicate and confuse any pursuit of the witch by bloodhounds and the dogs of the foresters.

Father Norbert supported Sergeant Garth, as he felt he should. He claimed that if the witch had time to assemble her magic and call on the powers of Satan all the temporal force assembled against her would most likely be powerless, whereas if she was surprised and driven from her charms and potions she would simply be a lame crone hiding in a forest and easily taken.

Sir Roger was unimpressed by these arguments and about to put his own plan into operation when he was undermined by a rebellion among his party. Some of them surveyed the knobbly summits to the east of Misperdale and were afraid that while they were engaged on strenuous cross-country manoeuvres they would miss all the fun of the arrest. Others in the party, daunted by the ominous waste of Slatterdale, the collapse of the constable and the increasing sense of the proximity of Sycorax, preferred to remain under the dual protection of the priests and archers.

As the troop entered the forest and negotiated the ravine that led to the hut of Sycorax the most godless felt a superstitious twinge and the most boisterous were sobered. Even Sir Roger seemed happy to submit to the sergeant's decree that the archers now lead the way, together with the priest who was carrying the largest crucifix.

Just before the hut of Sycorax was located the clamour of a large dog alarmed everybody and set up a medley of answering woofs and bays from the dogs of the expedition. It guided them to where they were confronted by the huge black dog, Satan, that Trissie March had described: tethered to the doorpost, straining towards the intruders and barking furiously, not at all intimidated by the odds against him.

At a command from Sergeant Garth the archers deployed into a line, fitted arrows to their bows and aimed. The order to shoot was largely lost amid the din of praying priests and excited dogs. Some of the archers were clearly fazed by the unusual ambience, for several arrows missed the target entirely, but most of them hit the dog and at least one made a fatal strike. Satan's last bark was transformed into what sounded like a yelp of outrage as he suddenly bristled with arrows. His hindquarters collapsed first, then he lolled on to his side and lay still.

Sergeant Garth ordered his squad to fit another arrow and stand ready. Nothing emerged from the doorway behind the slain guard dog. Garth loaded and cocked his crossbow. On an impulse Father Norbert took the largest crucifix from the priest who was carrying it and placed himself at the sergeant's side.

Everybody watched agog as the two men waded through the

choked, parched underbrush of the narrow glade and went into the hut. All the dogs seemed to sense the tension and stop barking except for the lap dog in its wicker cage, which went on yelping doughtily. The priests were now praying in muted union like a hive of bees.

After a few seconds the sergeant reappeared in the doorway and issued the self-evident news that the witch was not at home. Norbert came out behind him, crucifix aloft, declaiming exultantly:

'The Fiend has fled! His powers are futile against the holiness we bring! He has deserted the witch, giving her little warning of our coming. She in turn has fled in such panic that she did not even free her familiar – a mere mortal dog without the presence of the Fiend – but left it to be slain.'

Sergeant Garth respectfully disagreed with this last point. The witch was out gathering food and herbs, he suggested. She'd leave the dog to guard her property and give her notice of visitors.

There was further discussion, while the town constables ransacked the witch's hut, scattering her apothecary and searching for the treasure she was rumoured to have amassed. Sir Roger said that even if the witch's supernatural powers had failed to warn her, the racket of her dog, the other dogs and the priest would have done the job. He seemed freshly emboldened by the slaughter of the dog Satan and wanted to ride off in immediate search, together with other horsemen, but Sergeant Garth entreated him not to do so. The sergeant maintained that the best chance of catching Sycorax was by using the bloodhounds and that those beasts would be more effective if the trail they followed was as undisturbed as possible. Recent events having imbued the Lord of Dorsay with a sneaking regard for the sergeant of archers, he fell in with Garth's wishes.

After the specialist hounds had been primed with garments and belongings of the witch the entire expedition set off through the forest, with the bloodhounds and their handler now in the van. The official posse, fifty strong – archers, foresters, constables and other volunteers – followed in two roughly parallel lines. They kept pace with each other like grouse beaters, as far as the forest allowed, and checked the underbrush to ensure that the witch, endowed with Satan's subtlety, did not double back, elude the search party, cross her own trail and confuse the scent. The priests and the Dorsay contingent brought up the rear. All horses were either ridden at walking pace or led, all dogs kept leashed and reckoned redundant (apart from the bloodhounds) until the quarry should actually be sighted.

Snuffling the earth and straining at their leashes, emitting a lugubrious bass bay and displaying the utmost confidence in their own talents, the bloodhounds dragged the concourse north-eastwards, into the face of the breeze that was now a distinct wind travelling through the wildwood: funnelling between the boles of the trees and swaying and shimmering in their foliage.

It soon became evident that the breeze was carrying an acrid smell of burning. It was conjectured that the witch had set the underbrush alight in an attempt to obscure her trail.

At about this time the expedition against Sycorax became aware of another phenomenon. As they passed out of the denser copses and spinneys of birch and elder into the glades that were sometimes permitted by the grander trees – the elms, oaks, sycamores and pines – they observed that the daylight was fading, though it was late August and not yet noon. When they reached a glade that permitted them a sighting of the sky to the north-east they saw a grey-black mass in that direction, slowly swirling and thickly forming as it crept up from the horizon of treetops to obscure a third of the sky. It looked like either storm clouds or the smoke of a gigantic conflagration.

The smell of burning increased and seemed to contain other unpleasant odours, as when rubbish or potions are flung on to a fire. The whole line stopped, with the impatient bloodhounds in the centre, while Garth and Norbert conferred with the foresters, who were unhappy about developments. Sir Roger rode forward to join the conference.

The oldest forester said, 'If there's fire in t'forest, after all yon dry days, it were best keep clear on't. It were best go back now, this minute.'

It was Father Norbert who answered him. Norbert, a devout man of normally modest bearing, was taking a keen and conscientious interest in this mission, though according to some he had been reluctant to undertake it in the first place. His courage and fervour had become more marked as the expedition progressed. Fixing his eyes on the crucifix he had borrowed and was still carrying, he spoke out in the strong pulpit voice that he had used at the valley head and the witch's hut:

'Cannot you see that it is the wiles of Satan and Sycorax? They seek to terrify us and make us break off the pursuit. They know that they have no power to withstand the power of the Cross, or they would have confronted us and destroyed us by now. They seek to terrify us with stinks and clouds, for their only hope is to turn us into cowards and betrayers of God.'

The old forester did not look convinced by this, but as far as everybody else was concerned it settled the matter. Norbert's fellow priests let out a communal gasp of acclaim, then broke out spontaneously into *O Gentes Omnes Undique*. Sergeant Garth extended his right hand and pointed a heroic finger onward. Sir Roger let out an enthusiastic bellow and made his stallion prance.

The expedition moved forward: the bloodhounds baying, the priests singing, the hunting party tooting their horns. There were some in the gathering, though, who were not so braced by what Father Norbert had said but found the concept that Satan was causing the stink and clouds somewhat dismaying. Other misgivings were expressed by the old forester pursing his lips, the horses rolling their eyes, the greyhounds wrinkling their noses and slinking their tails between their haunches.

The trail turned east and then south-east, so that the burning smell was wafted at the left flank of the expedition for a while, which seemed less unnerving. But then the bloodhounds turned back into the face of the smouldering wind and at the same time entered what looked like another bothersome but shallow spinney. The expedition followed, expecting to soon emerge into more open forest. If the foresters knew better, they said nothing: either feeling quelled and defeatist after the earlier conference or hoping that the problems of the spinney might bring the party to a halt and make them reconsider.

The spinney proved to be extensive and the terrain became increasingly difficult: pits and knolls, banks and declivities, lakes of nettle and tangles of bramble, the boles and roots of fallen trees. It was impossible for the priests to carry on singing or for anybody to keep a semblance of formation. The hunting party all had to dismount, the women clutching up their long, expensive dresses to protect them from the thorns and twigs of the undergrowth. Some of the hunters shouted that they could not go on, but the impetus of the vanguard had got everybody to struggle so far into the spinney that the idea of going back seemed equally unwelcome.

The survivors I have interviewed agree on the weird and threatening aspects of the scene which now evolved. It was dark, what sky was visible being overcast, though a few shafts of sunlight were slanting eerily through the foliage from the south. The entire troop became dispersed through the spinney, like the remnants of a shipwreck struggling in the waves. All the while the breeze from the north-east, from Sycorax, was loud in the leaves, carrying a stink of smouldering, sulphurous corruption through the trees and thickets, stifling the nostrils of beasts and humans alike. Tiny motes of black and grey ash came drifting and meandering down through the trees to speckle the foliage.

The vanguard with the bloodhounds pressed on grimly and came at last to flatter and less tangled terrain, as though the spinney was likely to develop into more open woodland. There they were met by a stag and three hinds, which fled blindly towards them until a collision was imminent, then swerved off and disappeared with great bounds into the depths of the spinney. The wind was more consistent and powerful, the motes of ash larger and more numerous. The bloodhounds circled desperately, snuffled and sneezed, then stood baffled.

Sergeant Garth announced that the leading group would wait where they were. When the whole party had struggled up to them through the worst of this spinney, they would regroup and advance. If the hounds could not pick up the scent again, the best hope was that the witch was not far ahead of them and would soon be overtaken at last.

Nobody gave what he was saying much credence. 'Thoo could tell as it were mullock what he didn't credit hissen,' one witness told me. Nobody now believed that a lame woman had gone before them through that intractable spinney. Nor did anybody believe that the troop was going to advance in pursuit of her, into the billowing darkness, the stench and the din that was coming at them through the birches and elders.

The noise was a new phenomenon. Even before Sergeant Garth had finished giving his redundant instructions, Father Norbert, who was drooped over the crucifix which his weary arms had grounded, let out a great cry and cupped his hand to his ear. Those around him halted and listened. Distinct and terrible, above the racket of man and beast struggling through the spinney and above the billowing of the wind through foliage, they heard a crazy, evil multitude: shouts, laughter, the roaring of ravenous beasts, the crackle of flames. The noise was not just ahead of the expedition but to the right and left of them, indicating that they were already outflanked and almost surrounded by the fiends.

The Retaliation of the Fiend Sycorax

HE FIRST TO react was the black stallion of Roger Dorsay. This creature had been very reluctant to be dragged and coaxed through the spinney, once or twice planting its feet and resisting. Now it let out a great whinny and lunged forward, dashing its master to the ground. Swinging away from the evil wind in its nostrils it described an untidy semicircle in the spinney, plunging and jinking as it leapt over obstacles or crashed through twigs and fronds.

The panic of the black horse might have been infectious, but it is more likely that others came almost instantaneously to the same conclusions. Many of the dogs set up a melancholy howling, while others yelped and whimpered. Only the lap dog bounced up and down in its cage of wicker and barked indomitable defiance. The horses bucked and lurched, becoming impossible to control, and a couple of them broke loose at once and bolted after the stallion.

Among the humans it was marginally the Dorsay contingent whose morale cracked first, because of their involvement with the horses. Women lamented shrilly, men bellowed senseless orders and imprecations. Sir Roger, who had a dislocated shoulder, was wailing for assistance and being largely ignored. Then the rest of the expedition succumbed abruptly and as if a trumpet had blown retreat everybody turned and started struggling back through the spinney, following the bolting horses towards the south-west where bright sky was still sometimes visible through the foliage.

As soon as the posse turned back any hint of individual calm or courage vanished, along with any hope of order or discipline. The archers threw away their bows and quivers and some of them divested themselves of their leather hauberks as they fled. The priests discarded the crucifixes and other holy implements. The dogs and horses were left to their own devices, their reins and leashes threatening to snag on branches and trap them; the lap dog clamoured frantically in its cage that had suddenly become a condemned cell. Sir Roger was left supine, in agony if he budged, his demands for assistance becoming ever less peremptory and more imploring.

Everybody flung themselves back through the spinney: sprained in the underbrush, concussed on the boles and branches, flayed by the thorns. They were accompanied in their flight not only by their own animals but by creatures of the forest such as rabbits, voles, squirrels, partridges and pigeons. The clouds had now covered the sky so that it was midnight dark in the spinney but lit with the lurid, flickering light of the approaching flames.

The roar of the forest burning was behind them and around them, together with the clamour of the fiends of Sycorax. Now that the crucifixes of the clerics were flung aside and their prayers forgotten she was able to wield the full fury of her magic at last, taking revenge for the insults she had borne and the punishments she had received as Sukie Dobson and Sukie Trothers.

The fiends she unleashed on the eighty humans and their beasts were many and various. The heads of great serpents nuzzled up out of the undergrowth of the spinney and sank fangs into the ankles of the fugitives, either dragging them down into the earth or holding them trapped to await the flames. Birds like crows but the size of men flapped everywhere, sometimes bearing off victims whole into the darkness beyond the flames. Red and yellow goblins with pronged goads dashed from the flames that were their element, tormenting and jeering. Fiery dragons swooped from the air with scorching breath. The heat, noise and stench were the certified accoutrements of Hell.

Over four dozen of the four score humans perished in the rout: most of them in the spinney, for once they were out of it the nightmare was somewhat abated, if by no means over. They could move more freely and escape more rapidly south, so long as they could avoid or negotiate dense woodland while keeping ahead of the remorseless pursuit. Any that lagged or fell lame were gobbled up by Sycorax's rabble of fiends. The fire raced and raged amid the dry grass and parched trees of the more open forest as ravenously as in the spinney. The fiends rampaged and multiplied: some taking shapes that were personally appropriate to their victims. One witness was bitten in the neck by a fiend in the guise of his dead brother – when living his virulent enemy – whose red-hot fangs left marks in the flesh still visible today. Another saw Sergeant Garth destroyed by the fiery bolt of a shadowy, giant crossbowman perched in a blazing pine.

The residents of Beck Gap, together with numerous Dorsay villeins and folk from Nithermoor and Pickering, celebrated Mass (with the Dorsay chaplain officiating) when the expedition was gone, then dined off the remains of yesterday's sheep boiled into broth with carrots and onions. 'Then more ale were supped, an' we sang and danced some more while we waited for t'posse to get back wi' t'witch,' Trissie said. Some of those who were not simply committed to the self-indulgent pursuits of the holiday were engaged in claims and recriminations about the expenses and profits arising from the event. Others were simply looking forward to beating the witch to pulp, if it was permitted either by the agreement or the inattention of her captors.

At noon a breeze arose to flutter the pavilions and cool the dancers. A thick, black slab of cloud was seen to be ascending the sky to the north-east – a direction from which the weather rarely came. It was applauded as a sign that rain was on the way at last and made by some an excuse for intensifying their celebrations. It seemed to occur to nobody, at first, to connect the cloud with Sycorax, though it was universally known that the posse had set out in that direction to seek her lair.

By half past twelve the sky was entirely overcast with a porridge of thick, dark-grey rain-bearing clouds. A weird gloam had settled on Beck Gap, as at twilight or during an eclipse of the sun. There were flecks of lightning and growls of thunder, but the rain did not drop. The festivities continued warily.

By one o'clock there was drinking and music still in progress, but the dancers had taken shelter. Still it did not rain. A smell of burning came and the first motes of ash, so few they were hardly discerned, floated and twisted on the wind. A roaring hubbub was heard in Slatterdale and the neighbouring forests, advancing from the north like continuous thunder or as if a thousand dragons were being slain. It was accompanied by an eery, shifting light: at first as faint as marsh glow on the darkness, then unmistakably the loom of a multitude of flames. Hundreds of sheep ran down past the hamlet from Slatterdale, driven from the banks of Cropton Beck on to the moor by the blazing forest, then pursued down the valley of parched gorse and grass that the flames had eaten like tinder.

At ten past one the first survivor of the expedition arrived at Beck Gap: a Pickering constable and famous runner, whose account of what had happened – and what was approaching – put an end to the most determined drunkard's attempts at revelry, silenced the music and spread terror. Altogether nearly a score of survivors, all active young men, got into Beck Gap in advance of the enemy, together with several shepherds and a number of riderless horses and ownerless dogs. The rest of the expedition was deemed to have perished, though it was later discovered that a few had survived by their flight taking them deep into the south-east forest, out of the path of the flames and fiends.

Some left Beck Gap immediately, while others began collecting their beasts, gathering their families, trying to find transport for their belongings and making other frenzied arrangements. There were some, too, that decided they still preferred to cringe and shelter in Beck Gap rather than trust themselves to the open, where there was clearly going to be a stupendous tempest as well as fiends and flames abroad. The Dobsons and Marches were among these: Trissie says she had lost all kinship with the creature whose legions were approaching the birthplace of Sukie Dobson. 'We felt no different. We were scared daft like everybody else.'

The darkness was suddenly dispelled when East Copse became a great torch that smeared the hamlet with thick shadows and flapping light. Great flakes of grey ash and black soot fell on Beck Gap like snow. There was a roaring of hoarse monsters and the burning stench grew prodigious. Then Sycorax came.

She came down from Slatterdale in a wall of flame and smoke like an ocean billow. The flames licked flickering light on to the earth they were about to devour, while the smoke churned up to meet the low clouds and make a perfect blackness. Against the flames in shadow-graph, or illuminated on the black air, was a multitude of insanely active and deafeningly jubilant monsters. Many of these were foul chimeras formed by the coupling of reptiles, birds and beasts. There were legendary beasts among them such as dragons, griffins and salamanders. Then there were horned demons that looked as if they had been cut out of dark red leather and witches black as the sky who swooped and soared astride sacks of straw or the handles of brooms. Most of these monsters brandished in their claws or held in their fangs the charred and bleeding heads, limbs or other portions of those humans who had already become their victims: among whom those at Beck Gap recognized relatives, friends and acquaintances, as well as the gentlefolk of Dorsay.

Most witnesses describe Sycorax as riding a black goat with curling horns and beard, but there were claims that 'it were t'black dog Satan she rode, brung back alive by witchery an' swole to twice it size.' In any case, it is agreed that the animal flapped vast wings that kept the witch suspended among the smoke and flames. She appeared to one witness as naked, leprous white and skeletal, sprawled backwards between the black wings of her steed while she performed blasphemous obscenities with a crucifix: but this is an unsupported testimony that it is safest to discount as the product of a brain made fervid with terror. Most witnesses concur that the witch was splendid in a scarlet gown and great, horned headdress such as noblewomen wore. Her glittering eyes in her pale face were particularly remembered as awesome, along with her 'gummy gob spread wide in a mad gloat'. She rode astride with her arms outspread in mockery of Our Saviour on the Cross, except when she pointed with her right hand to direct her fiends and flames. Clutched by the hair in her left hand was the mangled but still recognizable head of the Lord of Dorsay.

The Triumph of the Fiend Sycorax, 1414

'HE FLIGHT FROM Beck Gap to Nithermoor was perhaps the most spectacular event of that infamous day. Nearly two hundred folk took part in it, of whom about half were actually residents of Beck Gap. It began as a disorderly retreat and ended as a shambolic scramble down the path beside the empty beck. Sheep, pigs, dogs, cats, cattle and poultry went with them, out of all semblance of control and contending with each other and the humans for priority on the narrow track. Those who tried to take substantial property with them, in wagons or meal sacks, soon felt forced to abandon them to add to the obstacles and chaos of the road. There were overturned carts, boxes, sacks and a spillage of belongings: weapons, household utensils, musical instruments . . . Quite a lot of livestock and a couple of geriatrics had actually been overlooked and left in Beck Gap to await the cruelty of the demons and the mercy of the flames.'

'I think it more elegant if the verb is left till the end of the sentence,' Prior Jocelyn remarked.

He was speaking not to me but to Brother Stephen, against whom he was playing at chess while I read to them. Neither of them had been giving me much attention so far, apart from scowling at their game as if it was being spoiled by the reading I was imposing on them. It was, of course, Prior Jocelyn who had commanded the reading, as a means of assessing what I was up to without having to plough through the manuscript himself.

Brother Stephen, a sandy, plump, freckled fellow, had followed Prior Jocelyn from Rievaulx and was shortly to be appointed Claustral

Prior at Byland, when Jocelyn became Abbot. I think he has little Latin apart from devotional and ceremonial, but all the same he nodded wisely at what Prior Jocelyn had said.

I allowed a respectful pause to acknowledge the Prior's words then carried on reading:

'The scene was so overwhelming both to the senses and the intellect that none of the witnesses interviewed has given me a clear and comprehensive picture. Some were blinded in the blackness and the smoky firelight, recalling everything in terms of sound: the bedlam of wind and flames, the terrified human and animal voices, the screams and roars of the exulting fiends. Others were preoccupied by the demons of Sycorax and unable to describe any other aspect of the event. Trissie March could not provide any details at all. "I were minding t'bairns. I were shit skeered" was all she could recall.'

Prior Jocelyn looked sharply round from the chessboard and said, 'Pardon?'

'I use the vulgar speech, Father,' I explained, 'for the direct testimony of my witnesses. I consider that direct testimony adds authenticity to my account but can think of no way of transcribing it into Latin.'

Prior Jocelyn's eyes met those of Brother Stephen across the chess board and they exchanged a derisive smirk at my expense. Neither of them made any comment about what I had said, so I went on:

'When the storm broke at last it brought even more chaos and terror. There was sheet lightning and deafening, instantaneous thunder. A great weight of rain descended from the darkness, hissing and smoking among the conflagration, churning the so far unscorched earth to mud. Yet it was the storm that saved Nithermoor from Sycorax and her fiends – and by first slowing then arresting the flames that were the element of the fiends it also spared most of the fugitives from Beck Gap who might otherwise have been their prey. After the weakness and sinfulness of man had permitted Sycorax and Satan such a triumph, the storm must be seen as the merciful intervention of God, countering the fire of the fiends with the opposite element of water and denying them the opportunity to further wreak their malice on His creation.'

Prior Jocelyn chortled, then asked, 'Is that just pious cant, or do you believe it?'

I looked up from my reading to see that he had turned again and was staring at me. Since I was not sure how best to answer him he decided that I had not understood the question.

'The fire was Satan's? The water was God's? Do you not think that forests can burn and storms rage without supernatural intervention?'

I was taken aback and could not muster a reply. This was probably as well, for Prior Jocelyn's tone and demeanour were those of a scoffing instructor rather than somebody interested in a theological debate.

'Do you not understand that the demons your witnesses described to you existed only in their minds? That Sycorax was a madwoman who set fire to the forest to save her skin? That the plague, the drought and the storm were natural occurrences for which we should neither blame God nor congratulate the Devil?'

He now waited for me to speak, but I did not dare. It seemed to me that Prior Jocelyn was embroidering the very sentiments that I had myself blurted out to horrify Abbot Fabian in the herb garden, when Sycorax was speaking through my lips and clutching her claws into my soul.

He laughed. 'You think I am uttering blasphemous heresy, Brother Edmund. I can tell by the way you are gaping. But you are mistaken. The Church has made no pronouncement on Sycorax and the events in Slatterdale. Only local ignorance and superstition have pronounced.'

I was considering how Abbot Fabian would have refuted his successor but said nothing. My obedience was now due to Prior Jocelyn. After a few moments he asked, 'Have you more to read?'

When I had first arrived with my manuscript in answer to his summons he had demanded that I read the last few pages that I had written. I now said that one more page remained, and he waved me to proceed. Turning back to his game he let out a squeal of flippant rage, seeing the move that Brother Stephen had just made.

'The storm raged through the evening and night, while the terrified survivors and their flocks took shelter in Nithermoor. In the morning the whole of Slatterdale and thousands of acres of forest were a sodden ruin. Neither Sycorax nor any of her fiends were to be seen. Not that anybody went to look for them. From that day to this it has been accepted locally that Slatterdale belongs to the witch.

'Two months after the event a squad of soldiers accompanied two priests into the burnt-out shell of Slatterdale. They went as far as Sycorax's hut and found the scorched skeleton of the dog Satan. Returning, they performed a ceremony of exorcism at Beck Gap. The next summer the meadows and moors were recovered and though the forest was full of dead trees the smaller plants were thriving as never before. But nobody moved back to Beck Gap or pastured sheep in Slatterdale.

'In an arrangement between Sir Roger's widow and the Steward of the Duchy, Slatterdale passed into the direct control of the Duchy of Lancaster, along with the main Dorsay estate and the manor farm. Since then nobody has been found to lease or buy Slatterdale at any price, not even the abbeys, for it is known that no local labour can be found to work the land. The Duchy has to bring foresters from Eskdale and even these soon become chary and remiss in their supervision of the Slatterdale region.'

'You were in check, clodpoll,' Prior Jocelyn said to Brother Stephen, 'so how could you move your queen?' Then he said to me, 'Go on.'

'That is all I've written so far, Father.'

'How do you propose to end it?'

'Abbot Fabian's intention was that I should conclude with a warning to all regarding witchcraft and the powers of Satan – and an exhortation to virtue and piety, since only by obtaining the grace of God will we secure ourselves against evil.'

'An unctuous notion from the old hypocrite!' Prior Jocelyn exclaimed, meeting the eye of Brother Stephen, who laughed complicitly. 'I'm afraid I have little sympathy with your admiration of Abbot Fabian, Brother Edmund, nor with the foolish book you have composed.

I do, though, agree with Abbot Bernard of Rievaulx that there is the makings of a prestigious manuscript in the work you have undertaken and the information you have gathered. Only it will need to be heavily revised, eh? It is couched in a dunce's Latin that cannot be endured. We can surely find a scholarly monk at Rievaulx, or borrow one from Fountains, who can produce a more elegant text, without any of those quaint passages in the vulgar, to be properly illustrated for the Rievaulx library.'

'My work is finished then?'

As ever in a creature incapable of firm convictions, my reaction was confused. Since the death of Abbot Fabian the task he entrusted to me has assumed great value: as personal contrition, commemoration of my mentor and defiance of the witch that slew him. It seemed to me now that Sycorax was defeating me through the low opinion that Prior Jocelyn had formed of my work. At the same time I felt great relief at the notion that I was to be released from the terror of my predicament. I was eager to find obscurity, out of the notice of both Sycorax and Friar Gervase.

'Yes, as far as I am concerned. But Friar Gervase has made a request for your services as a scribe on an occasional and extramural basis. He will explain the matter to you further next Sunday, when you attend the execution of the wench you have helped hang.'

The Bewitching of Brother Edmund and the Hanging of the Witch Alys

HE CATHEDRAL WAS thronged with ecclesiastics, pilgrims and devout citizens: lighting candles, waiting to confess, kneeling in prayer . . . The noise was of priests officiating, the mumbled responses of worshippers and the tinkle of censers.

The columns rose dizzily, the arches climbed and soared to a roof so distant, so wreathed with the smoke of incense and candles, that I could not tell if it was stone or timber imitating stone. The wooden chancel screen, miraculously carved, was itself the size of a small chapel. No windows were visible from where I knelt, except for a distant, multicoloured radiance high beyond the chancel screen, but candlelight illuminated the shrines in the aisles, the alabaster effigies and the paintings on the walls.

I could see Saint Christopher holding the infant Christ and trampling a serpent under his right foot. John the Baptist knelt headless while Salome held her laden platter close to her heart. My own saint Edmund was impassive under the assault of four archers, his smile fixed on martyrdom.

A thin, calm voice was speaking Latin from the pulpit in the chancel screen. I was delighted to recognize Abbot Fabian's tones. His long, starved hands rested on the shelf of the pulpit next to the lectern, and his mild face peered down at me. It came to my awareness that what he was reading was not the Holy Scriptures but an extract from this very history of Sycorax which I am writing. I therefore lifted my knees from the rush-work hassock and seated myself on the bench behind me to listen. It was not easy to pick out the words because of the noise in the cathedral from the many simultaneous ceremonies and acts of devotion, but I could discern that he was reading my account of the expedition to arrest the witch and the devastation of Slatterdale.

Another obstacle to hearing the Abbot's reading was the distraction caused me by the other occupants of my bench. I was surrounded by fair women in expensive and brilliantly coloured drapery.

On my right, at one end of the crowded bench, was the Virgin from the Byland chapel, come down from her plinth and sitting beside me in her starched wimple and blue robe. Her face was turned from me as she listened intently to the reading of the Abbot, but her white hand was laid on my arm in a calming and reassuring gesture. There was a fresh, cool aura radiating from her, as of a breezy meadow in spring. I could smell mint and lavender, warm milk and baking bread.

On my left was Rosamund Mowbray, the girl I had watched with helpless, hopeless yearning through one summer of my youth – observing her kneeling in church, riding to falconry, a couple of times at table reaching daintily for her meat – when she and her family were rejecting a proposed marriage to my brother Ralf. They were wealthy folk who slept on bags of flock. If she looked on Ralf with disdain, she never looked at me at all: I was too young and boorish to come into the orbit of her awareness. I now felt again the pure, forlorn pain of my love, seeing her narrow face and prim lips, the haughty blue eyes between the long lashes. She was clad in the most preposterous finery she had flaunted that summer: a linen headdress draped from a frame of what seemed to be antlers and a high-waisted, voluminous dress of velvet trimmed with fur.

Beyond Rosamund Mowbray other women were sitting: young, old and matronly, all elegantly clad, their faces hidden from me by their headdresses and wimples. Their conduct made it impossible for me to follow the reading and was scandalous in a place of worship. They chattered to each other with the utmost nonchalance and had jackdaws, kittens and lap dogs, which they teased and cajoled, and trays of dainties from which they fed themselves and their pets. Even more disgracefully, there was a wineskin being passed among them, from which they refreshed themselves generously as they chatted and played.

The wineskin came to Rosamund Mowbray, and to my surprise she accepted it, crooking her arm and tilting her chin expertly as she quaffed from it. Then she wiped her lips and chin with the back of her hand and belched. As she turned towards me to offer me the wineskin I saw that there was a hectic flush on her cheeks and her proud face was transformed so that I could hardly recognize her. Her eyes and lips glistened as she grinned at me. I could smell the heavy wine on her breath.

I shook my head, discomfited by her conduct and the turn of events. Rosamund thrust the wineskin at me insistently and seemed to be saying that if I did not want to drink myself I should pass it on to the person next to me. Unwilling to do this, I turned from Rosamund towards her to apologize for the appalling sacrilege: but she also turned, smiling, and I found that I was gazing into the compelling eyes of Alys.

She took her left hand off my arm and placed her right hand on to the yellow hose of my knee – for I was no longer in my monk's habit but in the popinjay garb of my predatory youth – then ran her hand up my thigh until it rested on the crimson corduroy codpiece I flaunted in those days. This manoeuvre brought her face close to mine. She winked at me, a slow, lascivious swoop of an eyelid, and at the same time peeped out her tongue suggestively between her slightly parted lips.

We would surely have kissed, for all my dumbfounded dismay, but Rosamund, on the other side of me, let out a squeal of jealous pique. She had somehow jettisoned the wineskin and hitched up her gorgeous clothing above her knees. Now she seized my right hand and plunged it among her skirts, so dragging me round towards her. She clamped her lips on to mine, jutting her tongue into my mouth and waggling it wildly as she guided my captive fingers between her thighs. Meanwhile Alys had slid her cool hand under my codpiece and was fondling my testicles, but other events were preventing my sexual arousal.

The cathedral was burning. The film of candle and incense fumes in the vaulted roof had become a boiling turbulence of dark smoke. Flames were spiralling up the columns as they had devoured the straight boles of the pines in the forest east of Slatterdale. The chancel screen, on the point of collapse, was bright as the embers in the depths of a bonfire.

And there was other evidence that I was in Hell. Abbot Fabian lolled from the charred pulpit, transfixed by arrows like Saint Edmund, or like the witch's dog in the forest hut, but in this case the arrows blazed and the old man's flesh smouldered and shrivelled as he whimpered with pain. Throughout the fiery fane the incantations of the priests were the rigmarole of fiends and the murmur of worshippers had become the groans of unshriven sinners in perpetual despair.

The stench of burning filth was as oppressive as the heat. The two perfervid women assaulting me had melted into one being. The tongue inside my mouth was the probe of some utterly alien creature and talons were tightening on my testicles. It was time to wake up, if I was ever going to wake.

The scaffold was erected in the castle grounds, for the convenience of the Duchy of Lancaster's soldiers who had been entrusted with the execution. It disappointed those who had been looking forward to the witch being paraded through the town, so that they could amuse themselves by pelting her as if she was in the stocks, trusting themselves not to kill her in the process and obviate the execution. Now she was simply carried from her dungeon to the scaffold by two soldiers, very much as she had been carried into court, with not a lot of scope for audience participation.

This was not the only disappointment on a morning when a large and expectant throng had filled the castle's inner court, crowding towards the scaffold that was sited between the chapel and the Devil's Tower. Alys was the first witch to be executed in Pickering for half a century. The hanging had made a special holiday of the Sunday, as was typical in the North Riding, where every circumstance is made an excuse for sottishness and Sunday is observed with less worship and decorum than anywhere else in the land.

The majority of the population of Pickering was assembled and many folk had come into town from neighbouring manors and granges. A lot of children had been brought along, either because it was felt they would benefit from the occasion or because nobody was willing to forego the hanging to tend them. Burghers and country gentry, with their wives and children, were accommodated above the rabble on a wooden platform built against the curtain wall and the keep. Castle residents and retainers, including the soldiery not being used for crowd control, lined the wall and the keep ramparts.

I saw nobody from Nithermoor, which did not surprise me. Relations between Pickering and Nithermoor are not cordial: it was unlikely that anybody from Nithermoor would venture into Pickering on the day that a native of the village was being executed as a witch. There were probably only a few of us in the crowd who had known Alys in her normal role.

Though the hanging was clearly intended as a spectacle, its purpose was improvement rather than entertainment and there was no distasteful enhancement of proceedings. The sobriety of the atmosphere was ensured by the fact that the event took place in the morning. Tumblers and musicians, judged unsuitable, were not allowed in the castle grounds. Nor were traders permitted to pester the mob, except for licensed sellers of holy relics and petty pardons. There were no officious proclamations or opportunist exhortations. Apart from the victim and her escort, the only performers on stage were two cowled figures: the almost inaudible priest and the discreetly efficient hangman. The only musical accompaniment came from a muffled and staccato kettledrum beaten by a soldier, from just before the entry of the witch to the moment when she was hoisted into the noose.

The biggest disappointment for the crowd was the performance of the victim. Those who had advocated that she should be allowed a longer period of recovery from interrogation were justified by her unimpressive contribution to the entertainment. Apart from the lolling of her bristly head, it was as if a half-filled sack of meal was carried to the scaffold by the soldiers, patiently supported while exhorted three times to repent and receive extreme unction, then held aloft precariously for the noose to be fitted. When the soldiers released her at last and she was supposed to writhe and cavort while strangling, she merely dangled like an already dead thing. It was a bit more satisfactory for the spectators at this stage, because what had previously seemed a squalid bundle of rags was at least now discernible as a human being, even a young woman. Apparently her hands and feet were crushed, since her limbs all terminated with a blunt bandage of brown sacking, but even the picturesque effect of this was lost by her hanging so limp and orderly.

The people, determined to find this holiday treat memorable and impressive, responded enthusiastically to everything, contributing their emotions generously to compensate for the lack of drama. They chattered with excited expectancy until the clunk of the kettledrum effected an awed silence. They raised a great outcry of dread and hatred when the witch appeared: the pious crossing themselves, the profane shouting obscenities. A vast and spontaneous cheer saluted the hanging, then everybody relaxed almost at once into merry babble and laughter. The grumbling came later, as the mob exited through the outer court, eager to get at the fairground stalls, the drinking, feasting and dancing.

I shared none of the crowd's emotions. Once I felt my presence had been noticed by Friar Gervase and other ecclesiastics, who were arranged on stools at the back of the scaffold platform, I was tempted to slink away but did not dare. Neither was I able to inspire my spirit with the dutiful satisfaction, recommended by the late Abbot, which might have made the occasion tolerable. The inert anonymity of the witch, that disgruntled everybody else, was an intense relief to me. I further mitigated my ordeal by shifting my gaze from the scaffold whenever I could bring myself to do so.

This brought me to study the faces and comportment of my fellow spectators and to arrive at an appalling concept. I conjectured that

Sycorax and all her minions and familiars were among the crowd in the inner court of Pickering Castle, sent by Satan to honour the death of the witch Alys. I saw faces in that crowd that were gargoyles depicting deadly sins. I saw faces that resembled all manner of brutes: men like dogs and pigs, women like cats and ferrets. There were fiends, too: dragons of wrath, witch-like crones, goblin children gaping their lips in glee.

'You should be rejoicing at the hanging of the witch who tormented you, Brother Edmund. But you seem sad, as if you had lost someone dear to you or a valued colleague.'

I might have suspected malicious humour in this remark if I had heard it from anybody but Friar Gervase. Humour was not a notion easily associated with him, nor was there any trace of it in his solemn eyes. There was no trace of intimidation, either, yet the menace in his utterance was impossible to ignore.

'I am deeply grieved that the witch did not repent,' I said. 'I hoped that my denouncing her, as well as rescuing me from her sorcery, would in the end save her from Satan and win her back to God.'

'It was unfortunate,' he agreed. 'But there was not the remotest chance that the witch Alys would repent. After her trial she never spoke again, nor uttered anything except the occasional exclamation of pain.'

'You would say then that Satan had a secure hold on her soul?'

'I have examined seven witches since God appointed me to my work. The others were in the Ripon diocese when I served the Bishop there. I can assure you that the witch Alys was entirely remarkable, both in her stubborn endurance of pain and her failure to be impressed by either the threat of Hell or the offer of Heavenly Grace.'

We were sitting at the table in the room next to Friar Gervase's cubicle in the Archdeacon's residence. I had dined with him there on my previous visit, but on this occasion I was housed and fed with a number of lesser clerics in a dormitory and refectory at the rear of the building. Nor was I offered wine: a jug of water, which we both ignored, was the only item on the table.

He went on: 'Her strength indicates the investment of Satan in her and in all this region. It is why I have need of you, Brother Edmund.'

He smiled at me without showing his teeth. Not for the first time, I felt a cold thrill of antipathy towards this calm, healthy, handsome man. I told myself it was the evil in me that feared him, but this did not help me to fear him less. I could not understand why he felt so in need of my literary powers, when a number of adequate scribes must have been available to him.

'I dare say you are wondering why I have such need of your literary powers, when a number of adequate scribes are available to me? It is because you know about Sycorax. The research you have done has made you the greatest expert on Sycorax that has ever lived.'

It was not the first time he had worked his disconcerting mind-reading trick on me, but all the same the shock of it meant that I took several seconds to collect my wits. I was going to blurt out that I only knew about Sycorax what I had been told at least twenty years after the event by unreliable witnesses – but I managed to restrain myself in time. It was only his notion that I was valuable that was keeping me from the rack and noose.

'And Sycorax hates you,' he went on. 'She has worked her sorcery on you, with the aid of her accomplices. She will slay you, as she has slain your Abbot, unless we slay her first. We have need of each other, Brother Edmund.'

I pretended to calmly inspect the backs of my fingers. They were quivering slightly. I was about to be very brave and put myself in jeopardy.

'I will help you gladly, Friar, asking only that Malkin and Luce are not arrested and examined.' He had told me earlier that these two tormentors of my dreams had been located near Sheriff Hutton, where my brother Ralf now held the family property. 'Nor any of the other girls I told you about, if they should be found.'

Now, if ever, there was a faint light of humour in his mild, brown eyes – or was there? He wiped his forefinger slowly round the rim of the water jug as he spoke. It occurred to me that we were engaged in an intricate game, like the chess that Prior Jocelyn had imported to Byland from Rievaulx.

'You are in no position to propose terms, Brother Edmund. I represent your only hope of survival. Not only do I spare you daily, by withholding investigation of your infected soul, but I am the only person on earth who can save you from the malice of Sycorax.

'Let us speak of something more congenial. The last time you were here I began an account of my personal history. My purpose was not just to give you information which you might use in the course of your chronicle of witchcraft in the North Riding but also to present you with my special credentials, permitting you to see that the authority by which I demand your compliance comes directly from God and is irresistible. Today I wish to continue by relating my infancy and boyhood: instancing the qualities that distinguished me from other children and furnishing a number of remarkable and edifying anecdotes to illustrate these qualities.'

Somebody was walking ahead of me carrying a spluttering flambeau. It flickered red light on to walls that loomed in on me, hairy and glistening with moss, studded with iron fangs which bit and bruised my flesh as I groped past them. The torchbearer was holding the torch in front of him so that all I could see of him, outlined against the red flare, was the shadow of a hunchback in a pointed cap. Looking beyond him to the portion of the narrow corridor lit by the torch I could see that the walls and ceiling were of uncut stone: the protrusions that plagued me were metal pegs that had been driven between the stones to accommodate rags and links of chain.

The door at the end of the corridor was bound with black iron like the scullery door at Byland. From behind the door could be heard the ferocious barking of a huge dog. When the torchbearer kicked open the door I expected the dog to leap out at us, but it did not do so, though its clamour became deafening and even more hectic.

The torchbearer set the torch into a bracket on the wall of the room inside the door and gestured me to enter. I saw that it was Simkin, his face ashen and his eyes glazed with dread. I moved forward charily, fearing the dog, only to discover that there was no dog in the room.

It was a small, windowless cell constructed of the same stone as the corridor. The only item of furniture was what I at first took to be a type of rack, on which the figure was strapped that was emitting the canine din. Then I saw that it was simply a heavy wooden bed. Although the occupant's hands and feet were tied at the four corners of the bed there was no apparatus for stretching or other torture.

The creature on the bed was Sycorax. She was naked, as she had never appeared to me in any previous dream or vision. I saw that whereas she had the head of an old crone her body was that of a fiend from the Easter mummers: dark red in the torchlight with purple nipples and pubic hair. Her flesh was hard like leather armour and her hands and feet were talons. A long and slender caudal bone twitched and flexed as the witch arched her body and contracted her limbs with a force that threatened at any moment to tear her free or collapse the bed. All the while her toothless jaws were wide agape and the voice of an enraged dog was belching and roaring out of her.

Simkin, in a dither of terror, handed me a sharply pointed stake. He contorted his features in an attempt to communicate with me, but his voice, drowned by the barking, came to me faint and unintelligible, as if hailing me from afar across a troubled sea. The frantic gestures that accompanied whatever it was he said made it clear that I was to transfix and slay the Fiend with the stake before she freed herself and we were lost.

It would have been helpful if I had been provided with a hammer to drive the stake home, for I was not sure that the force of my muscles was enough to penetrate the tough hide of the creature. The writhing and bucketing of Sycorax, as well as the dreadful sight and sound of her, made it difficult for me to aim the stake, but the fact that I seemed to have no alternative made me resolute. Aligning the weapon with my left hand, while my right hand rested on the butt ready to apply all the weight I could muster to the thrust, I placed the point on her belly just below the rib cage, aiming up beneath the ribs towards the heart. This forced the witch to keep her body still, but her thews still bulged as she strained at the cords that bound her talons to the corners of the bed. The barking became a ravenous, slobbering snarling as her alien gaze met mine.

I swooned. I was blind and deaf. Almost simultaneously, I regained my senses. The dog noises had ceased. Tethered spreadeagled on the bed was a shepherd wench in a grey woollen gown that left her calves and arms bare. She was biting her nether lip in apprehension and staring up at me with green, bewildered eyes.

I would have relaxed from my tense crouch and removed the point of my spear from where it rested against her belly, but Simkin grabbed my arm. What he shouted at me now was loud enough but still made no sense: terror was rendering his thoughts into gobbledegook. Yet I absolutely understood what he was trying to say. The apparition of Sukie Dobson was a ruse of Sycorax. It was to make me hesitate long enough for the witch to free one limb and strike me dead.

I shut my eyes and thrust upon the stake with all my weight and might. Hearing neither a human shout of agony nor the uproar of a fiend, I opened my eyes again to discover that the shepherd girl had received my blow in complete silence. She was by no means dead, the point having not reached up to her heart but embedded itself in her entrails. Her eyes were shut and her mouth was shaped into an oval 'O', as if she was planning to make a lot of racket as soon as the pain eased to permit it. A bloodstain, black in the red torchlight, was drenching the grey woollen frock, spreading rapidly from the point of entry of the stake.

I thrust Simkin aside and left the room.

In the dark corridor I was gouged and torn by the iron that jutted from the walls, but horror flung me on. I understood almost immediately that Sycorax had tricked me, first into merely wounding her, then into flight. She would have freed herself by now. Then she would deal with Simkin. Then she would be after me.

I groped for a long time along stone conduits and through doors that creaked open to my pressure. Sometimes there was no doorway and I had to feel with my hands along the blind wall until I came to an aperture in the stonework through which I queasily thrust myself into reciprocal darkness. Since I could hear no sound of pursuit my panic subsided into a duller, more desolate dread.

I was helpless and despairing when I saw the Cross of Our Saviour against an illuminated rectangle, floating above me and beckoning through the dark. The cross proved to be composed of the transom and mullion of a small window that illuminated a cell sufficiently to show its proportions and contents. The proportions seemed exactly the same as those of the cell I had left. The only content, over yonder, muffled in the gloom, was a mound of rags chained to a vast iron staple that was embedded in the wall.

Was it Alys? I could dimly make out a boyish crop of dark hair such as she wore when I first saw her. Resting my hand gingerly on the contours of a shoulderblade through tattered sacking, I started to babble concern, contrition. A female voice, husky with pain, hungry for sleep, interrupted me.

'Hush. Never fret. We aren't to blame, none of us.'

There was a clatter of chain, a rustling of cerements and the creature unfolded like a weird flower. I gave a little sob and put my head between soft breasts. She leant back against the cell wall with her arms harbouring me, the way my mother sometimes cuddled me after my father had thrashed me.

Putting my hand inside her skirt, on to her inner thigh which was smooth and warm, I felt my member stirring. Immediately I asked myself, *What if this is another ruse of the witch? What if it is Sycorax that holds me?*

She opened her legs and took me in. Her mouth engulfed mine so that I could not breathe and her heels were crossed on my spine like my brother Ralf used to grip and hurt me when we wrestled. There was no slippery friction, no sinful bliss, only a stifling, strangled dread from which I threshed awake.

The Expedition Against the Fiend Sycorax, 1431

'YCORAX HAS BEEN found. A lame old woman with a stick has been spotted north of Beck Gap. Her footprints have been found in the snow. Finally, smoke has been observed rising from one of the huts in the deserted hamlet.'

Only now that we were actually on the road, in a lowering winter dawn, was Friar Gervase giving me information. All I had been told by Prior Jocelyn was that Friar Gervase had requested my urgent presence in Pickering yet again. I had assumed, aghast, that it would have to do with the examination of Nance, Luce, Malkin or any other lass unlucky enough to have featured in my dreams. When I reached Pickering Gervase had quite uncharacteristically refused to speak to me until the morning, and nobody else was able (or willing) to tell me anything. The secrecy had become more intriguing when after Prime and Mass I was kitted out by servants of the Archdeacon with breeches, boots and leggings suitable for a foot traveller in difficult winter terrain.

'With the Archdeacon's cooperation I have hired Randal and Loll from the Ripon area who are intrepid and remorseless in the pursuit of witches. It is these who have discovered the whereabouts of the witch – with the help of Forester Tomson, who is conversant with Slatterdale though himself a native of Eskdale, far to the north. But it is I, because of my belief in Sycorax and my belief in my own fatal part in her story, who am really responsible for her being found.'

The trodden snow on the track between Pickering and Nithermoor was dark grey in the dawn light but would be slushy brown if the sun came out later to shine on it. It seemed unlikely that this would happen.

Tiny flakes were already beginning to fall. On either side of the track the world was still white from the last downfall.

There were just five of us: all stoutly clad in boots, leggings, padded jackets and breeches. The friar and I had the jackets over our habits; the skirts of the habits were divided and bound to our legs with string, so that we walked as freely as Forester Tomson and the two constables from Ripon. Randal and Loll bore crossbows and the forester carried a sack.

'To go against Sycorax is mortal danger,' I said. 'And any local will tell you that to venture into the moors in midwinter is folly. To combine the two risks is lunacy.'

I was surprised that this candour did not annoy him. In fact he smirked as if he had foreseen my objections and had been waiting for the chance to unleash his arguments.

'You are speaking to an expert on winter weather. I am from a region in the Pennines where the winters are harsher and bleaker than here and am accustomed from infancy to making my way through snow. Forester Tomson yonder, who is himself from the wilder northern moors of this shire, will bear me out when I say that winter is an over-rated obstacle in the Pickering region.

'I have in fact been eagerly awaiting this extreme weather, in order to put into effect my master plan against the witch. It is winter – this particularly white, cold winter – that has brought Sycorax back within range of us. She would still be lurking in the forest depths to the north-east if this exceptional weather had not plagued the mortal crone that harbours the Fiend, driving her down to the edge of civilization. The coldest winter for many years has provided an opportunity of capturing the witch, and it is fortunate that it coincides with my coming to Pickering and my awareness of such issues.

'The brilliance of my plan resides in our moving to apprehend her not – as one might facilely assume – when the weather abates but in the very thick of the worst of it. For the snow and cold will act as a defence against Sycorax, preventing those fires that were the vehicle of her fiends and her chief weapon against the last attempt to arrest her. Therefore Sycorax will be deprived of a main element of her magic – and on a more mundane level, the witch Sukie Trothers, a lame old hag by now, will be rendered less mobile by the snow than we are.'

I was bewildered by the ease with which he switched from the supernatural to the natural, regarding our quarry as a magical fiend or a powerless old woman to suit his argument. Even more seriously, there was a complacency behind his flawed though agile thinking which made it difficult to know how to reason with him.

It fleetingly occurred to me that I might save myself by abandoning this unpromising expedition, counting on Friar Gervase meeting his doom from either the witch or the weather. But now that we were out on the Nithermoor road between the swathes of snow it would have been very difficult for me to defect from the party against the wishes of Gervase, given the two thugs with crossbows that he had at his disposal.

In any case, Gervase turned to me at that moment, shook his head chidingly and said, 'Do not even consider it, Brother Edmund. Even if I do not return myself to deal with you, I have left instructions with the Archdeacon regarding your case.'

I was left with the unpromising resource of trying to get him to reconsider his strategy. 'Have you heard nothing of the last expedition to capture Sycorax, Friar? When so many priests and archers, cavalry and infantry failed, why do you suppose that the five of us will succeed?'

He smirked again. 'The last expedition, Brother Edmund, has been very much in my mind when planning this present venture. If there has been a degree of secrecy about our preparation, it has been to avoid the sort of fiasco that took place then.'

He adjusted his stride more closely to mine, so that he could talk almost directly into my face. 'The number involved in that attempt was a preposterous folly. If they had encountered the mere mortal Sukie Trothers, there would have only been the need for a couple of stout villeins to arrest her – as she was arrested when she was a young woman. Since the witch was able to summon the powers of Satan to her assistance, a whole army would have been insufficient to prevail against her unaided by God. The numbers resulted in confusion, incompetence and a great aggravation of the eventual disaster. And the religious observations throughout the expedition were ignorant and chaotic.'

I was impressed by the extent of his knowledge of past events in Slatterdale, which seemed hardly inferior to my own. I was intending to ask him what role he envisaged for me in the action he had contemplated so painstakingly and to try to convince him, even at this late point, that my terror of Sycorax and susceptibility to her power could only be a handicap to his enterprise and even put it in jeopardy. But I was prevented from this by coming to understand, as I listened to him, that he did not regard me as a functioning member of his expedition: neither as a valuable expert on Sycorax, nor even as a sort of bait, a vulnerable victim, with which to lure the witch. He simply had need of me as an audience for his pronouncements, a witness of his talents and, he hoped, the historian of his glory.

'On this mission, which you clearly do not feel privileged to have joined, Brother Edmund, I am making none of the mistakes of our predecessors. Nor am I relying entirely on my stroke of genius in employing these winter conditions against the witch. All the proper authorities have been consulted, all proper preparations have been made. Every crossbow bolt, to give you an example, has been both blessed by the Archdeacon and dipped in holy water. We have no animals with us, for they are particularly sensitive to the aura of the witch and the history of Sycorax abounds with instances of her power over them. The three men with us are all strangers to the region. I have chosen Loll and Randal because they are men without imagination or compunction, who can be trusted to handle the physical transactions, while the spiritual battle against Sycorax and her Master is a task for which I am uniquely gifted and have been preparing all my life.'

I understood by now that I was headed for a situation of extreme danger, under the absolute control of a fool. Yet even now I was incapable of a clear and firm response. My compliance was not only from fear of the consequences of non-cooperation. It occurred to me that my own personal peril from the malice of the witch – the persecution I had suffered in dreams, the terror that had arisen in me since the death of Abbot Fabian – might all perhaps be resolved by a confrontation with Sycorax at Beck Gap. And unlike Abbot Fabian, when I met the witch I would not be entirely alone.

A couple of dogs plunged in the snow, yelping and snarling, as we plodded into Nithermoor, but nobody came outdoors. The village was swathed, the doors and windows boarded with wood and stanched with sacking. The thatches were laden with snow, even on buildings that had smoke issuing from their chimney apertures. The main path through the village was obstructed by drifts.

To my horror, Randal led us to the ale house I knew so well and eased the door aside, without the formality of knocking or hailing, to usher us in. Terrified, long before we reached Nithermoor, at the prospect of being recognized there as the accuser of Alys, I now kept my features concealed in the cave of my hood: having the excuse that the interior of the ale house was not much warmer than the snowy village.

A smoky little fire in the central grate had been prepared in our honour and a repast of umbles and stale bread laid out on a trestle table flanked by benches. Though the ale stake was still above the outer door and had presumably led Randal to arrange matters here, there were no other tables, no barrels, nor any furnishings of the ale house of the previous summer. There were no customers either: we were the only people in the building until the ale wife followed us through the door with a jug of ale.

A hand seemed to leap from my heart and rise in my gorge, clutching me by the throat. The ale wife was enveloped in rags and wrappings like a shelterless vagrant, even as I pictured Sycorax from the many accounts I had heard. Around her head, fashioned into a sort of wimple, was the scarlet scarf that Alys had surely worn during the mumping dance the previous summer. The arthritic creep with which she approached our table was exactly how Alys had moved her broken body in the Pickering courtroom. When she raised her downcast eyes to us, they were not the eyes of Sycorax but faded, bleary grey, like those of Alys might have been after a century of pain.

For a few moments of panic I surmized that my victim had somehow survived hanging and been returned to Nithermoor. In those moments I understood my own worthlessness clearly and for ever. I understood that I would sooner Alys was dead, unshriven in Hell, than that I should be confronted, claimed by the wreck of her.

My shock subsided as I saw that the ale wife was Alys's mother, whom I had hardly noticed on my previous visits to Nithermoor, to the extent of not even knowing her name. Presumably the rest of the family, with the infant Gog, were in the dwelling next door, or it might be that Jackin had gone back to live with his parents and taken his child with him. My composure was assisted by the perception that her tentative gait was partly the result of poor eyesight: she was unlikely to recognize me, in the present circumstances, unless I gave myself away. I sat with my back to the room and my eyes on my companions as we picked at the untempting food and drank the flat, watery ale.

Friar Gervase seemed marvellously disguised by the sheepskin cap which covered his ears and the jacket collar which hid his dapper beard. Only his brown eyes were recognizable, as they gleamed with that calm and tender light which I was beginning to think was distinctly misleading. The two constables wore black leather caps. Randal was gaunt and melancholic, with grim slits for eyes and lips and a bony beak of a nose. Loll was squat, hairy and choleric, with round blue eyes and the jaws of a dog. These were both in their late twenties, but Forester Tomson was at least ten years older. He was little and shrivelled, a younger version of Simkin, his countenance wrinkled and stained by weather within a helmet of dark green wool.

Even while we were eating our glum repast and I was making these observations, Friar Gervase was talking tirelessly to his chronicler. Perhaps not aware of the coincidence of our meal stop, he made no reference to it, and I was not disposed to do so. Instead, having exhausted the topic of his wisdom in the present instance and the subsequent infallibility of our expedition, he reverted to his autobiography, with which he had regaled me on my last two visits to Pickering. As on the previous occasion he continued where he had left off with no sense of intermission.

'When I came to manhood I remained no less distinct. I have never known drunkenness, nor felt the faintest stirring of animal lust such as stupefies and enslaves most young fellows. It was evident to me that there was no profit to be had from the daughters of Eve one might encounter on the hard, snared road to Salvation. But neither did my body betray my judgement and persuade me that pleasure might be got from such creatures. I rejoice that the concept of copulation with a woman seems to me akin to bestiality and fills me with such disgust that I am tempted to vomit. I am even made queasy by the notion of carnal contact with members of my own sex. It is evidence that God has a higher purpose for me, and while it is a reason for gratitude it is at the same time a heavy responsibility. For it is clearly insufficient for me to be conventionally virtuous in order to fulfil my duty to the Saviour. I am intended for higher things and am to be judged by more rigorous standards than other men.'

The Triumph of the Fiend, 1431

HE FOUR-MILE journey between Nithermoor and Beck Gap took us longer than the eight miles from Pickering to Nithermoor. It was a route hardly used since the events of 1414 and the vestigial track now lay hidden under untrodden snow. Keeping the frozen beck close on our left gave us confidence that we were never far from the track. We were also sometimes guided by the two-day-old prints of the forester and Randal, made when they descended from Beck Gap with the news of the sighting. But we had to move very slowly. Plodding forward too carelessly put us in danger of twisting our ankles on rocks, cavities and vegetation hidden under the snow. Our progress was further obstructed by the thickening snowfall, coming from the north-east, like the fire-laden wind of the famous catastrophe: drifting into our faces with such weight and persistence that it had soon filled all the old footprints that were helping to guide us and even made it difficult for us to judge the line of the beck and keep ourselves parallel with it.

The exertion required to maintain any progress prevented Gervase from making me the recipient of further information or opinions. Apart from the physical effort, we had to keep our wits. The weather almost prevented us from moving away from the beck at the point where the track turned towards Beck Gap.

As we struggled into the white hamlet I saw that the cross that I had propped up on my last visit was cast down again and almost buried by snow. I took it as an awful omen, though I can see now that it had probably tumbled because I had not set it securely, rather than been overthrown by fiends. It focused the terror I was feeling on entering Beck Gap, and

I tried to speak of it to Friar Gervase, even to suggest that we pause to raise the cross. But he was too preoccupied with his own sensations to give me any attention, and I was not prepared to undertake the task alone and be left by the others.

The forester and constables brought us to the hut from which Randal had seen the smoke of a fire rising two days earlier. I do not know if it had once been the family home of Sukie Dobson. The falling snow made it difficult to judge whether smoke was now issuing from the chimney hole; but a sack across the doorway, whitened with the downpour, distinguished the place from all the other buildings in Beck Gap, whose doorways gaped wide. In the snow around the building there were tracks which the fresh snowfall had not yet had time to obliterate.

No giant black dog defied us. Randal simply pushed the sacking aside and we entered the hut.

A grey cat rose from the hearth, with arched back and wild eyes, then leapt up the wall to disappear into the roof. Otherwise it was a strange anticlimax. The hut was evidently empty: the immediate sensation was not disappointment at having failed to trap Sukie Trothers, nor relief at having been spared an encounter with Sycorax but simply pleasure at finding shelter from the fluffy, sticky snow.

There were two rooms in the dwelling; the main room showing several signs of habitation. A mound of ancient sacking in one corner looked very much as if it was being used as a bed. In another corner there was a broken mattock and a small pile of roots. Next to the hearth in the middle of the room were a couple of old pots, one of which contained the bones and feathers of a small bird. The other pot had a few roots in it, chopped and scraped clean. There was nothing else: no clothing, no possessions, no furniture.

The stones of the hearth were still warm. There were a few twigs and logs laid ready to be fuel, but the fire had been doused with snow not long before our arrival. The place stunk of excrement, which was easily explained by a number of turds, in various stages of decomposition, in the corner of the second room. There was also a rudimentary channel which had been gouged to let urine run out under the wall.

While we made these observations Gervase was standing with his eyes shut, mouthing silently some purifying or exorcizing prayer. He then said, 'Randal, build a fire and prepare this dwelling to shelter us when we return with the witch. The rest of us will set out on her trail immediately. If the cat, the familiar of Sycorax, should reappear, be sure to either arrest or destroy it.'

I said, 'Friar Gervase, that fire has been deliberately doused. How could the creature have known of our coming, unless it is indeed Sycorax, with powers far surpassing ours? I do not think that we should venture out against her.'

This was the first time I ever saw a chink in his composure. Perhaps the heavy snow was troubling him more than he cared to admit. Perhaps he was more nervous than he seemed about the projected confrontation with Sycorax. Whereas he had previously sneered at my objections without letting them impinge on his complacency, he was now furious. His eyes flashed and a lip curled up to reveal a triangular expanse of white tooth.

'I have suspected you of several things, Brother Edmund, but not of such stupidity. Yet if you are not stupid you are in league with the enemy.'

I was hardly listening to him, because I was suddenly fascinated by his hands, which were belying the calm, stilted tenor of his voice by shaking uncontrollably, as if with cold, though he had only just taken them from the snug sheaths of their mittens. He now chose a stick from the firewood and grasped it in both hands, so preventing their involuntary dancing, as he spoke with even more exaggerated patience:

'If she was Sycorax she would not have fled from us. If she is still Sukie Trothers, we must take her before she becomes Sycorax. She is a lame old woman who cannot go far, but we must follow her immediately, before the snow covers her tracks.'

The stick snapped. He threw the pieces into the hearth and

returned his hands into his mittens as he confronted me, at close range, with his stark face and burning eyes reminding me of the cat.

'Do not dare to speak again,' he hissed, 'or do anything that hinders my purpose.'

We found tracks that Forester Tomson said were recent, but they were fast being filled, like those we made ourselves, by the swift, thick snowflakes. Forester Tomson declared them to be the prints of a lame woman with bandages for boots and a stick for a prop, but this was not evident to me. The trail led away from the hamlet, up into the forest, which at this point was open, deciduous and swallowed in snow. The experience was taking on a dream-like aspect, engendered by the whiteness of everything and the soft hiss of the flakes, which had taken away my terror along with my belief in the outcome. I stumbled and waded along, mostly deaf and blind, in an oblivion that seemed to cocoon me, for the time being, from responsibility and consequences.

But it became clear that events were not having the same effect on other members of the party. We had wallowed on, at Gervase's urging, for several minutes after the last trace of footsteps had vanished, when Loll suddenly halted.

'That's it fucked for me, Father. I'm off outa this.'

Gervase was sufficiently swathed in snow-laden protective cladding for his reaction to be mostly concealed. Standing very still for several seconds after Loll's announcement, he could not help but have an impassive look.

'You cannot! I shall not permit it!' he called. It was now necessary to talk loudly to each other, if our efforts allowed us to talk at all, because the wind had risen and was driving the muffling snow between us at a shallow angle.

Gervase's voice was a little more shrill than usual, but this could be ascribed to the cold. His disturbing reaction to my earlier, feebler mutiny made his present response seem disproportionately meek, a mere petulance. Yet the rebellion of Loll was surely more devastating to him than mine. And more surprising: for if he was like me he had not really thought of Randal, Loll and Tomson as people at all but simply as utensils.

Loll said firmly, if with a note of apology, 'I'll be back at th'ut wi' Randal, Father. We'll bide for thee an hour.'

'I shall not permit it!' Gervase cried again.

After another embarrassed pause Loll shrugged and turned away.

'Very well,' said Gervase, so sharply that Loll swung back towards him. 'But leave us your bow and bolts, otherwise we are unarmed.'

Loll handed the crossbow and quiver of bolts to the friar. 'Best if we all of us fuck off back, eh?'

Gervase did not respond to this. Loll shrugged again and turned again downhill, his back to the snowfall.

I was feeling giddy by now and could just about stand upright in the snow. I watched fascinated as Gervase plucked off his mittens, fitted a bolt to the crossbow, took careful aim and fired at Loll as the latter trudged away from us.

Loll stopped as if struck by a sudden thought, stood motionless for a moment, then fell forward on to his face, slithering several yards downhill before coming to rest.

'Do not go to examine him,' Gervase called commandingly. 'He is quite dead. The bolt has pierced his spine and heart. It is a bolt that was blessed by an Archdeacon, dipped in holy water and guided to its quarry by God, for I have never fired a crossbow in my life and am even unacquainted with the mechanism.'

At this dire moment Forester Tomson and I exchanged a glance of mutual understanding – complicity in plight. That flicker of profane human contact was later to save my life.

'God's expedition against Sycorax will proceed,' Gervase proclaimed. As he spoke he reloaded the crossbow, with more difficulty than previously, as if to prove the point he had made. 'It will proceed in better spirits, with more direct purpose, now that the error of dissent has been corrected and the commander's resolve made manifest.'

We climbed into the whiteness, following no trail that I could discern. My jacket was now saturated with snow, though the heat of my exertions was still protecting my body from feeling the cold. This was not the case with my hands and feet, which despite their wrappings were frozen numb.

The wind eased a little, temporarily, and the flakes were sparser and lighter. Gervase glanced over his shoulder, then halted and laughed, an uncharacteristic falsetto. I saw that Forester Tomson was no longer with us.

'Sycorax is cunning! I have chosen my troops from among the minions of the witch! Another cowardly mutineer, another traitor to God, must be corrected!'

He spoke with tetchy playfulness, like an irritated schoolmaster. I believe that he would have set off then after the footprints of Forester Tomson, bent on shooting him down, if I had not gazed beyond him and seen something that forced a great shout from between my jaws.

'Sycorax!' I pointed an arm at what I had seen.

The witch was sitting ten paces from us, partly in the lee of an oak tree's bole. She sat erect and composed, watching our advance with the baleful stillness of a predator. I was made to think of a bird by the way her head was reared up on her long neck, and I remembered witnesses who had described Sukie Trothers in those terms. Her garb seemed to be composed entirely of ancient sacking such as we had found at Beck Gap, including an untidily wrapped headdress or bandage that hid her hair and shadowed her features. The left side of her face and body were out of the shelter of the tree and white with snow, which gave her whole aspect the look of a crude cartoon, a heraldic figure daubed with a stick of tar on a blank, white wall.

I did not dare fall to my knees to pray, knowing that once I was off

231

my feet I would not rise again. When I joined my mittened hands to pray where I stood I discovered to my horror that I could remember not a word of Latin. Nor was I able to close my eyes to concentrate my mind, for my whole being was transfixed by the apparition of Sycorax at last.

Gervase let out a shout of triumph. 'The pride of Lucifer has delivered up his minion! They think that our force is weakened enough for her to confront us – but they have miscalculated! We have only lost the dross.'

He aimed and fired the crossbow. The figure of the witch was undisturbed.

'Missed!' I yelled, hoarse with panic.

'It is impossible for me to miss. The bolt has passed through the witch and paralysed her forces, without entirely destroying her. A second shaft will bring us victory.'

Despite his confident tone, his fingers were frantic as he wound and loaded the bow. Gazing again at Sycorax I saw that she had not moved but that a portion of snow had been dislodged from her left flank, either by the passing of the bolt or coincidentally from its own weight.

I called out, 'Wait! It isn't Sycorax! It's the stump of a tree!'

'I must tell you once again that you are either a fool or in alliance with the witch, Brother Edmund.'

He fired again. This time the bolt struck with a splintering thwack and a cascade of snow. It became evident that we were staring through pestering flakes at a tree stump, a branch of the oak that had sprouted from near the base of the bole then been broken off.

Gervase looked from me to the bow, to the tree stump, then back to me. He then spoke in a reproachful murmur that hardly reached me through the snow. 'I read your mind, Brother Edmund. I read how you are despising me and triumphing over what you consider to be my error.'

I laughed at him in my despair. 'You are correct as usual, Friar Gervase, in your assessment of my thoughts. I despise you almost as much as I despise myself. I think that you should fire your next arrow at me, or at yourself, for if Satan is anywhere in the vicinity he is in us rather than in the tree stump yonder.'

Gervase laughed, too, a free and virile laugh that put my effort to shame, then raised his voice as if in exultation. 'I have underestimated the strength of Satan in you, Brother Edmund. I have underestimated Sycorax, too, for she can clearly survive these holy bolts. She can even retain sufficient magic power to transform herself into the semblance of a tree stump in an effort to get me to desist from my service to God.'

He tossed the crossbow aside. 'These bolts, however blessed, will not do the trick. It is by naked faith that she must be destroyed.'

Plucking the fleecy cap off his head he flung it after the bow. 'Faith like mine is sufficient to counter fire and snow and all the guile and power of Sycorax and her Master.'

His voice became muffled as he pulled off the padded jacket, then his habit and vest. When his head emerged he was saying, 'I am minded to wrestle hand to hand with the Fiend, in the old style. A man of God needs only God for protection.'

His head and torso bare, he crouched to untie the cords that bound his boots and breeches, his fingers amazingly nimble in the cold. 'I want you to witness this most avidly, Brother Edmund, and record it scrupulously as the conclusion to your history. It is for this that I have spared your scrofulous and cowardly life. We have reached the climax of this story, the decisive battle between the Holy Church that I represent and the Empire of Satan championed by Sycorax.'

Heaving himself out of the breeches he stood naked in the snow. His skin was rapidly turning grey-blue, apart from the brown pelt on his chest, and his chattering teeth now interfered with his diction, but he otherwise looked and sounded serene. I was impressed by the size of his sexual organ, which was mysteriously erect.

'Yet it is only one story, only one of many battles, for Satan is served by a million witches that befoul all Christendom with their sorcery. It is my delicious destiny to slay them all, sparing nobody, least of all myself, until I am glorified among the servants of the Church Omnipotent and take my place among the Saints in Paradise.'

The last sentence was scarcely audible, for he had produced a small crucifix and gripped it in his teeth, in order to leave his hands free for conflict. He dashed into the snow towards the oak tree and flung himself on to the stump, laughing.

I did not witness the sequel but turned and ran down the way we had ascended, my back to the snow which was now swooping down thicker and heavier than ever on the swelling wind. I understood everything. The friar's madness was overwhelming proof of the proximity of the witch and her power.

I was fearing pursuit as I ran, peering over my shoulder, but I would have fallen in any case, considering the speed I was attempting over the treacherous surface. I seemed to fall in a slow arc, into a deep bank of snow: twisting as I fell, so that I lay looking back into a dark wind, feeling the million motes as they crowded towards me and lit on me.

Winter at Byland

‘ E IS CALMER now, Father.’ Brother William sounds ill at ease, like somebody exhibiting an animal that has a flaw. ‘We bleed the emunctories and apply enemas. His urine is pale with phlegm.’

Abbot Jocelyn lets out a chortle and shrugs but approaches me warily just the same. He has been in awe of me since they brought me back from Pickering and I bit his elbow.

‘Why have you removed him from the infirmary?’ he asks. They discuss me in my presence as though I am unconscious.

‘His turbulence was distressing the other patients.’

Brother William, who usually works in the infirmary, has been assigned to tend me. As well as having some medical expertise, he is sturdy and muscular for his years and not easily shaken from his composure. He escorts me to meals and prayers, then back to my cell and sleeps in an adjoining cell.

‘I see he still has his wretched manuscript,’ says Jocelyn. He waves his manicured hand at the desk and writing materials that were transferred to the cell when Brother Clarence, who is now in charge of the library, refused me access there.

‘He works very sluggishly,’ says William.

I am distracted from sustained mental effort by the mischief of Sycorax. Whenever she snaps her fingers I lose track. She creaks a windlass in my left ear, freckles my vision and puts spectacular insects into my beverages. She commandeers my pen so that my writing turns into an obscene or foolish doodle. Sometimes she takes entire possession: so that I am unable to prevent myself from shouting lurid rubbish or becoming playfully violent, slapping the tonsures of my brothers . . . biting the Abbot and tipping Brother Vincent into the carp pond are the worst manifestations of this affliction so far.

'I am not sure that it is wise for him to write,' Jocelyn says. 'The work has little value and perhaps exacerbates his morbid condition.'

'I think, with respect, Father, that it is beneficial that he has an occupation. He is slowly becoming calmer and strives to be obedient.'

'He talks to you?'

'Only in confession, which I hear once a week.'

I confess absolutely everything to Brother William, even my perception that he is a nincompoop and the instrument of Sycorax. His counsel is bland. He says I must not commit the fatal sin of pride by holding myself to blame for anything. Only the Saints and Angels are strong enough to resist Satan.

'At other times I try in vain to engage him in therapeutic conversation. He usually listens submissively but only speaks if I insist and then it is to complain about the cold.'

'Ah yes. The cold.' Beyond Jocelyn's spurious grin and arched eyebrows, through the window of the cell, I see snow falling.

Just as Sycorax swept down Slatterdale into Beck Gap fifteen years ago, the witch has now extended her empire throughout the North Riding. Her first assault was fire and storm; this time it is snow that drops implacably from a yellow sky, burying farms and blocking roads. Perpetual winter surrounds us here in Byland Abbey: snow heavy on the guttering, capping the parapets, muffling the lancet window and the tracery on the west front, smothering the herb garden Abbot Fabian loved. The cloister garth is a snowscape of trodden brown paths, smooth drifts and shovelled mounds. Accompanying the constant snowfall is a zero cold that bites to the bone, so that I am swathed in sacks and woollen scarves yet my teeth chatter. The ink has not yet frozen in the inkwell, but when I unglove my fingers to grip the pen I can hardly keep the script legible.

Abbot Jocelyn leans towards me, though keeping out of range of my fangs, and addresses me directly for the first time. It makes me think of Forester Tomson peering down at me after he had dug me out of the snowdrift in Slatterdale and slapped me awake. 'Brother Edmund, listen carefully. It is not cold. It is midsummer. There is no snow in Byland.'

I manage to prevent myself snorting disdain. The conduct of my fellow monks is an outrageous part of Sycorax's teasing and proof that the empire of the witch is now total over the denizens of this region. For in the coldest of weather and the thick of the downpour the brothers wipe their brows, protesting about the heat, and walk out shod in sandals into the icy slush of the courtyard. Brother William is constantly bringing me drinks of cold apple pulp, consuming them himself, when I refuse them, with every pretence of pleasure.

Abbot Jocelyn puts his face closer to mine and adopts a more authoritative tone. 'This is your Abbot addressing you. It is hot today, Brother Edmund. I wish you to acknowledge the heat.'

He wipes his hand across his brow, says, 'Phew!' and stares at me commandingly. I remember his face screwed up with pain and dread, his mouth a childish rectangle, after I had bitten his elbow. Then I see Abbot Fabian moving famished lips, urging me that if I obey my superiors I make them responsible for my sins.

I nod obediently, puff out my cheeks and pretend to wipe the sweat from my icy brow with my mittened hand.

'Remove your mittens,' the Abbot orders me.

I stare at him appalled.

Brother William murmurs, 'With respect, Father, I would not advise it.'

Jocelyn frowns, then his face clears and he gives his jolly chuckle. 'He is perhaps not so calm as you claim?'

'With respect, Father, I said calmer, not calm. He is still much tormented by the malice of the witch.'

I have confessed in vain to this clodpoll that it is not the malice of Sycorax that afflicts me. She craves me, has craved me from the first. She herself put the idea of a book, a history, into the head of Fabian, in order to bring me into her sphere of influence. Both the tragedy of Alys

and the grotesque death of Gervase were to blend my destiny insep-
arably with hers. She adores me and will not rest until I reciprocate.

Abbot Jocelyn moves to the door, and Brother William follows with
prompt deference. As they exit Jocelyn says loudly, intending me to
hear, 'Your calm and patience do you credit, Brother William, but the
results of your approach are not spectacular. Unless Brother Edmund
shows encouraging progress soon, something more drastic may be
needed to bring him to his senses.'

I remove the right-hand mitten, pick up my pen and gaze at the
page on which I was working when they interrupted me. Then I tuck
the pen back into the ink well. Through the narrow window I watch the
thick, soft flakes slanting down. After a minute I put my head into my
hands, shut my eyes and await Sycorax.

Soon I am in summer, warm and young. The bracken is tall, and the
carved tips sway almost imperceptibly against the blue. If I half shut my
eyes the sun makes yellow and orange lines of light, like distant flames.
Before long I come out of the bracken and into a meadow where sheep
and lambs are blundering and bleating, finding each other and losing
each other again.

I am carrying a rabbit pie in an earthenware dish, the way Gib the
miller used to do, but I know for sure that I am Edmund Cresswell. I am
wearing the rust-coloured doublet and hose, the leather boots I was so
proud of when I met Malkin at Nunnington Fair. All the same, Gib the
miller used to bring Sukie Dobson rabbit pie, such as the one I carry,
then they used to fornicate amid the ferns, on fine days.

This seems an agreeable prospect to a foolish young man, so I look
round eagerly. Yet at the same time I am afraid. I remember my fierce
old father thrashing me with rope and Luce's husband, in the water
meadow by Sherriff Hutton, raising his blood-spattered stave to strike
me again and again. I see Abbot Fabian purse his lips with disrelish as
he insists how women are beastly instruments of Satan, disgusting to
the senses and dangerous to the soul.

A girl comes towards me through the meadowgrass. She has a grey gown and a white wimple, such as Luce wore, but I know that it is not Luce because this lass is loose-limbed and slender, walking through the meadow with limber grace. She is accompanied by a black dog that wriggles and bounces around her, obstructing her progress as it leaps up barking to lick her face. I am apprehensive of the dog, being sure that at the very least it will snatch and gobble my rabbit pie, but the girl calls to the creature in a clear, cool voice and it goes to heel.

The girl comes close and I see the grey eyes and mirthful lips of Alys. She is younger and slighter than I have known her. Plucking off the wimple with an impatient gesture she flings it into the grass. Dark brown hair falls lank to her shoulders. The woollen dress she wears, exactly the same shade of grey as the sheep, leaves her shins and fore-arms bare and is belted with string.

'Pie, yum yum,' she says. 'Grass cat, i'n't it?'

'Rabbit,' I say. Grass cat is her name for a hare. My voice catches in my throat as I speak, because I am so glad to see her looking blithe and well.

She pulls a disappointed face then says, 'It's 'appen best. If they catch thoo scoffing grass cat thoo loses a thumb, sithee.'

Linking her arm in mine she leans against me, firm and warm as Nance in the cider orchard, as she leads me into the bracken, which is now silky and shimmering, the boudoir of an enchantress. Insect noise is louder than the faraway flock. She gives her dark and mischievous laugh.

We have reached the point where a succubus would lift its skirt and spread its thighs. I look into the face of Alys, and we both smile. Squeezing her hand in mine, a timid and decorous pressure, I feel the friendly response of her fingers. Would I be content to go on merely holding her fingers like this, in innocent happiness, without compulsion or aftermath?

'Never thoo fret, Feyther, eh?'

I gaze into her eyes. Seen so close, her irises are a complex shade of grey with a tinge of green. I can see myself mirrored in her pupils, suddenly old and anxious, a tonsured head against an empty sky.

'You mustn't call me Father, child.'